Edd King;   *A Law Unto H*

A LAW U

HIMSELF

A lawyer recruits fraudsters to help him steal his clients' cash to support his failing business and put the blame onto a new employee. But he encounters problems.

Copyright © Edd King 2024

The moral right of Edd King to be identified as the Author of this work has been asserted by him in accordance with the Copyright, Design and Patents Act 1988 and any amendments thereto or renactments thereof in so far as they enhance or preserve the Author's rights. All rights reserved. All names used in this book are fictional and made up by the author. No offence is intended if they happen to be real people is purely accidental. No part of this publication may be reproduced stored in a retrieval system or transmitted in any form or by any means without the prior written permission of the Author or his Agents or be otherwise circulated in any form of binding or cover other than that in which it is published and without a similar condition being imposed on any subsequent purchaser.

This book is a work of fiction. Names, characters, businesses, organisations places and events are either the product of the author's imagination or are used fictitiously . Any resemblance to actual persons living or dead events or locates is <u>entirely coincidental.</u>

This book is dedicated to all the convicted innocents, victims of the vengeful spirits of their pursuers, of incompetent lawyers and the sometimes corrupt police officers who fail to undertake any worthwhile, investigations into the alleged crimes. The police are supposed to be neutral, not biased in favour of the prosecution, not to 'high five' on a conviction. And to wait sometimes years to get to trial is cruel in the extreme and destructive of a defendant's mental health, possibly rendering him unable to give a good account of himself. And there are too many cases where information helpful to the defence is not disclosed. But you have redress through the Criminal Cases Review Commission, don't you? Er … no. Although the CCRC was a laudable addition to the justice system, its successes are limited, and its independence from the Appeal Court questioned. Read Jon Robins book, *'Guilty Until Proven Innocent – the crisis in our justice system'* [Biteback, 2018] a book described by the Secret Barrister as 'a no-holds-barred insight into the serious and often overlooked miscarriages of justice that stalk our broken justice system'. And the journalist Catherine Baksi called it 'a book that informs, shocks and demands a response. It demands justice.'

Too many people are in prison, over-crowded, rat-invested insanitary hell-holes, and shamefully, many incarcerated beyond their sentences simply because they will not admit to their crimes, if, indeed, they committed any in the first place, a modern-day equivalent of the witches ducking-stool; if you drowned you were innocent. There is no education, often no work and no rehabilitative processes between the walls. Many resort to drugs, too plentiful in prisons. This is not the way a so-called civilised society should treat anybody, where for many their only hope of freedom is suicide.

Even when released, just with the clothes they stand up in and a few pounds in their pocket, they may have nowhere to go, abandoned by family and no job until, possibly, their 'rehabilitation' period has expired, and even then, few employers will take them on. So it is little wonder that the dry, the warmth and food is only obtainable back in prison.

It is shameful that despite this state of affairs being known to the prisons' minister, to the PM and to the public at large, we are doing nothing about it. The UK criminal justice system and all it's component parts was the envy of the world, now reduced to a rubble-strewn desert of failures, ineffective provisions, cruelty and not even within sight of the high principles upon which the system was founded. It should be scrapped and reconstructed and operated in some measure along the lines of those of our European neighbours. In the meantime, we hope for divine intervention; after all, there's little else available.

Edd King

Would be very happy to share your experiences

of issues you have with the UK criminal justice system.

Good or bad.

We cannot fight these injustices on our own.

Coaster747@gmail.com

Other fiction works by Edd King:

'Nelson's Law'

Former Army officer Ed Nelson starts his law training to discover that his principal is one of the country's biggest money launderers and people traffickers.

'Set Up!' [sequel to Nelson's Law]

Things go seriously pear-shaped when a Spain-based gang of smugglers try to take over a UK haulage company to shift all their gear. But they reckoned without the boss's widow and her ex-flame accountant who have other ideas..

'The History of Victor Clément'

A young lad is trafficked into the arms of a team of neurosurgeons who carry out an operation which they do not believe will work. But it does ...

'Target; Victor Clément' [sequel to 'The History etc']

The people traffickers need to find Victor and send out teams to find him before he blows the gaff on their operations. Their brief is to get him dead or alive and at any cost.

'Victor Clément – the Final Chapter' [sequel to 'Target; Victor Clément']

Victor joins the RAF but MI6 pick him up and engage him on a badly organised mission to track international arms smugglers. But when it all turns to worms, Victor uses his experience to make a daring escape from enemy territory to safety.

'Unfit to Practice'

A look at corruption in the police force and the legal profession. A lawyer thinks he and his bent copper associates can fool all of the people all of the time, but they didn't bargain for their new partner, Ed Blake.

'Bishop's Move'

The world is a chessboard; you are born into it with no choice as to gender, colour, race or whether you are a pawn, king or queen. You'll have to deal with the behaviour of people towards you. Bishop learned that from an early age that sexual abuse was not on. And she dealt with it.

Non-fiction works by King & Cochrane also on Amazon.

The Will Writer's Handbook

HM Forces Summary Justice system

Criminal Behaviour and Prison Reform in the UK

Professor Holly Slater was pleasantly surprised at the number of delegates who had turned up to hear her latest offering in her series *'Focus on Law'* lectures, this one entitled *'The infallibility of the law and lawyers; shattering the myth.'* As she approached the lectern, a wave of applause filled the venue. She was well known for her robust views of the law in general and in particular her take on what she was repeatedly drawing attention to, the appalling state of the UK criminal justice system.

"Thank you, thank you ... as usual I am probably going to offend some of you here this evening, and others are going to be buoyed-up and, I hope, reassured at what I am going to say. You know ... society in every country in the world is riddled with corruption to a greater or lesser degree, it is like the veins in a chunk of Danish Blue cheese. Here in the UK, I am concerned about the corruption in the UK criminal justice system by its signal failing to perform the roles for which it was established, evidenced by incompetence, laziness, ignorance stupidity and prejudice inter alia. But worst of all is the appalling performance of the appeals system, and in particular the Criminal Cases Review Commission ..." There was a smattering of applause, and 'Here Here's' before the bulk of the audience rose to its feet, clapping loudly. Slater raised her hands to acknowledge the appreciation of what she had just said. "Well ... well, I seem to have touched a raw nerve there! But at least I have not been in jail for a crime I patently did not commit!" There was some more applause.

The professor's offering drew to a close. 'Let's kill all the lawyers; the law is an ass, an idiot. These are not the rantings of madmen. The first was Shakespeare; 'The first thing we do, let's kill all the lawyers', from Henry VI. He may have been making a joke when his character Dick The Butcher suggests one of the ways the band of pretenders to the throne can improve the country is to kill all the lawyers, his rough solution to a perceived societal problem and criticism of how lawyers maintain the privilege of the wealthy and powerful, how lawyers stand in the way of violent mobs and criticism of bureaucracy and perversions of the rule of law. The second was Dickins, who often portrayed lawyers as dishonest and socially awkward, and this not-so-flattering assessment of the law you'll find in Oliver Twist. Then Trollope. He portrayed lawyers as caricatures as evidenced by such names as Alwinde, O'Blather, Slow & Bideawhile, Haphazard, and Chaffanbrass. He was outraged that barristers put loyalty to their clients ahead of the search for truth and justice.'

'Yes, the law is a business like any other. They have an eye on the bottom line, and no pun intended, they also have issues with sexual abuse of their female staff with judges, head of chambers and the barristers all at it. And bullying. Anyway, very few lawyers will ever turn down a case by suggesting a client has no hope; how can some lawyers almost guarantee to get their clients off a drink-driving charge; why do others take on cases against the government repatriation policy and others drafting an illegal immigrants back story? Because it is good business for them! They have already been paid around a hundred and fifty million pounds by the post office to fight claims from the wronged sub-postmasters Horizon affair. For goodness sake, didn't anybody ask why the cases were approaching seven hundred in number? Of course not; it was good business! And if any of you are thinking about divorce, lawyers are the most expensive but most useless therapists. I have a special supplement on divorce in the booklet." She indicated the table stacked with the free offerings. "You know I have been around the law for most of my life, and I believe that the legal system in the UK is crumbling; lawyers are not paragons of virtue; the criminal justice system is not fit for purpose; the appeal process including the - justifiably - much-maligned Criminal Cases Review Commission has long been on its knees. And finally, thank you all for being here tonight, and please collect your free booklets covering tonight's lectures with additional comment. Thank you."

In the front row, Mike Maynard and his wife Karen were there courtesy of Maynard's dad who had seen the lecture advertised in his local paper, law section, and had bought tickets as he knew his son was looking for a permanent role as a solicitor now that he had managed to rid himself of his other businesses. His son and daughter-in-law had bought a new house paid for with bank of Mum and Dad, and the proud father was keen to do all he could to get his son settled. Maynard junior had done some research on Slater, and decided it was going to be a worthwhile few hours to attend. The woman was actually attractive, and he imagined that anybody who tried anything on with her would, according to her web site, very soon realise their mistake. He would read a book about some girl, Bishop, who was equally determined to not put up with abuse of any kind.

After the short break, Slater returned to the lectern and turned to face the three people seated at a table behind her.

"May I introduce my guest speakers this evening. Firstly, Edward Nelson, who now works with the military court services. He has an amazing tale to tell about how his principal during training turned out to be a serial money-launderer. Next to him is Tracy Bishop, who works with Edward, and she will talk about her experiences which made her and others establish the SwanFly operation for reporting abuse of any kind, and working with Soteria Bluestone, set up by the National Police Chiefs' Council but first let's hear from a former member of the Criminal Cases Review Commission, Ainsley McGeorge". The gentleman stood and took the lectern.

"Thank you. I want to begin this evening by touching on what is probably the most appalling episode in the history of the criminal justice system, apart of course from capital punishment, and that is the number of people who claim to have been wrongfully convicted of a criminal offence; of them, many actually have been. The injustices arise for a number of reasons; fabricated evidence or evidence withheld that should have been made available for the defence; lawyers overworked, underfunded and incompetent and a defendant being advised to plead guilty for an offence or offences they did not commit just to get a lighter sentence. I'm sure any of you who have been in a criminal practice know just how true that is ... but I also wonder what if anything you did or tried to do about known cases. I appreciate that it is very difficult to contradict the advice or even question the activities of your principals' without seriously prejudicing your careers, and later in this lecture I will bring up other issues again overlooked or ignored when action is needed but rarely if ever followed through. Now, there will be occasions when I might ask you via a show of hands if you have been or are aware of the sort of behaviour I am alluding to. I think looking at you, especially the young ladies, quite a few of you are right now dwelling on your various court experiences. We'll get to it later. If you are one of the many, have you managed to have the conviction overturned or did try but failed." Ainsley continued. "Many professionals engaged in the administration of justice feel that delay in bringing cases to court together with incompetent solicitors and barristers and corrupt police officers or sloppy investigations too often results in a gross disservice to defendants in that they are convicted whilst in fact innocent or to victims of crime who do not see justice done. Where a person is wrongfully convicted, the consequences of the conviction can last a lifetime, and for myriad reasons fighting for justice can be a lengthy, frustrating and expensive experience and in many cases an applicant may never achieve satisfaction, and where he is genuinely innocent of any crime it remains with him forever. The system of appeals is based on certain principles and procedures which do not, generally, allow for an argument challenging a case which, legal niceties aside, 'just does not add up'. A further hurdle is that after a certain period all documents relating to cases are destroyed. This is a disadvantage to any appellant, but should not mean that the case can never be revisited ... the justice system is facing a sea-change. The police, legal aid, probation service, courts and both branches of the legal profession in short the entire criminal justice system have all been deliberately underfunded by successive governments. A properly funded criminal justice system is the bedrock of a civilised society. Ours used to be the envy of the world and copied by many. Now it is broken and is probably beyond repair. No doubt, as always, the ministry of Justice will blandly claim that 'all is well' and continue paying the ukulele as the ship finally sinks."

ONE

Chris Goodrich was already having a bad day trying to complete his last transaction of the week. It was a Friday, completion day for all the houses in the UK to change hands, and the lawyer was trying to get another firm to agree to go ahead with a purchase so he could deal with the related sale then wrap up for the day. It was the middle of August, the room was stiflingly hot and he couldn't open the office widows to let in a little cooling breeze because the busy, traffic-clogged streets below meant he couldn't hear himself think. In addition, it buggered up his dictation and the traffic fumes made him ill. Then his office door suddenly opened in a manner signifying a violent entrance and it crashed against a chair parked behind it, knocking a pile of old conveyancing files onto the floor.

"What the ... !" It was the expression on the face of his senior partner, Ian Collins, which told him that something was obviously up.

"It's that bastard Sam! Arsehole! He's walked out! Just dumped all his files onto Debbie's desk then walked out! I knew he would do …!" Chris Goodrich had no sympathy for his partner, as, ever since he had become involved in the business with Ian Collins, and against the better judgment of his wife, who constantly reminded him that he was a pig-headed moron who deserved all the problems which Collins had generated for their lives. But on occasions he was not averse to fighting back.

"Well, what the hell did you expect? He's been threatening to do that for ages and that letter you sent him can't have helped … blaming him for all the problems! How he managed to put up with you for so long, I do not know! And telling him that you would sue him for the agency fees and the salary you paid him, just does not help! I told you not to send it! And when you want to open the bloody door, use the handle, it's a damn-sight easier!" Collins ignored the point. He never listened to anybody anyway.

"He wanted more money! I was not …!"

"Ian, I told you! Why don't you just close the bloody office. Between them, Sam and Maggie, the woman you are always insulting, hardly earn enough to justify keeping the place open, and then with you constantly ringing up and asking if Sam has sent out any invoices, what the …"

"Chris, how many more times? I cannot sell … I signed a ten-year lease only a couple of years ago, there are eight years to go, I signed a personal guarantee … and there's a non-subletting clause! Shit! What am I gonna do?" Chris knew that the guy was too damn proud to take advice and close the office as it would signify a very public defeat.

"Ian, that is your problem! I told you to let me see the lease before you signed it, but you …!" He was wasting his breath, as Collins was not listening. "Get another lawyer in, this time a real solicitor, not a bloody para-legal! Now piss off, I've got some work to do!"

"You could be more helpful, couldn't you? For God's sake, say something positive!" The lawyer turned and walked out of the office. Goodrich pushed the door shut with his foot, and whilst waiting for some good news from his related purchaser's solicitor, gazed out of the window and into the middle distance. He had for a very long time now wondered why he put up with Collins. Ever since he and Collins had set up the practice, done on a wave of euphoria seven years ago with cash borrowed from Collins' ailing mother, they would, according to Collins, be made for the rest of their lives, rolling in cash. But Collins' attitude, a refusal to take on any caseloads himself, and treating staff and clients like shit, had soon given all three of their offices a bad name locally. Effectively, all the profit they made, and that was not much, had all gone back into Collins' pocket supposedly to repay the cash he had borrowed from his mum, who had been applying pressure on him to repay her, but Goodrich knew damn well that Collins was keeping it all for himself, and as her dementia had worsened, he was keen to get her taken off his hands which would have meant into care, but as she owned the substantial property they both lived in, Collins knew it might have to be sold to pay the care-home fees and at two grand per week, and him as tight as wallpaper when it came to spending his own money, he could just not let that happen.   Another pain was that Chris knew his own wife was getting pissed off with Collins' constant bitching to her about his problems, as though it was her husband who was the entire problem. It was okay for him. He lived with his mum, treated her very badly by all accounts, and professed to have a girlfriend whom nobody had ever met and, into the bargain, had the most improbable name. The whole office knew everything he bragged about especially when the subject of sex came up, was all bollocks, and the story kept changing by the week, and into the bargain Collins was in no way physically attractive to any normal female, and he was mentally incapable of holding any normal conversation. In fact, the whole Collins package was a total turn-off principally because he refused to behave normally in any sense of the word. What he actually did for sex was not a subject anybody wanted to know about, but it was known that once he had a few drinks inside him, he became even more objectional and had been barred from many local pubs because of his forthright and thoroughly unpleasant views on everything under the sun. He seemed, according to Mrs Goodrich's expert opinion, determined to be regarded by all who encountered him as a wealthy, highly-respected business owner, a man of the world, but the charade was so thin that everybody saw through the veneer like it was a piece of glass. In short, he was widely known as 'Mr Bullshit'.

Chris Goodrich turned his attention to the problem in hand. He knew that the shattered office which Sam occupied had been a thorn in their sides for a while now. It had never really made a profit because Collins was too damn mean to pay decent wages or provide decent equipment. And although Chris had himself thought about leaving the partnership to work for another firm, he knew damn well that the firm Collins and Goodrich had such a poor reputation, even though it was principally due to Collins, that nobody local would want to employ him anyway. Basically, he was stuffed. As far as the immediate problem was concerned, he thought the only solution was to get another lawyer to take over Sam's work. He picked up his phone and dialled the number of Century Legal, the agency he'd used many times before to replace staff who had left the office principally because of Collins behaviour. He got straight through and spoke to the boss.

"Hi, mate. Chris Goodrich here again. I'm afraid we need you to look through your books to find another person to take on our Green office. The same office you supplied Sam for. He's just walked out and frankly, I can't blame him either. But for Christ's sake, can we this time go for a qualified solicitor? We're getting fed up with having to clear up after Sam with the mess he made. He just dumped the files on the office desk. Didn't say a bloody word. And as for bloody Collins, he went bananas when he found out about it. He's really tearing his hair out. So can we look for a qualified solicitor, say five years PQE? Let us know what you reckon we should pay him. And what your commission will be. I must tell you that this is quite urgent. Do your best for me, mate, OK? You take care. Cheers."

Chris put the 'phone down. Next time Collins barged into his office, he'd tell him what he done. He didn't see there's any option because he knew damn well there's no way Collins would pay eight years rent for an empty office. He was himself beginning to get pissed off with the whole business, being too young to retire, he had to speak to his wife to consider his options, few as they were, if any, and as he did and had done far too often. Maybe think of another way, either moving to another part of the country. Or something else? He reckoned it wasn't too long before he'd probably finish up in the looney-bin. His disturbed meanderings were interrupted by his 'phone ringing. It was his related deal. The news was good, so he released the documents and cash held in escrow. Job done. He stood up, pulled his jacket off the back of his chair, and left the office for home. He knew that as soon as he told Pauline, she would again go into all the reasons why Collins was a sociopath, and as a psychiatric nurse, she knew what she was talking about, and if he were to broach the subject, it would be the topic for discussion for the whole weekend. At least he'd get a break from Collins. Chris knew he was trapped. He'd been lucky to get a mortgage on a new-build that they could barely afford, but which they regarded as their forever home, and Chris was thinking seriously about starting a home-based business, possibly a franchise, for estate planning, but he'd have to get the owner of the franchisor to take him on. He had told nobody but his wife of his plans, distant as they were, and he knew that as soon as Collins knew about them he would do all he could to scupper them. Whatever else the bloke was, he was certainly a bully. He knew the guy had been an Army policeman, and when his mates refused to work with him due to his extremist views in particular misogynistic and racist, he was transferred to the dog section. What Chris also knew was what one of the guys Collins had served with told him that he and a number of his mates hated him so much that they been working on a plan to kill him. Maybe, he thought, he would actually do it himself. It had crossed his mind before, and reckoned he could plead extreme provocation. It would be a sudden, unplanned attack with a hammer while he was using the tool to fix something in the office. He knew loads of people who would come to his defence, but that he would never do it, but he hoped that at least the bastard could have an accident one day when driving back from the pub. But hope is a revolutionary patience. Another matter that pissed him off was that Collins constantly referred to himself as the senior partner, which was not true although he reasoned that as he had put in most of the money to get the offices up and running, he believed that he was entitled to call himself the senior partner. And Chris read that a meddling boss, one who micromanaged everything, gave his co-workers a higher than average risk of heart attack and strokes. American professor Lisa Berkman had said that working conditions were important social determinants of health, and when workplace conditions and work-family conflict were mitigated there was a reduction in risk of cardiovascular disease. He remembered the report almost word for word, after his wife had cut it out of the Times a few years ago. What he would not admit to himself, was that his working time or a good chunk of it, was dealing with getting round Collins' bloody stupid behaviour. Oddly, their junior partner, Arnold, seemed unaffected by it all but the kid was a virtual alcoholic anyway and a known crack-head but for all that, he was efficient, quiet and very good at this job in probate, trusts and succession. Maybe, thought Chris, I could find salvation in similar addictions.

As Goodrich left his office to go home, he heard Collins on the phone, and from what he was saying Chris knew he was talking to Debbie, the secretary from the office Sam had recently abandoned. He was shouting and even from where he was, he could see the spittle spraying over his desk, and him waving his free arm around as though to accentuate what he was saying. Chris slipped past him to the receptionist, and scribbled a quick note about his chat with the agency.

"Hannah love …" he addressed the girl, a work-experience candidate from college, as he scribbled a note, " … when Ian has finished on the 'phone, can you give him this please?"

"Yes, of course, sir." Goodrich made for the exit, hoping he could escape without the idiot seeing him. He felt sorry for the girl who would no doubt get back to college to tell her friends that all lawyers were nutcases, and instead she wanted to do anything in life but go into the law. It was not without good reason that everybody who knew Collins referred to him as 'the Dick Head', another soubriquet, many far worse, sometimes a lot worse, most unrepeatable in good company. But Collins held the purse-strings, and anyway, most of the people who worked for him had history which made them virtually unemployable elsewhere including a number of ex-police officers whom he used to undertake supposedly covert operations such as using their contacts and use of the police computers to check-out the criminal record bureaux on certain 'clients' on whom he could apply pressure, and indeed did.

Goodrich drove to his river-side home, wondering every inch of the way how he could disentangle himself from the Collins web. It frankly made him ill. He knew that he would have to go to Sam's office to deal with the files the guy had left with Debs, and that would double his workload. He banged the steering wheel in his frustration. When he arrived home, his wife could see he had had a bad day.

"Collins again, love?"

"Yeah, and how! I've just about …!" The phone interrupted

him. "I'll get it!" He knew it was Collins. He reached for the handset. "Yeah!" He was right. It was Collins.

"Hi. Next week can you … you can cover Sam's office? I don't think …"

"No I can't! I've got too much …"

"You'll have to, mate …" Goodrich hated being called 'mate'.

"Why can't you cover the place? I've already asked Nick to find us a real lawyer, and …"

"I know you have. I got your note. It'll be yonks before he finds anyone. I can't do it 'cos I've got my own clients … like the accounts, the leases, the annual returns for the law society, and not forgetting …"

"Ian, if ever there was a sophistry …"

"A what?"

"Oh, for God's sake! It's a deliberately invalid argument displaying an ingenuity in reasoning in the hope of deceiving someone … maybe forget the ingenuity bit, 'cos that would invest in you a skill you do not …" Goodrich was about to suggest that Collins was not in any way capable of ingenuity, but decided it would make the bugger break into a stream of obscenities. "…you know damn well that's bollocks!" And Collins knew it.

"Well keep your bloody fingers crossed that Nick comes up with someone soon! Like Monday!" Before Goodrich could comment, Collins put the 'phone down.

"Arsehole!" Pauline called from the kitchen.

"Ian?"

"Who else!"

"Why don't you just kill him!"

"I think about it every day!"

"Well, the way you two are going, he'll damn well kill you first!"

"Yeah, it's possible! What's for dinner?"

"Spaghetti Bolognese, and for you also a bottle of wine! Then we'll sit down and watch a decent film, then an early night. Take some Nightnurse to get rid of that lingering summer-sniffle and get a good night's sleep. I've made up the spare room so you can have a decent lie-in tomorrow. And I've got a report to write up and then in the afternoon we can go to Waitrose for a big shop."

"Sounds good to me."

Back in the office, after Collins had slammed the 'phone down on his partner, he ordered a take-away to be delivered to his home, then left the building. He reminded himself, talking aloud, to get that girl Hannah to give the offices a good clean on Monday morning. He hated the idea of anybody wondering around the offices once the staff had gone home, in case they stole something or worse, found and kept any cash lying around. It was something very much in his own mind, as during his articles he had once lifted a couple of thousand quid he had found hidden in a conveyancing file.

Collins home was a large, converted farmhouse, owned outright by his mum. His father was dead. Collins had been at home when his dad had collapsed with a heart attack, and instead of calling for help, he just drove to his local then returned a few hours later to find his dad dead. He had already done wills for his parents, and as he had watched the emergency services take his father's body away, he knew that the lasting powers of attorney he had prepared for his parents gave him power over his mum's affairs. His worst fear now was that his mum would be moved into a care home, so it was in his interests to keep her at home. Her care was sorted by an arrangement with an old mate who has assigned a couple of illegal immigrants to come in twice every day and were paid in cash, and far less than was the going rate. With the mate also running a couple of immigrant sex workers, which Collins knew about, the guy had no choice but to do a deal on the cheap. And with Collins now having access to his mum's substantial savings accounts, the whole business suited him down to the ground. The only possible fly in the ointment was that he has got Goodrich to sign the LPAs as certificate provider and witness to the documents without his mum or dad being present, which was fortunate as neither of his parents had actually signed them; Collins had. Ergo, he could not afford to upset Goodrich too much, even though he thought maybe the bloke didn't really know enough about the documents to cause any trouble. Collins' brother, Mark, knew about it and about his using mum's cash to support his business, and had made it abundantly clear that bro had better replace it. Mark was a prison officer, well used to finding ways of getting most of what he wanted, and had further boasted, in a rare drunken moment, that even arranging a hit-job was easy. Collins could not be so stupid as to be unaware of his personal failings, and it was always possible that making himself thoroughly objectionable when any opportunity arose was an auto-defence mechanism, clearly indicating that he had not received counselling, or if he had, then it was a waste of time. As a child he had always been difficult and inclined to turn any situation to his advantage, howsoever small or large, and over his years at school and beyond, he just accepted the fact that he really pissed people off but he was utterly immune to their discomfort, and the more they reacted, the more he preyed on them. And he recognised when people were vulnerable to bribery, to the promise of a quick buck and that they could be exploited

TWO

When the 'phone rang, Mike Maynard was in the shower, but by the time he had grabbed a towel and made it to the bedroom, the thing had stopped ringing. He finished the bathroom business, got dressed then sat in the kitchen with a mug of coffee and returned the call. It was his agent, Nick from Century Legal Staff who answered.

"Nick?... Mike, Mike Maynard. You called."

"I did, and it's good news. We might have found just what you are looking for."

"That was quick. As you know, I don't want to continue as a locum, looking for a permanent position. I've managed to dump most of my other interests …" As he spoke, his eyes rested on the bookcase jammed with his old business files. Once he had sorted out his tax matters he would probably dump the lot into the nearest canal. "… so I can spend more time at home rather than having to stay at the London flat. Anyway, my wife also has another job. I assume you got the message?"

"Yeah, we did. And the office we're looking at is, as you stipulated, almost within walking distance by comparison … about four miles away from where you are now."

"Sounds good. What's the firm?"

"Collins and Goodrich … heard of it?"

"Can't say I have. Tell me about it."

"Three offices, three partners. Looking for a solicitor, at least five years PQE to do manly conveyancing. Right up your street. Salary not all that encouraging, but I believe there will be increments with time." Nick knew that had not been mentioned, but he didn't want to lose a job.

"I suppose I'll have to drop into their office for a quick look?"

"Of course. However, wait until the partners have seen you. I don't think you'll have any problems … they need someone as soon as. The guy who is leaving is not a solicitor, just a licenced conveyancer. Anyway, I'll pass your details on to them. Their main office is about an hour's drive max from you. Okay?"

"Sounds good. Let me know. Thanks, Nick." Maynard opened his PC and looked up the firm. Nick was correct, the office was only a short distance away. He heard his wife come into the house. "Karen?" Who else would it be. His wife appeared at the kitchen door, carrying a loaded shopping bag. She dumped in onto the table and bent down and kissed her husband.

"Yes love … any news on the job?"

"Yeah. All fixed up. I'll no doubt have to go for an interview, and the location seems perfect!"

The following day, a Friday, the agency called back with the interview details, time, location and name of the contact, being a Mr Ian Collins, the senior partner. On the appointed day Maynard nosed his Mercedes 'A' class hatchback out of the garage and pointed it towards the Collins and Goodrich head office. It was conveniently close to a multi-story car-park, but their head office turned out to be in a rather unimpressive block, the lawyers' offices on the first-floor, accessed via a main door off a busy pedestrian street, only a few hundred meters from the city's main thoroughfare and conveniently close to the courts. There were, Maynard noted as the main office door swung closed behind him, four separate offices, a reception area and a small kitchenette visible through a door close to the receptionist's desk. The girl's name was Hannah, as evidenced by a small cardboard sign propped up on a mug bearing the 'Nescafé' name and, incongruously bearing mind it was mid-summer, a bright Christmas decoration.

"Hello, Hannah. I'm Mike Maynard and I have an appointment with your Mr Collins. I'm a little early." The girl smiled at him. She looked a bit young, but he guessed she was probably on a short work-experience assignment.

"Oh, yes. I'll tell him you are here." She slipped out of her chair and disappeared briefly into a room at the far end of the corridor. Maynard looked around. The place gave the impression of being a little shabby, unloved, the carpet somewhat care-worn. It was not overly prepossessing. He heard a few voices from behind the door, then the girl re-appeared. They won't be a minute. Would you like a coffee or something?" Maynard declined. Apart from the fact that he really did not want one, he knew that there was some debate about the protocol of dealing with a drink at an interview. Like asking for one then not drinking it, and apparently interviewers can tell a lot about the candidates who leave a full cup of cold coffee as their legacy, a coffee left untouched is an opportunity wasted. An undrunk cup of coffee might show that you are afraid to speak your mind, or you were nervous, with the smallest disconnect bringing your authenticity into question. Or it is a great prop to slow things down a little. If your communication style is pensive and relaxed, it may encourage the interviewer to mirror your behaviour. When they ask a question, take a sip of coffee and then launch into an amazing answer. A drink helps to create natural pauses. If you do this, the interviewer will feel able to do the same. There were other protocols regarded as essential by those whose job it may be to prepare you for the shit-hot interview, but no doubt spilling the drink would be a disaster, or it is a crucial weapon in any job seeker's toolkit. He actually wondered who undertakes all this research, if indeed there was any, or was it just a topic dreamt up by some under-worked psychiatrist. Like the one whose research concluded that all the time taken by chambermaids in hotels neatly folding the edges of the toilet rolls amounted to the entire working-life of one chamber maid.

However, by the general state of the office first-impression, he doubted the interview would swing either way by how he disposed of his coffee, unless he threw it at the wall. Just as he finished his musings, the door ahead of him opened and he was summoned into the interview room.

"Mister Maynard … Mike … please come in." He entered and was shown to a chair. There were three people in the room. Two seated, and the other standing, his back to the window, his bum against the radiator. He introduced himself as the senior partner, Ian Collins. He pointed to a man seated immediately in front of him as Chris Goodrich, and another at the end of the table, as Arnold. No surname. Goodrich then seemed to take over, as Maynard sat down and slipped his small file of documents onto the table, stuff he assumed the interviewers might like to see. Goodrich smiled and addressed the visitor.

"Mike … tell us about yourself." Maynard launched into a brief he had used on all his assignments, a note about when he qualified, his time as a locum, his preferred disciplines, family life.

"Why are you looking for a permanent post now, Mike?"

"Family reasons, mainly, and I had been running a few businesses most of which I have now sold with the last few in the process of being sold-on or shut-down …"

"What kind of businesses?"

"My dad ran a haulage company, and I started an agency for drivers … initially, for dad's goods' vehicles, then expanded into chauffeurs, van drivers, Europe deliveries … then got into film and TV work. It was hard graft!" Maynard was not being entirely honest. The truth was that his dad had sold the haulage business together with all the spin-offs he had involved his son in, and had shared out the proceeds between his three children. The shares were substantial, and allowed him to invest in realty, with the idea that his dad would survive for seven years so reduce his inheritance tax liability to zero. Anyway, it was no business of either Goodrich or Collins to know that.

"I bet it was hard graft, too! And now …?"

"As I said, all gone. I want to concentrate on the law, only the law, not any more businesses. Then there is a few family reasons, like new babies."

"Have you approached any other firms?"

"Yes. Cruwys and Atkins …" It was a big, local firm. Radiator-man, senior partner Collins responded.

"Them! Ha! I wouldn't go near them!" Collins was dismissive of all other law firms, especially those who had been stealing his clients, usually the ones who at some stage Collins had upset by his well-known habit of being unable to control his mouth. Apart from these interventions by the senior partner, he seemed to take very little interest in the interview process, and Arnold had said nothing at all. With the formalities over, such as they were, Maynard suggested that he might pop into the office he was to take over to see the retiring fee-earner, but this proposal was not well received. On reflection, that was the second hint that maybe things were not quite as he might have hoped they would be. Not really a problem as he reasonably assumed that he would meet him when he was briefed on the hand-over. It seemed that the interview was now finished. Maynard slipped his slim file off the table.

"Well, anything else you need from me?" Goodrich stood up, and Collins pulled his arse off the radiator. Maynard stood up as well. Window man again.

"Nope! I think that's all. We'll get in touch with the Century people. Give us your address as well, so we can contact you direct, okay? Thanks for coming in." Maynard scribbled his address, Boothryen House, and the postcode on the pad Goodrich had slid across to him. Maynard smiled all round, and let himself out of the door and waved briefly as he passed Hannah then down the stairs to the multi-story car park across the road. He thought the interview went well enough, but he was not too keen on the rather shabby state of their offices.

When Maynard had gone, Collins picked up the pad on which

the visitor had scribbled his address. It seemed to be more or less local. He tore the sheet off the pad and stuck it into his pocket. He would drive up there to give the place the once-over.

"Well, Ian, what do you think!" As with every new meeting, even with what few clients he dealt with, Goodrich knew Collins' first reaction would be one of dislike. However, his reply was simply, 'He'll do.' Goodrich was surprised. From Collins, who for for many reasons, jealousy, a craving for attention from others, or because he is constantly unhappy with something in his own life and putting others down somehow makes him feel better and which is never okay, it was by comparison a resounding endorsement for the guy, praise indeed. Goodrich looked at him sharply.

"Really? Well maybe you ought to give him a thumbs-up and get a start date before you change your mind! What do you think, Arnie?" In his slow, ponderous way, and as though struggling to pull himself out of a catatonic state, indicating to any casual observer unfamiliar with his normal state a lack of critical mental function, a level of consciousness in which he is almost entirely unresponsive except to intense stimuli such as pain. But Collins and Goodrich both knew that with Arnold it was a false diagnosis. The guy was as sharp as a pin. He he raised his head, in the same way a tortoise would, as though it had a bad headache, and shifted his gaze from Collins to Goodrich, then delivered his verdict. It was one word, three syllables.

"E'sokay."

"Well, mate, that's another resounding positive! But make sure you don't let him see you snorting coke off your desk!"

"Fuck off, Chris" Arnold never expressed any sentiments sufficiently forcefully as to deserve an exclamation mark. He rose and returned to his room. Collins called after him.

"Hey, how are you doing on the Fish case? Any progress?"

"No. Looks like we'll have to hold onto the account for months, probably years! Anyway, it's Lady Fisher!"

"Really?" Collins ignored the correction. I asked for a sum, not her bloody life story! How much will it be?"

"Once we've sold the house, probably seven hundred and fifty thou." Then Arnold pushed his office door closed, and pulled another beer from his bottom drawer. It was fortunate that the office was within easy walking distance of his flat. In fact, that was one of the reasons he accepted the job in the first place. Back in the interview room, Collins made up his mind.

"Okay. Call the agency. Let's get the bugger into that bloody office!"

Back in the car, Maynard weighed-up his feelings about the interview and generally about the deal he was considering, and would in any event, discuss with Karen. Pros; the office was very local, a short drive or bike-ride. It was a small firm so, he assumed, no office politics. Mainly conveyancing. The Chris guy seemed okay, possibly under Radiator man's thumb. He could then think of no more pros. Cons; head office shabby, but his office might be okay; small salary, not a problem, as he was not short of cash anyway and did not want to have to sell his soul and probably his life in order to secure a huge salary with all the headaches that would go with it; the Collins bloke ... couldn't make him out, but he might be an OK guy or a pain in the butt. So, pros matched the cons. He voted to go with the pros. What he would also do, once offered the job, is insist on visiting the office before a final acceptance. He worked out exactly what he would do and say to Radiator Man to make it happen. He pulled up and parked outside the double-garage, next to Karens little Fiat, then entered the house via the garage side-door, leaving his shoes on the mat in the utility room which formed part of the extended garage, convenient for taking off wet or muddy clothes or dumping the prams and lifting out the babies. Or letting the dogs dry off before letting them into the house proper after washing them in the over-large sink. Once inside, he called for his wife.

"Hi love, I'm back!"

"And I'm in the kitchen! Come and let me know how you got on!"

"Wilco! Just change first!" He must stop using his dad's old military flying expressions. But at least, he had learned the phonetic alphabet, always useful when telling people postcodes or spelling awkward names. Maynard pulled on his running kit then entered the kitchen. Karen was feeding Theo, their latest addition to the family. His wife looked up.

"Go on, is it a yes or a no?"

"A yes … in fact only by a casting vote. But only on condition of being able to visit the office and meeting the staff. For some reason the senior partner, Collins, seemed a bit reluctant to okay it today. Anyway, I can deal with that. Now I'm off for a run. I'll go along the river and turn round at the motorway bridge. See you later!" He tweaked baby Theo's little rosy cheeks, kissed the top of his wife's head and made for the door. Running alone was a good way to clear his head and concentrate on pressing matters, like in this case the new job. The run would last for about two hours, and by that time he expected to have mulled over most of the issues.

By the time he turned round to head for home, he had made up his mind. Firstly, he liked the challenge of a new job and if he didn't like it he could always move on. So, decision time. Go for it provided he could do an office recce first, meet the staff and was otherwise able to put his own mark on the office if, as he believed, he would be the employee in charge and able to make what he considered to be essential changes. And with the office so close, and if necessary, he might be able to WFH on occasions if Karen was unable to rope in the child-minder if she was tied up to a particularly difficult shift at work. Job done. He was bathed in sweat when he walked into the utility room. He stripped off, chucking all his clothes into the washing machine, then padded barefoot into the master bedroom en-suite for a good hot shower. Once clean and shaved, he donned his pyjamas and slippers and made it to the kitchen. He could smell the dinner Karen was cooking. He sat down, grabbed the copy of the Times, as yet unread, and relaxed. In their three-aspect kitchen, the sun was now mostly in the west, and the light and warmth made him soporific, and inclined him to nod-off. He shifted himself from time to time to fight the tendency.

"Hey, love … you might have walked into Elaine just now when you came out of the utility room! She might have seen you in your birthday suit!"

"She might have been unable to control herself and dragged me into the bedroom!"

"Maybe, but I doubt you could afford the consequences if you obliged her!"

"Yeah, I know … and you would have slapped me or done a baseball-bat job on me! Does Elaine like the place?"

"You can bet on the baseball bat job! Yes. She's happy to stay here with the kids when we're both working. And she said that if we baby-proofed the little annex, she could probably take on three of four more clients! Now come here and sit down, your dinner's ready!"

"Thanks … maybe after dinner you can look out my suits and suitable shirts in case I get the job. Want to create a good impression on my first day!"

"Yes, will do and dig out your briefcase and the few legal textbooks you still have. Need to shift all that junk out of my bookcase please!"

At the same time that the little domestic scene was playing out inside the house, a powerful motorcycle was approaching the property. The rider quickly realised that the neighbourhood was one of substantial, expensive homes. The Thames was only a few strides away, and the frontages were Impressive. According to his I-phone compass, rear the garden would be south-west facing, ideal for catching most of the afternoon and evening sun. Nice. There was an integral double-garage, a generous drive with two new cars sitting on the gravel at the front. Clearly, Maynard had done well. Collins roared off. He would make some 'phone calls from the office tomorrow. As he headed homeward, his mind was working overtime. How could he turn this to his advantage? Tomorrow couldn't wait. As soon as he parked his bike outside his garage, he got onto his PC and looked up the address, did a street-view and a plan of the property. It was more impressive than he had first estimated. Zoopla put the asking price at two-million plus.

The following day, Collins made some 'phone calls, and learned from the several estate agents that that houses in the same road as Maynard's appeared to be selling for in excess of two and a half million pounds, just as had Zoopla. Radiator man's brain went into a frenzy of activity. He knew that whatever else, he had to engage the guy, whatever his demands. He opened the drinks cabinet and poured himself a tumbler of brandy and lemonade, equal measures, sat on the couch and put his legs up onto the coffee table. His mother was, as usual, in bed and the care-agency account was on the table in an envelope. He had some serious thinking to do.

THREE

The Maynard's little black Cocker, Scottie, by his usual furious barking announced the arrival of the postman, then pawed open the already-ajar door to the lobby, picked up the mail and dropped it at the feet of his master, looking up expectantly for the usual reward. The other dog, Buster, just and as always, watched the almost daily pantomime from afar, her intertest only being that she and Scottie would get some treats. Not always, but it was certainly worth keeping an eye open for them. Both dogs knew if they would get lucky, because the treats were kept in the utility room, and when their master moved in that direction, mail in hand, both dogs made it to the door before him, heads up, tails wagging furiously. It was definitely treat time. Maynard did his bit, then returned to the kitchen and opened the three letters. One was from Octopus energy, another from the water-board. It was that time of the month. Those he dropped onto the desk in his office, which had effectively taken up bedroom four; the third letter was from the Century agency. He slit it open, dropped the dead envelope into his waste-paper basket, and unfolded the letter. It told him he'd got the job, starting salary thirty-thousand, with increments depending on performance, which to him meant nothing. There was no definition of 'performance' so he didn't whoop with joy, just ignored it. Thirty thou was okay for the time being. But the main advantage was the vastly reduced commuting time and the added convenience for Karen, giving her more flexibility to cope with her job as a lecturer at Bucks university. He returned to his office, paid the two bills on line, then called Collins and Goodrich office. Hannah answered.

"Hi, Hannah. Is Mr Collins in please? Could I have a word with him? ... its Mike Maynard?"

"Of course, hang on." He imagined the girl trotting to the boss's office. She was back in no time. "Mister Maynard ...? Just putting you through now."

"Thanks ..." There was a brief pause. Then he was on the line.

"Mike ... good to hear from you. How can I help? I assume you have heard from the agency!"

"Yes, thanks. All I'd like to do now is have ... I'd like to drop into the office and suss out things like the parking, shops and possible take-aways, you know, that sort of thing, then once happy, just sign on the bottom line, if that's okay?" It was not quite what Collins was expecting. But the urgency of the situation meant that he had no choice but to agree.

"Er … Chris is covering at the moment … I'll ask him to expect you … when … when do you think you can get there?"

"Could do this afternoon … any time before say, four-thirty?"

"Okay. I'll tell Chris to expect you. Thanks." The line went dead. Collins then burst into Goodrich's office. "Chris …" he didn't wait until his partner had finished scribbling on his pad… "…that bastard wants to …" Goodrich looked up. His look said, 'Oh for Christ's sake, what now?' But he limited his question to 'Just who is 'that bastard'?

"Maynard. Wants to meet you in the office, Sam's office that is, at about four thirty. I suggest you get there by about three, call Debbie to tell her you're on your way and go and sort the place out. And remember, no talking about Sam or anything, okay? Remind the girls!"

"What if he asks questions? About Sam I mean?"

"Ignore them. And tell Maggie and Debbie, the same. They know zilch about the guy or why he left, okay?" Goodrich gave a sigh of resignation.

"Okay, if you insist."

"I do insist! If the guy gets put off by Sam's buggering off, and he doesn't take the job, then you'll have to cover until we find another replacement!" That was what Goodrich expected Collins to say, but was not happy about it.

"Oh, very well!" He looked at his watch.

"Grab yourself some lunch and get over there now. If you've got any urgent jobs to do, finish them when you get back, okay?" Collins backed out of the door, without closing it after him. Goodrich thumped the desk-top with clenched fists. He was wishing he had a hammer in his drawer.

"Yeah, okay! I'll have my lunch now!" He was talking to

himself.

Maynard approached the address he had for the office he was to occupy. It appeared to be in a modest-sized block, with apparently four parking spaces behind allocated to the firm. There were other parking spaces, free to occupy, which he assumed would be available for visitors. He pulled into one of those, checked his watch. He was a little early, but still climbed out of his car and made for the door. It was a common entrance, and on seeing a small board listing the four occupants, he saw that the lawyer's firm occupied one half of the first floor. He noted that the office would be facing roughly south-west, so warm in the afternoon. He was always conscious of any property orientation. There was no lift, not that he would expect one in a two-story building, but he did wonder if the firm lost wheelchair-dependent clients. He took the stairs two at a time, then opened the door to the lawyer's office. Immediately inside, he saw a girl sitting in front of a small PC, and along the other wall a few chairs and a small table with a few magazines. He took this as being the reception area, looked over by a secretary. She glanced up as he entered.

"Hello! You must be Mister Maynard?"

"That's right. To see your Chris Goodrich." She stood up and offered her hand for a shake.

"Good. I'm Debbie, secretary and general dog's-body. Follow me, please. Chris is waiting for you." She led him to the far room, there being two rooms each side of the short corridor. She pushed open the door. Goodrich was sitting at a desk with a small pile of files, one of which was open and the one he appeared to be working on. He stood up and extended his hand across the table.

"Mike … welcome. I see you've met Debbie! Our two fee-earners are both out currently, but I'll show you round." Maynard's first impression was good. The place was fairly new, better furnished and better décor than in their head-office. He was, though disappointed that he would not meet the guy he was replacing. After a whizz round the offices, the two men returned to the first room.

"Right, Mike. While Debs is making the coffee, let me give you a few ideas of how we operate." Goodrich started as though he were introducing property conveyancing as an entirely new concept. He was clearly trying to give the impression that what he was saying was of interest, and that he was enjoying what he was doing. Maynard was not fooled. He just knew that Goodrich was trying to justify his being there, and wanted to escape back to the head-office as soon as possible, and without giving Goodrich the impression that he wasn't interested in the shit he was spouting, Maynard chipped in with some relevant questions.

"Thanks for that, Chris. Now what is the monthly turnover and how does it compare with the business plan targets?" It was clearly a question the man could not answer. But he picked up his coffee ... the tables were now turned. It was the interviewer who was playing the coffee trick, basically having a rapid think.

"Er ... good question. Er ... we have two fee-earners in this office. The family-law side and the conveyancing. I do not recall the two separate figures, but we look for roughly a turnover of three times the combined salaries ..." Nice one, mate, Goodrich was thinking, "... and that covers the non-fee-earners, plus running costs and rent." And in case his new man was thinking it was perhaps not reasonable, he added, "... of course, that is flexible. Depends on the time of year, naturally."

"Of course." And so as to not disappoint Goodrich after his inventing the figures, he added, "... seems reasonable enough." Goodrich's guess was pretty good, but the division of one third to the earner, one third partner profits and one third on overheads, indicated to Maynard that the head office was not apparently doing well at all. Even a brief dip into the subject of expected earnings was a fifteen-paragraph summary. He also wondered about the staff turnover, but he knew that would put Goodrich in a spot. High staff turnover is an indicator of something wrong as it loses out in a decreased capacity for billable hours, reduces expertise, wastes startup costs and recruitment fees and lost clients. Goodrich looked at his guest, as if to say, 'anything else?'. Instead,

"Well, I have an appointment in the other office now ... maybe you can get Debbie to have a chat about her side of things, I mean what she does to assist on the conveyancing." He stood up. "I'll leave you to it then. Let me know how you wish to proceed. I'll call Debbie then be on my way." That was it. He was out of the office like a rat down a drain. Maynard finished his coffee, then Debbie walked in.

"Mister Maynard ..."

"Call me Mike, please! Will I meet the guy who is leaving?"

"Mike. No That was Sam Cottrell. He left over two weeks ago. I don' t suppose Chris or Ian told you that!"

"No, they didn't! But they gave me the impression that he was just away today ... they didn't even tell me his name!"

"Sam. Sam Cottrel. A really nice bloke, and he ..." Debbie turned away. She was clearly upset. "I'm sorry." Maynard changed the subject.

"And Margaret?"

"Oh, she's in court today. She should be back soon though. The girl seemed to have recovered, then the 'phone rang. Debbie moved to answer it, and Maynard moved away to let her get on with her job. He was both surprised and annoyed that he had not been told the truth. Maybe he could find out later. Debbie finished the call and made a note in the incoming calls log. "And I have Sam's number. He told me he'd be happy to talk to you at any time. I think there is a few things he would like to discuss!" Maynard thought that was distinctly possible.

"I'm okay with that. In fact, give him my number, as I don't want to call him at any inconvenient moment."

"Good idea!" Debbie picked up a pad of post-it notes and a pen. "Shoot!" He gave her the number. "Right. I don't suppose there would be any problem if I were to call you? I mean, maybe out of working hours if we encounter any problems?" Maynard was warming to the girl. She was being honest and if he did take the job, she might be useful. And if the whole business folded, he could possibly engage her as staff in his own office, if, that is, he went down that route.

"No problems with that, Debbie! Anyway, can you show me where I would be working? I mean Sam's old office?"

"Yes. I sometimes sit in and do Sam's work while Maggie keeps an ear on the 'phone. Let me show you all the rooms. Neither Chris nor Ian ever come in to help out, so I have had to do it all. I've been doing it for quite a time anyway!" The girl went up in his estimation. He imagined from what he'd seen of Collins that he was probably a bit of a misogynist. The office was neat, an uncluttered desk, and as a bonus it was light and airy. The furniture was a bit care-worn but otherwise okay, but the largest room, the interview room, was well furnished with a large table and comfortable chairs, eight of them in all and not looking a bit cluttered. "This is where Ian and Chris hold their various meetings ... far more impressive that the head office! And sometimes I have to act as hostess, like making coffees and fetching lunches from the nearby take-away!"

"Actually quite nice! And what about your PC, Debbie? It looks a bit ancient!"

"Oh, it bloody well is! But when they have some offers in the computer store, I could swap it for a better one!" Maynard felt that the girl was a bit reserved about her comments, but he put it down to their being unfamiliar.

"Well, maybe that's something we could look at if I take the job!" Debbie looked up at him, sharply, in fact she seemed alarmed even.

"Oh, you must! Er ... I mean it would be nice to have you here with us!" Just then, like a ship in full sail, Margaret walked into the office.

"Oh, hello! Debs, aren't you going to introduce me to your friend?" The new arrival looked Maynard up and down, approvingly.

"This, Madge, is or could soon be, our new lawyer! Mike Maynard!" She extended her hand and took his giving it a damn good shake.

"Maggie aka known as Madge, Madge Bell. I sincerely hope you will be! You look like you could handle me and our Debs, and sort out those two plonkers from head-office! Sam left in rather a hurry, and frankly unless someone comes in pretty sharpish, Debs and I will be having Prozac with our coffees, *nes-pä*, Debbie? You know, Fluoxetine, the antidepressant of the serotonin reuptake inhibitor used for the treatment of major depressive disorder ..."

"Yes, Madge, we know your new client is an expert on the stuff and took a lot of it according to all the evidence about the abuse she suffered over too many years, and has now found it was about time she dumped her old man, but I thought you were on it already!"

"So you have said on numerous occasions, love, but may I remind you to tell your boyfriends that it does not treat premature ejaculation!" Maynard laughed.

"Wow, Margaret, I bet you go down well at parties! I don't mean flogging drugs either!"

FOUR

On his way back home, Maynard made a decision. He would take the job. Yes, he had nagging doubts, but the negatives, although outweighing the positives, he could handle. Half-way through his journey, his mobile rang. He connected via his hands-free.

"Hello!"

"Hi. Is that Mike Maynard?"

"Yes. How can I help!" Maynard knew it was Sam.

"Sam Cottrell. Debbie gave me your number. Can you talk?"

"Yes. However, I'm driving at the moment. Can I call you back as soon as I get home? Be about half an hour."

"No problem. I look forward to your call." It took no time for Maynard to arrive home and park up. His wife was out, but a note on the kitchen table told him that she was out doing a big shop with the kids. He made himself a lemon tea with a squirt of honey, sat at the kitchen table and called Sam.

"Sam. Mike Maynard."

"Hi, Mike thanks for getting back to me. I suppose you have met Ian and Chris? And Maggie and Debbie?"

"Yes. The girls seem to be pretty switched on. Can't quite fathom Collins, but ..."

"Yeah, I think he's a bit of an oddball, but you'll be dealing with the Green office as I call it ... an abbreviation of its location obviously. I expect you'd like to know why I left?"

"Well nobody has told me ... I assume it was a pretty hurried decision?"

"Yes, it was. Let me tell you why. I have a nephew, nice lad, and he worked for a firm of solicitors for a while, as a clerk. He'd been there for about three years when he was suddenly sacked. Anyway, it all became very messy and I agreed to look into his case. I won't go into any detail, but I have on my hands a personal emergency ... my mum has had a few bad turns, and I have agreed to look after her, become her full-time carer, and I mentioned it to Collins but frankly, Mike he ignored me. When I reached the deadline, I just left. What I'd like you to do for me is perhaps look after my nephew's case. You are a solicitor, and you may well have some experience of criminal law, certainly more than I have as a conveyancer, and all he needs is advice … for the moment. Thing is, he lives with his mum very close to the office. His name is Nick Forrester. He can fill you in with the details if you agree. At the moment, he's unemployed, but is a good worker. I can have him drop off the file for you to look through before you agree to take it on, of course. He can pay, 'cos he has just sold his house …" Maynard recognised a pleading tone in Sam's voice.

"Sam, okay. Let me see the file. Then I can decide. Of course, I'll do what I can to help, and I'll do it on a pro-bono basis if he can cover any expenses. Anyway, any concerns about this office? I mean the Green?"

"No, not really. Debbie is brilliant, looks after everything very well, and Maggie is great company. There's plenty of work. And if you need anything from me, just ask. If you take Nick's case, I'll be mightily relieved."

"Okay, get the file to me … and I'll let you know. Thanks Sam. And look after your mum. Cheers." Maynard leaned back in his chair. He didn't want to sound too negative to a guy who had a problem, nor did he want to take on something or someone who would prove difficult. He was very aware of how things could creep up on a person, just as that Nelson bloke had said in Professor Slater's talk, and more especially in the little handbook he was given after the lecture. He was doubly wary because he was once turned-over by a bloke who worked for him, and the business had acted as guarantor for his car and the small house he was given to live in, and the bloke turned rogue, paid nothing and cost the firm a good few thousand pounds. It was a cheap lesson for him, but he'd never let himself be caught again. He heard his wife come into the house. She had two bulging shopping bags and two hungry children.

"How can you manage a big shop and the kids? You must be worn-out!"

"No, not really! I had Elaine with me and we even managed

to have a drink and stickies in the little café there. I dropped her off on the way back. How was your day?"

"The office is pretty okay, better than their head-office and I'm minded to take the job. I've suggested that I can probably do a few WFH sessions if I need to look after Theo and Robyn ... and the secretary there, Debbie seems well clued-up! And I spoke to Sam, Sam Cottrell, the guy who's leaving ... correct that, the guy who has already left!"

"What was his case?" Karen was talking as she put all the shopping away.

"His mum. He's having to look after her full-time. Saves him having to put her into full-time care I expect, and at about two thousand quid per week, it makes a lot of sense to me, and where the carers are paid bugger-all I cannot imagine dumping you into care when you finally lose it!!"

"No chance ... you'll go first!!"

"Well, if I ever get to that stage love, I'll top myself to make sure that you and the kids get to keep the house!"

"Right! I'll start working on that! How do you want to go?"

"That's easy ... I can eat myself to death on your cooking!"

After his evening meal, Maynard went to his little office and sent an e-mail to the Collins and Goodrich office and copied to the agency, saying that he accepted them assignment, and asked for a start date. The following morning, his 'phone picked up the replies. The agency had obviously heard from Collins. An ideal start-date was the coming Monday.

Back at the head-office, Collins once again burst into Goodrich's office.

"We've got him!!" Goodrich looked up.

"Explain!"

"The Maynard bloke! I've asked that he starts on Monday. So if you can liaise with Debbie and between you deal with any completions until then, it might be a good idea!"

"Well, that will be say, Wednesday, Thursday and Friday … I'll have to be pretty smart about it … do Debbie's then dash back here to do mine!"

"Yeah! I've already told Debs. Anyway, I'll leave the way you do it entirely up to you. Gotta go … seeing Arnold now!" Collins left the office, leaving the door open. Goodrich lifted his eyes to the ceiling.

"Yeah, fuck off, why don't you!" He spoke under his breath.

At the Green, Debbie put the 'phone down after getting the news from her boss. She shouted over to Maggie.

"Maggie! It looks like that nice Mike Maynard is going to be working for us! Break out the Champaigne! Downside, misery-guts Goodrich will be here on Wednesday to Friday helping me to do the completions!"

"Yeah, that's great! And I think if you shared an office with Collins you'd be a misery guts as well! I feel sorry for the bugger!"

"Yes, I do feel for the bloke. But he seems to put up with it so maybe Collins has something on him."

"Possible. That's why Arnie puts up with it … snorting coke is the answer … ! Hey, there's someone in reception!" Debbie backed out of the office to go to reception. She recognised Nick Forrester.

"Nick! Hi … What …!"

"Oh, hello, Debbie. Sam asked me to drop this off for Mike Maynard. Is that okay?" The bloke was young and very good-looking, and the girl knew that he was in some kind of trouble that Sam had been helping him with. He had also helped out in the office from time to time.

"Of course, no problem. How are you keeping? Your mum?"

"Thanks, both fine. I've put my number on the outside of the envelope. Mike can call me any time if he needs to, is that okay?"

"Of course. Do you want a coffee or something?"

"Would, but I've left mum in the car so I suppose I'd better

leave now. Thanks anyway." Then he was gone. Debbie slipped the envelope into her desk drawer. She didn't want Goodrich to get hold of it. She sent a text to Maynard's 'phone.
'Am told you will be joining us on Monday! Glad you decided to come and work with us. Maggi's delighted. Nick dropped some papers in for you to look at. He was here sometimes working with Sam. I have put the stuff away so Chris doesn't get hold of it. He'll be here for the next three days helping me with the work. That okay?' The response was almost immediate. 'Thanks. Yes, I agreed to have a look at the stuff. Maybe you could have a whip through it so we can both keep an eye on it. See you soon.'
"Will do. I'll maybe take it home tonight rather than having it floating all over the office here. I have no idea what it's about, but it's nobody else's business. See you on Monday!" Debbie pulled out the envelope and shoved it into her shopping bag. It should not take too long to whizz through it as Mike suggested.

At home, Debbie shoved a standard fourteen-inch pizza into the oven. Her excuse for eating one per week at least was because as a pizza expert, she knew it was an excellent source of calcium and protein with bioengineered food ingredients and real cheese, two hundred and fifty calories, low cholesterol and fifteen percent fat. Wouldn't kill her! She set the timer once the oven had reached the selected temperature, slid in the pizza, then sat at the kitchen table and opened Nick Forrester's envelope. The top page was blank, and she estimated that there were probably forty pages in all, held together neatly with a treasury tag. She turned the page and was instantly hooked. The page started with dates, the first over three years ago when Nick started working as a clerk for a small Reading firm. Further dates gave dates of charges for theft, trial and of imprisonment and release. Other pages were accounts set out how he was accused and convicted then jailed all on fabricated evidence and names of the police officers, solicitor and barrister involved in his defence. As Debbie read on, she became very emotional. In her mind's eye, she could see the guy, barely a man, and knew instinctively that he was not only innocent, but was incapable of committing the crime. Now, according to the law, he would never be able to follow his chosen profession. She ignored her pizza, and instead went to the lounge and poured herself a stiff slug of brandy. In bed, she was unable to sleep, tossing and turning until at last she dropped off, waking again at five am, and again started to cry, tears rolling down her cheeks onto the pillow. She rose at five thirty, had a long, hot shower and breakfasted on toast and coffee, then removed her pizza from the oven and sliced it into pieces and bagged it up to take to the office with her. She would share it with Maggie. She stuffed the Forrester file into her bag and walked the half-mile to the office. She was the first one there. She put the papers into a separate file and hid it in the back of the bottom drawer of a filing cabinet. As far as she recalled, neither Collins nor Goodrich actually knew that Nick Forrester ever visited his uncle at the office, and she certainly did not want to find either of the partners leafing through the file one day. She did know that Collins used to drop into the office at odd times, including evenings and weekends, but she had assumed he was probably just checking that everything was neat and tidy, but then she discovered he was going through the accounts cards as if trying to find lost cash. The office account was always in the red, and it must have been tough on the guy knowing that he was effectively reigning over a bankrupt business, but he only had himself to blame, and according to Goodrich, any money he did make would always go into his pocket, not to pay off any overdraft. The alternative explanation was that he was paranoid that the whole world, in his case conveniently compacted into his life, the offices and his neighbours, were conspiring against him and that with every turn he would uncover a series of actionable plots, and the Green office was at the centre of his paranoia, actually making millions without his ever knowing, but that his constant snooping would eventually prove that his suspicions were well-founded. Well, as long as it kept him happy.

At about nine am, Debbie sat down with the current conveyancing files, checking all was ready for the Friday rush. Mortgage funds applied for; bankruptcy searches done; completion statements sent to the clients. All in order ready to press the button on completion day. All the time, the Forrester case kept coming to mind. She made herself a coffee and recovered the file, to read through it once more. She would also make a cast-list, names and roles of every person mentioned. She could then do a search on them to see what she could find out about them. Once the new guy had found his feet, she would brief him. She wanted to be in on the act, not leave it all to him. At ten the 'phone rang.

"Hello …"

"Debbie … Sam. Nick tells me he has given you the file, the one which the new guy, Mike is going to look at. I think I ought to tell you that I have not told anybody else about this, neither Ian nor Chris, of course. However, I think the lad was the victim of a shameful, deliberate conspiracy by other parties involved, and it upsets me terribly and poor Nick is beside himself …he walked into a trap! I would …"

"Sam …! Don't worry. I have the file and I'll help Mike deal with it. I promise you, it will not fall into the hands of anybody else, I promise!"

"Thank you, Debbie. I'm sure you'll know what to do to help Mike. He or you can call me at any time to update me. Thanks you again."

At head office, Arnold crept into Goodrich's office.

"Chris … how are we doing on the Fisher sale? Any progress?"

"Not really. The agents have had some stupid offers, and they will not agree to them in case the heir-hunters find family, and they then bitch about the house being virtually given away! Last thing they or we want is a bloody inheritance battle! I reckon that bearing in mind the lady's position, the contents alone could probably be auctioned-off for more than the last idiotic offer! The agents reckon it will be bought by a builder who will spend a few thou on the structure, decorate it and sell it for over a million! Anyway, what's the rush?"

"Dick-'eds chasing me for some reason. I think he's up to something. You heard him say that he wants to dump the account into the Green office … all the danger signals are flashing up! I reckon, Chris, that we ought to keep an eye on the bugger before he lands us all in the shit!"

"Where is he now, anyway?"

"I think he's gone to see his brother. I tell you, mate, something's in the wind! Keep an eye on him. I don't like his brother too much, either, and neither of them are on my Christmas-card list!"

"Let's put him on out letter-bomb list!" Arnold laughed.

The fears Debbie harboured that Mike would not pitch-up on Monday were unfounded. He arrived shortly after Debbie and Maggie and they were both overjoyed to see him.

"Right, maybe I ought to go through the work-in-progress files. I have no doubt, Debbie, that all is in order. Does Ian just let you get on with all the conveyancing? I mean when nobody else is in the office?"

"Yes! And I don't suppose he'd take the blame if I screwed everything up! Right, Madge, if you boil the kettle, I'll spend time on the conveyancing files with Mike."

FIVE

Collins' mobile rang. He could see it was his brother. He knew he could not ignore the guy forever.

"Yeah!"

"Where were you last night? I thought we had arranged to meet?"

"Yes ... sorry. Got called out on an urgent matter and left my bloody 'phone in the office. Have to ..." Mark knew his brother was an accomplished liar.

"Come now, then, it's my last day off for about two weeks. We're very shorthanded here these days. Be here in an hour. I'll feed you, okay?" Without waiting for a reply, he cut the connection.

"Your brother is an arsehole."

"I know that, Emma, so does the rest of the world, but we have to sort mum out. He's had about, I dunno, three hundred grand off mum, setting up his shit law business, and he's gonna have to sort it out. I ... we ... need some dosh if were gonna sell this place and move on. I'm not happy commuting to Winchester every bloody day, so we're gonna have to move!"

"That'd be good! Reading's a shithole!" His wife put the mug of lemon tea onto the arm of the sofa. Let's move as far away from your brother as possible. How about Australia?"

"Yeah ... go onto the internet and see what they've got going out there for jobs. Oz rather appeals to me!"

"Later. I'm going shopping now. Anything you want?"

"No thanks. love. I'll wait for bro to arrive. See you later!"

Back in the office, Collins scrabbled around for his Bellstaff motorcycle kit, and pulled it on. As he passed Hannah's desk, he told her to tell the others that he had an urgent court appointment, which even she thought was odd as he was wearing his motorbike kit, nor did he have a briefcase with him.

"Yes, of course Sir. When will you be back?"

"Tomorrow I expect!" Then he was gone. It was only forty minutes later that he pulled up outside his brother's house on the Oxford Road in Reading. The front door was open, with Emma dragging some shopping bags through the door into the kitchen. She had seen him arrive. Collins walked in, leaving the door open behind him. Emma tut-tutted as she quietly shut the door. She decided to sit in the kitchen while her brother-in-law was in the house. In the lounge, brother Mark had seen the guy arrive. Collins stood in the lobby and called for his brother.

"Mark?"

"In the lounge! Come in and make yourself at home. Coffee?"

"Yeah. One sugar please." Bro disappeared into the kitchen to see the kettle was already on. He fixed the cups.

"Emm, love, when the kettle boils, can you bring the coffees through please? Don't have any arsenic, do we?" Without waiting for a reply, he returned to the lounge and closed the door behind him. "Right, Ian, what's happening with mum's dosh?"

"Bloody hell, Mark, I've already told you …!"

"Well, tell me again!"

"I'm working on it. I've got this big deal coming off soon. It's a half-million pound job …"

"Ian, for fuck's sake, you're a lawyer … lawyers like you do not do half million pound jobs. Unless you're planning a bank heist!"

"No, Mark, really. It's a one-off … !" Then Emma entered with a tray of coffee and a plate of biscuits. She had heard the last exchange, and carefully placed the tray onto the small table, then turned to face her bro-in law.

"Ian … the whole world knows you're a fantasist! You expect us to believe that crap? Let me give you some ideas. What about this woman you are supposed to have known for over thirty years, the one in a senior position in government, the married one whose husband doesn't know about you! Is he brain-dead or something? Then all the other so-called ladies you're intimate with? Then the girl-friend, Trisha Slush? Or something like that! I mean, what kind of name is that? Sounds like a kiddie's lollipop or a children's hero character, a kiddie's story, like Harry Potter …!" Then she turned left the room, leaning against the doorframe, facing her husband, and looking at the back of Ian Collins' head. For a long time, nothing was said. Then,

"Well, Ian? What do you say?"

"What can I say? I mean, all that about my lady-friends is true …!"

"Bollocks! The problem is, Ian, you probably believe all that shit yourself. I mean, if I had a girlfriend for thirty years, virtually everybody I know would have met her, and I'd also suggest that you would have met her husband. Even a corpse would know by now that his wife was fooling about with somebody … unless she were married to a person who didn't actually have a brain. Look, mate, if you are going to come out with all this shit, make it at least remotely realistic, like a trillion-to-one chance! Then, what about this Slush girl! I mean, who made up that name? You know, Ian, I don't think you would recognise the truth if came up and slapped you in the face! Let's get down to the reality of the situation. Take the powers of attorney you did for mum and dad. Who gave you the idea that …"

"It was Arnold who did them for me. He's an expert and I just did what he said …"

"Ian, there you go again. You and I know neither mum nor dad signed them … you did. And neither mum nor dad would appoint you as their attorney, Ian, 'cos they have the same concerns about you as I and Emma do. Why didn't you do powers for health and welfare as well? Without one, the social services could remove her to a care-home, and you'd have no say in the matter, so goodbye two or three grand a week! And I doubt dad even signed his will either, 'cos any decent will-writer would have given the survivor a life-interest in the house, which, incidentally, they owned as tenants in common when dad died, and I suppose you know what tenants in common means? Well now mum is so far gone that I see a care-home looming up on the horizon, and because she is the sole-owner of the house, we could lose the whole fucking lot. Everything. Let's go a bit further back into your history, shall we? Even your degree … what did you get your degree in? Journalism? Education? Hair and make-up? You know I did all your assignments. You know why the Army sent you to University, Ian? Because nobody wanted to bloody-well work with you! Then they chucked you out! What do you say to that?"

"Everything you say is rubbish! You can't prove it! I know what I did …"

"Look, shall we stop beating about the bush. You, mate, are living …"

"Mark, you are talking …"

"Will you shut the fuck up! You will listen to me, after all, you have never listened to anybody else! The prisons are full of people who have said just what you have said that it's all lies and I can prove it, and I know that because it is my job. You are a law unto yourself, your behaviour … you ignore laws, rules, and conventional ways of doing things … you are living in a bubble, a bubble called 'Me'! On the inside it is a mirror, and wherever you look, front, left, right, behind, up or down, you see yourself. From the outside people see you, an introverted figure of fun, of ridicule, a person living in a fantasy world, shared by no-one except your own alter-ego. I feel desperately sorry for Arnold and Chris. Arnold retreats into his own little drug-induced world, and Chris just has nowhere else to go. You know how the Army wanted rid of you, but you are not entirely stupid, after all you did pass your law exams, and you also know that I gave you some serious help! I sometimes wonder, Ian, if you and I share the same parents, whether we are even half-siblings. So, while you finish your coffee, let me tell you how it's gonna be. You borrowed or maybe just took cash from mum to set up your law business. You have never had a decent trading year yet, not since you started. You have barely …"

"Mark! That is not true! I have been very …"

"Ian! Shut up! The time for bullshitting is over! Your behaviour makes me sometimes wonder if you should be sectioned …"

"What? What's 'sectioned'?"

"Oh, Jesus, I thought you were the lawyer? Section three of the Mental Health Act allows for a person to be admitted to hospital for treatment if their mental disorder is of a degree that requires treatment in hospital necessary for their health and or for the protection of other people! We are in reality street now!"

"That's just stupid!"

"Shut up and listen!" Collins was beginning to get the message. The first time since his sergeant once threatened to give him a good hiding because he would not shut his mouth and listen when he had been found planting evidence on a young recruit. He shut-up.

"Thank you! Now, you will, by this time next year, pay to me two hundred and fifty thousand pounds. That's number one. Number two. As mum's attorney, you and she will add your name to the deeds of the house, and immediately put it into a trust. She will have to assent to it 'cos otherwise it can't be done, and you will list yourself, and me and my kids and yours, if you've got any, as beneficiaries. You will appoint me, Emma and your Chris Goodrich as trustees. Then …"

"So, you been talking to him? Chris, I mean?"

"Not about you, no, but of all of you, that's of him, you and Arnold, I think he is the only one with any sense. Arnie is a bloody coke-head, that's obvious, after all I see them every bloody day, 'smy job, and Chris … he's gonna be the only guy I talk to on this. Now, it's not all uphill for you, because, and listen carefully on this, 'cos I won't repeat it, however you decide to do it, I do not wanna know, but I have at my disposal several hundred guys who can provide advice on just about every business, legal or otherwise, so let me know how you intend to go about it, and I'll send some blokes to see you. Make sense?" Collins knew he had no option. He also knew exactly what his brother was talking about.

"Yeah."

"And one last word. When you are with them, no bullshit about your women, I don't care about them, nor do I care what you are doing with, or to, those young girls who look after mum, but that will not be discussed with my blokes, okay? And, if you come to any agreements with them, stick to them. If you don't, you could finish up in the ICU …"

"The what?"

"Intensive care unit, like hospital. And you will not meet with my guys at mum's home. Only in one of your offices, and only when there is nobody else there, okay? You know, Ian, it's a great pity that you didn't come to your big brother when you were setting up your law firm. You could, by now, really be a millionaire, not facing bankruptcy! And you might actually know something about the law! Now, do you want a bite to eat?"

"No thanks. I've got to meet with some important people now."

"There you go again. Ian, remember this. The only other people in your life are your alter-egos, and if …"

"My what's? You said that before!" To Collins junior it sounded awfully impressive.

"Oh, for fuck's sake, Ian. An alter ego means an alternate self, believed to be distinct from a person's true self. Finding your alter ego will require finding your other self, one with a different personality. What I'm saying, is that when you attend these fanciful meetings, just pause and look into a mirror … it will be yourself you'll be looking at!" Even so, to Ian Collins it still sounded impressive. "… now, before you leave, remember this. You will keep me informed about what you are doing. You will also let me know when and if you need any help, what you need help with, either legal or more likely illegal, and I'll find the right person or persons. Do not try any of your usual bullshitting. Do not go back on any agreement you make with them …"

"I know, I know! You've already said that! I won't!"

"And anyway, my guys will keep me updated. And if you breach any of those conditions, I will go to the Public Guardian about those powers of attorney and the cops about your theft of mum's cash, and you never know, mate, you might even meet with a serious accident!" Collins stood up. Even he knew it was time to go.

"Right … I'll see yer then!" The front door closed behind Collins, and his brother watched as he mounted his motorbike and headed for home. Emma stepped in again.

"You know, love, I don't think you two are related. I wonder if it would be possible to do a DNA job on him!"

"Not a bad idea …maybe I could arrange for that. We'll see."

"And I tell you, Darling, the guy's a psychopath or a sociopath … or both!"

Back home, Collins checked on his mum. The young carers had gone. He climbed the stairs to his mum's room. She was sitting up in bed, asleep, a book lying on her stomach. He shook her into wakefulness.

"Mum? Mum? Wake up! This is urgent! There have been some burglaries in the neighbourhood! I'll have to move all your jewellery to a safe deposit box! Mum, where is all your jewellery?" Collins knew that whatever his mum had, it would be a start.

He left home late the next day, and drove to the office. He was in a black mood, smarting from the tongue-lashing he had from his brother.. He ordered a coffee from Hannah, and took a spare mug from the kitchenette. He spoke to nobody, but shut himself in his room and pulled his brandy bottle from the filing cabinet.

Hannah delivered his coffee. He took one sip, then shouted for her to make another one.

"There's no bloody sugar in it! Do another one! And get it bloody right!" Hannah was no push-over. She'd heard a lot of shouting from him, but today he seemed to be in a shit mood. She made a new coffee, and placed it onto Collins' desk.

"Sorry about the first one, sir. I'll …"

"Go! Just bloody go!" The girl clocked the brandy bottle. It was about half-full, and a glass next to it was about a quarter full. Then she left the office. Collins buzzed Arnolds number.

"Yeees?"

"Arnie … how are we doing on the Fisher file? Sold the house yet?"

"No idea. Call Chris. He's the guy in charge of the sale. Or call the estate agents."

"Okay." He buzzed Chris and asked the same question.

"Heard nothing, Ian. What's the hurry?"

"Wanna get the account paid of course. What are you charging for the sale?"

"About four thousand, why?"

"What's it on the market for?"

"Seven fifty."

"You're charging too little. Double it. Haven't got any estate beneficiaries yet, have we?"

"No, but …"

"Okay. Double it." Collins cut the line then called Arnold again.

"What are you charging for the probate job? Excluding the sale?"

"About five grand. We've got more than that in the account now. Do you want me to transfer that to the office account?"

"Yes." Collins took a gulp of his coffee and emptied the brandy cup as well. He was thinking, what's two-fifty minus nine. He concluded it made bugger-all difference to the money his brother wanted. He decided to do a check on the office account, to see if the overdraft was down. Last time he checked it was seven thousand in the red. It was now eight over drawn, and he has the Century Agency bill to pay them for finding the Maynard bloke. He phoned his third office and asked to talk to then fee-earner there to come up with his work-in-progress figure. It was not encouraging. Then he called Debbie.

"That new bloke turned up?"

"Yes he's here. Wanna talk to him?"

"No. How many cases has he got on for completion this week?"

"Between now and Friday, seven …"

"What's that worth?" Debbie knew the answer because he always wanted to know whenever he called. It'll be seven times two and a half. Thou."

"What's that in pounds shillings and pence!"

"Call it seven times five, that's thirty-five and half it … seventeen fifty, okay?"

"Yeah, thanks." Then he was gone. He buzzed Arnold again. "Put all the Fisher estate total monies into the Green client account please. Then do the same with the house funds. Like ASAP. As soon as it's sold."

"Yeah, okay. I'll tell Chris." Arnold might be keen on snorting coke and drinking, but he was no fool. He slipped out of his chair and dropped in on Chris. He pushed the door shut behind him.

"Hey, Chris, what the fuck's Colin up to? He seems to have some fixation on the Fisher money? Wants it all to go into the Green client account!"

"Dunno. Maybe he wants to open a trust account there but frankly, I don't give a shit what he does with it. Don't worry about it! Not your problem, mate! But if I were you, I'd keep a note of exactly what the bugger wants! And I'll do the same!"

Hannah was not happy being shouted at. She had heard her boss shout at other people in the office, and that upset her as well. She was supposed to be there to learn about the law, not how to answer a 'phone and clean up the office. She slipped into Pam's office, where all the documents were produced on the word-processors.

"Pam …"

"Yes love?"

"I am not coming back here tomorrow. Mister Collins shouted at me, and it's not right. And all I've done here so far is answer the 'phones and clean up the office, and I should be learning stuff about the law. I want to be a legal secretary not a skivvy!"

"I think that's a fair point. Leave it with me … maybe I can get you into the green office, where Debbie works. You've spoken to her haven't you?"

"Yes. She's nice. Thank you. So I'll leave tonight, and if I give you my mobile number you can let me know if Debbie wants me!"

"I'm sure she does! Leave it with me, love!" As soon as Hannah left then typing pool, Pam called Debbie and set out the problem. Debbie agreed that it would be okay for the girl to turn up in the morning and she'd look after her.

"It's really not fair! The man's an animal! No, Pam, tell her we'd be delighted to see her. And thanks." The secretary scribbled a note with the Green office number and that Debbie would be delighted to see her, and slipped the paper onto Hannah's desk.

"Here, love! Get there tomorrow. They would all love to see you. You know where the place is?"

"Yes … in fact it's nearer to my house, a lot nearer! Thanks." Pam also slipped a twenty-pound note into her hand. That's from all of us in the pool. Good luck, and keep us informed about how you get on!"

"Oh, Pam …!" The girl was close to tears. But she was also not going to let Collins get away with his behaviour towards her. Towards the end of the afternoon, she did her usual round of collecting the dirty cups and cleaning the kitchenette. She cleared Collins office when he had slipped into Goodrich's room and she saw that the brandy bottle was almost empty. It gave her an idea. She knew Collins drove a black double-cab Ford Ranger. She nipped downstairs to make a note of the vehicle registration number. Then she called her dad's mobile number to talk about her day and about Collins.

"… and this afternoon he drank a lot of brandy, probably getting on for half a bottle!"

"Okay, thanks, Han! Leave it with me." Detective chief inspector Mike Ellis had every reason to believe his daughter. He swivelled round in his chair and beckoned to one of his traffic officers. "Ted … look after this one for me please… just had this come in. Stake out the vehicle and stop him on the slightest infringement and do a breathalyser … its good info. He'll probably be heading home so find the address from the DVLA .. usual stuff Okay?"

"You've got it Chief!"

SIX

By three pm, Debbie and Maynard had dealt with all the WIP files, and Debbie had taken two new instructions from a local estate agent. She dumped the two new files onto Mike's desk.

"As soon as I get the sale particulars through, I put them into the files and start the searches and ask for a deposit against disbursements. I doubt the office account here will bear those … Colin keeps or tries to keep it at balance zero, putting all spare cash into his head-office account, so any payments I get I keep on the client account to keep him away from it."

"Makes sense … what do you want to do now? Look at Nick's file?"

"Good idea. But first, let me give you a brief on the case so far. I can tell you, it stinks!"

"Okay, let's go for it!" The two sat in the conference room, with

Debbie setting the slim Forrester file on the table.

"Right, by all accounts he, Nick, managed to nick about a hundred and eighty thousand quid from his firm while he was there for his articles. That was a period of just under three years, in fact it was thirty months. I did some sums. It meant that he apparently stole six grand per month, which is fifteen hundred quid per week. Per week! Three hundred pounds per working day. Apparently, it went unnoticed until the thirtieth month of his being with the firm. How are we doing so far?"

"Er… hang on a minute … firstly, I assume it was supposed to be from the clients' account?"

"Correct. Secondly, how could that amount of money go missing without any clients complaining. As far as I can tell from the file, that is also correct, and if any clients had raised an issue of missing dosh, then then standard protocol would kick-in, and if the firm could not deal with it then the firm or the client would get to the Law Society?"

"Also correct, Debbie. Something is not right!"

"You can say that again! And, Mike, it gets worse, a lot worse!"

"Maybe I ought to take the file home and read it then tomorrow we can have another chat. Is there any information on the firm which apparently lost the money?"

"Yes there is. Sam made some notes on it. By all accounts, it was a small firm, one office, which mainly worked for one or two property-developers, who referred all or most of their buyers to that firm, and according to Sam, they took a rake-off from the lawyers' money they were paid for the jobs. Look, Mike, it's all in the file. Take it home and see what you make of it, okay? And then we can chat tomorrow. Possibly."

Back home and after dinner and getting the kids to bed, Maynard sat at the dining table and opened the Forrester file. Someone had obviously taken a lot of time to compile it, and it had been set out in chronological order, listing each event as it occurred. He had a notebook at his side, and commenced reading and making a series of notes and questions where he thought further information should be sought. The first questions were how and why, as an articled clerk, did Nick have access to the clients' accounts if indeed he did, secondly, was it alleged that he used cheques or internet-banking to shift money and thirdly, there was no information as to where the allegedly stolen money went to. As he read on, Maynard found some answers. In all, he spent two hours reading and making notes, and decided that it would be necessary for him to have a meeting with Nick. The whole deal just looked wrong. He hoped that the lad was able to deal with the issues he had raised in his notes. Even in bed, he was plagued with issues buzzing around in his head. There was a great deal of work to be done. The involvement of the Criminal Cases Review Commission intrigued him. He remembered the words of Professor Holly Slater; '... *the appeal process including the much-maligned Criminal Cases Review Commission has long been on its knees.*' He remembered the booklet he was given at the event, and determined to dig it out and see the professor's full take on the CCRC. Then he fell asleep.

At the same time as Maynard was working on the Forrester file, Collins had been in custody for two hours, locked in a cell. He was not happy.

"Do you want to call your lawyer, sir?"

"No! I am a bloody lawyer! This is an outrage!"

"Sir, calm down! You have been arrested and charged with drink-driving. You blew well over the legal limit in the intoximeter, and we stopped you because you ran a red light and we ..."

"It was not red!"

"Sorry, that's a matter for the magistrates. We cannot let you go ... "

"Why not?"

"If you'll let me finish! ... Unless you arrange travel to your home, but your car will be retained by us for the time being! Now, do you wish to call anybody?"

"No. I'll take a taxi home! And I'll need my car ... my mother is in need of care and I cannot ..."

"Then call a family member!"

"No! I'll deal with it myself. I'll take a taxi home!" Collins knew he was screwed. He also knew that on his appearance in the magistrates' court, the press would be there, and his case would be all over the papers. "Er ... look, sergeant, can't we deal with this here and now? Can't you just fine me and get it over with? I'm a busy man, and will need to get back to the office first thing tomorrow ..."

"No we can't. You will be ... if you are convicted in the court you will also lose your licence for a while, of that I am certain. Now, sir, order your taxi please, and go home." It was clear to the police officer that he was annoying Collins, but that didn't bother him in the least. When the lawyer had left the station, a wooden box was placed on the custody-sergeant's desk.

"What's that?" The PC opened the lid.

"Looks to me like a collection of jewellery." The sarge looked at it.

"D'you reckon it has been nicked?"

"No idea. Maybe that stroppy lawyer can tell you! Would be nice if it was!" They both laughed. It was not until Collins arrived home that he realised his mum's jewellery was in his car.

"Shit!"

Collins had a bad night. In the morning he 'phoned Pam to ask her to pick him up and take him to the office. She was not happy, but agreed on the basis that he would pay for her petrol. She did not ask why she was required to pick him up, but she resolved to raise the question when she collected him. She arrived at shortly before ten in time to see the two young carers get dropped off for a day's work with Mrs Collins. He did not see Collin's car. As Pam drove away from the house, she raised the question.

"Where's the car, Ian?" He had clearly not thought about how he would answer the obvious question.

"Er ... I lent it so someone yesterday, and he's not returned it yet."

"Okay. By the way, Hannah has left. She said it was because you shouted at her and that she was supposed to be training as a legal secretary and not just ..."

"That's bollocks! Anyway, good riddance! Now I suppose you'll have to find a replacement?"

"Me? ...Why don't you use the Domino Agency? That's where I come from!"

"What's the Domino Agency?"

"You know! It's Arnold's girlfriend's business ... it was meant to be called the Domandoff Agency, meaning domestic and office, but that sounded silly so it was shortened to Domino."

"I knew nothing about that!"

"But you did ask Arnie to organise the staff ... said you were too busy!"

"Oh, Jesus!" It was getting too much. His brother, the drink-drive job, his mum's jewellery ... the cops will have it all by now .. then his staff leaving. It surely can't all be his fault, could it? "Better get someone in then I suppose!"

At the Green, Debbie welcomed Hannah to her new role.

"Welcome, Hannah! You will be in with me now, and we'll share the 'phone work and I'll also give you some little tasks to do. Firstly some filing tasks, then I'll a give you a book so you can write some wills, then we'll move on from there. I assume you have a word-processor at home?"

"Yes, of course!"

"Right, come and meet the staff" When she met Maynard

again, Hannah asked if he was related to Karen Maynard, a lecturer at her college.

"Vaguely ... she's my wife! So I hope that she now tells all her friends about me so I can earn some money!"

"Oh, I'll do that! Don't want them to go to Collin's office, do we! I don't suppose you have spoken to him today, have you?"

"No, I haven't but Pam spoke to me today. For some reason he had lost his car or something ..."

"I think something is more appropriate!"

"Do you know something we don't?"

"Possibly. My dad told me he's been caught drink-driving. He asked if it was my boss, so of course I had to tell him. I expect it'll be in the papers soon."

"What does your dad do, Hannah?"

"He's a police officer!" Debbie immediately thought of the Forrester case. She'd have a quiet word with Mike to see if they could ask if Hannah's dad knew the officers involved in Forrester's case.

When Collins got to his office, he saw the nearly-empty brandy bottle on his desk. He called Pam to make him a coffee so he could drink what was left of the brandy and drop the bottle into the bin. It suddenly occurred to him that the stop last night was somewhat questionable at best. Then he got to wondering. What if ...? He picked up the bottle and looked at it. He wondered again, this time if anonymous tip-offs about alleged wrongdoing were actually legal. He convinced himself that they were not. Maybe he should get one of those lawyers who guarantee to get you off any drink-drive charge. He had an overwhelming feeling that he was being victimised. Suddenly, everything was going pear-shaped. Nothing was his fault, but he failed to realise that the mouth is the insight into your brain. It was what he said that turned people off him, but it was his own doing. He decided he had to get moving with his plans. He went to Arnold's office.

"Hey, you didn't tell me you ran an agency for domestic and office staff?" Arnold didn't even look up.

"I don't. And anyway you didn't ask."

"Pam told me you did!"

"She might have done, but she was wrong, I don't." Collins could see that he was going to get nowhere with this. He changed tack.

"Have you put the Fish monies into the Green account yet?"

"No. We might have a problem with the house sale."

"Why?"

"Ask the agents. I think there's a right-of-way dispute with the neighbours or something, and the estate might be liable."

"What exactly?" Finally, Arnold looked up. Collins was being more tiresome than usual.

"Ian, there's the bloody file … if you want to take on the job, take the fuckin' file and get on with it!" Collin's day was getting worse. He still had no idea when or how he was going to get back home after work. He backed out of Arnold's office and made himself a coffee. Pam intercepted him.

"Ian, do you want me to take you home later?"

"No."

"When then? When will you get your car back?" The whole office now knew he had been picked up for a drink-drive offence, but nobody was going to let on.

"What time do you usually go home, Pam?"

"When I finish … I could do five if that's alright."

"Yeah, okay. That'll do." Collins knew he would have to face the beaks in due course. He had called a firm of solicitors and without giving his real name, but sounding as though he was going to engage then anyway, he asked what sort on information they would want for a plea in mitigation. He said that he was a lawyer, but from a town a long way from his actual location. He thanked them for the information, promising to get in touch later. Then he hand-wrote his plea, read it over then stuck it in his jacket pocket. Then he went to Arnold's office again. Pam had told him that they needed a new receptionist-cum cleaner as nobody else in the office had the time or were even prepared to do the job.

"Arnold …"

"What?"

"We need to talk …" Arnold knew what the guy wanted, the Fisher money and a new receptionist, but let him ramble on.

At the Winchester jail, Mark Collins called on one of his warders.

"Chuck … go and fetch Smudge for me will you? I've got a job for him."

"Righto, boss. Hopefully he won't still be suffering from his overdose. God only knows what it was he was taking, but the reaction was clearly not what he was expecting!" The warder disappeared to fulfil his mission. Smudge was a habitual offender, but he had certain qualities which made him useful to prisoners and warders alike. He was actually highly intelligent, and had a mind like a sponge, absorbing information and contacts like he was a computer. Life for him was easy. He exchanged information for whatever it was he wanted, be it fags, drugs or 'phones. Most of the time he was barely conscious, but when he was alert his services were in great demand from all. His cell door opened.

"Smudge!"

"Hey, Chuck, it's Mister Smudge to you! You ought to keep up with the prison-service protocols, mate!"

"Yeah, sure! Mark wants a quick word. Like now." The con sensed a deal coming up. He could do with a few favours now, like getting his 'phone back. After all, no 'phone put his business on hold.

"On my way! Let's go!" The meeting was as usual to be held in the office of the prison library, which was usually empty when the library was shut.

"Pull up a chair, Smudge. Right. This is the deal. I'm looking for a couple of cops, local, who might be of some use in assisting a mate of mine, I use the term loosely, to nick some dosh from his clients." Smudge knew straight away who the boss was referring to.

"Yer brother, right? Just been fingered for a drink-drive job, yeah? The lawyer?" That was something Mark Collins did not know.

"What? You serious?"

"Yeah ... d'you mean he ain't told you yet? Hell, man, that brother of yours, he ain't too well liked, y'know! And he's gonna get you into trouble one day!" The guy was genuinely shocked, and Smudge could see that.

"Well, brother or not. I need help. This is the deal ..." Within fifteen minutes, Smudge had the message.

"Two? Both Reading? Detective Sergeant Ronnie Dent and Detective Constable Johnny Forbear. They done it before. Now me 'phone please." Collins passed the phone. Job done.

Back in his office, Mark Collins called his brother's mobile.

"Ian? Got some info for you. Working on the deal we discussed. There'll be a Ronnie Dent and a Johnny Forbear wanting to see you. I've given them your 'phone number. All meetings will be after hours, to meet at the Green. And by the way, when you've been pulled up for drink driving job, please let me know! You'll probably need a driver for about a year now!"

"How did you ... ! What the hell are you on about? Where did you ...!"

"From an unimpeachable source, mate! Do you need a driver or not?" Collins knew he was lumbered.

"Yes."

"I'll give you details. You sort out the insurance!"

"Of course!" Collins was dying for a pee, so he left the office and passing Pam's office asked her to do a quick coffee for him.

"Yeah of course! But if you shout at me, so help me, I'll pour it over your head!" Collins was nonplussed. It seems that over the course of just a few days, he had become the subject of abuse and disrespect. Or that was how he looked at it.

SEVEN

Maynard sidled into Debbie's office.

"When you have some time, could we go through the Forrester file? I've made some notes."

"Good idea. Then I think we ought to get the lad in and ask him the obvious questions. I must admit, there are quite a few what I would call loose-ends, but I'm sure he can answer them."

"I damn well hope so! I'm thinking that maybe we ought to do the meetings away from the office in case Ian turns up, as you say he is wont to do. That'd be rather embarrassing! Do you live far from here?"

"No, only a short walk actually. And you have Nick's address, again he is sort of local."

"Right then, how about we get him to set a date and we all meet at my place, then I can run you home. Karen can feed us and we can take as long as we need, but as you say, you and I need to talk first, okay?"

"Yeah. And I let Sam know what we are doing."

"Okay. I'm kind of done for the day on the conveyancing files, and if Hannah is able to go through the little tasks you set her then maybe she can keep an ear out for the 'phone?"

"Yes … and by the way, we had two new jobs in today … from the college, with another on the way from the golf club. It looks like your little campaign is paying off!"

When Collins got back from his comfort-break, the coffee was on his desk, and his mobile showed a missed call. He got up again, closed the closed his office door, sat down and dialled the missed call.

"Yeah!"

"I think you called me just now. Ian Collins here!"

"Yeah, I did. You want a job done, yeah? My name is Johnny. Me mate Ron is here with me. What do you want done?"

"Well, I can't talk now, but maybe we could have a meet somewhere?"

"Yeah, of course. But even if I scratch me bum on your behalf, it'll cost yer. Our fees are a hundred an hour. Each. Payable on completion of the job. When do you wanna meet, and where?"

My Green office ..." Collins gave the address and postcode. "I have a quiet office there. I'll make sure that you get fed and watered, okay? How long do you think we'll need?"

"'Ow long is a piece of string? Dunno. Depends on what you have to tell us. And by the way, we're pretty busy now, so lookin' at Ron he's saying next Friday? Say six in the evening?"

"Yeah, that's okay!"

"Have to be mate! Right, see yer then." And the line was disconnected. Collins decided he didn't want any cock-ups. These guys sounded pretty rough diamonds. He called Debbie in the Green office.

"Debbie, Ian, Ian Collins. I have an important conference next Friday, so can you please make sure the big room is free and clean? If you want to earn a few extra pounds, I'd like you to do the hostess bit, you know, do the coffees and drinks ... I'll bring a few beers, and then we can order a take-away from the place just down the street, if that's okay?"

"Sounds good to me. What is the start time and how long will it go on for?" Collins did not want her to be hanging around for the whole time. He wanted the food and stuff first then she can bugger off and he and the cops can get down to business without having her ear-wigging all the time.

"Dunno. If you deal with the take-aways as soon as we arrive, you can then just go home. Hope to start at six-ish."

"Okay, do you want me to do the nice little place cards? It looks very professional."

"Yeah ... one for me and one for Ronnie Dent ... er ...Ronnie D ... "

"Is that just a 'D' or a D E E?"

"Just a D. And a Johnny F Just an F please."

Okay. I'll hang around until they've had their pizzas then go home."

"Great." Collins left a message on Ron's mobile telling him what he had arranged. Almost immediately, he got a call.

"Ian, for God's sake! We cannot have anybody else present! It has to be just you and us! And nobody must know who we are! So, please sort it out ... nobody else to be present!"

"Okay, Ron, consider it done!"

But the damage had been done. As soon as Debbie had finished on the 'phone to Collins, she rushed through to Mike's office.

"Mike ... Collins is arranging a meeting on Friday, here in the office ..." Just then, her mobile rang. It was Collins again. Debbie answered and put the device on loudspeaker. "Yes Mr Collins!"

"Debbie ... we will not need your services on Friday ... just make sure there's enough stuff for coffee ... neither Mister Dent nor Mister Forbear will need anything more than that." As soon as he said it, Collins knew he had cocked up. But it was too late. Maynard looked up sharply. As calmy as she could, Debbie replied.

"Okay Mr Collins, no worries!"

"Hell, Debbie, those two names ... weren't they the names in Nick's brief? The two police officers?"

"That was what I came in to tell you!"

"Right! We need to act fast! Let's pop into the briefing room! I think we ought to set up some surveillance kit! Cameras and voice recordings." Maynard had a quick look around. It appeared to him that there were not all that many places where he could fit any devices without it being too obvious. He opened his 'phone. And after a few seconds, dialled a number. "Adam! Mike Maynard!" ... yes, fine thanks. Need an urgent job please. Could you get one of your guys to pop round to see me? ... Today if poss. Address?" Maynard gave the office address. "Thursday at the very latest ... who will you send? ... Oh, yes, the same guy who fixed up dad's yard to catch those drug smugglers! Yes of course I remember him ... okay, look forward to meeting him again!" Then to Debbie. "That was a security firm, ANWisecurity. I'm going to get them to fix something up! This is an opportunity we cannot miss!"

It was close to four-thirty when Terry Thorne pitched up at the Green office.

"Hi, Mike! Nice to see you again. What can I do for you now?"

"Terry! Glad you made it! Follow me. ... Debbie? You want to sit in on this one?" She did. Right, we need, like urgently, to set up cameras with voice recording to cover the whole of this room, basically ..." Terry gave the place the once-over.

"Ah ha! We'll need a bit more cover ... could you fill a couple of those empty shelves? Books will do – that's for starters. Can we stick a clock onto that wall? That should get anybody who walks into the room ..."

"I can fetch the clock from reception ..."

"No need. I've got a couple in the van. Next, maybe a couple of smoke alarms? I reckon that'll do it. Also, something in reception ... I saw plenty of opportunities there! Right, Mike, if you can give me a hand to bring some kit from the van, I can get started. This stuff can be transmitted to our base and then processed by us. Transcribed if necessary with original recordings, and if even questioned it can all be supported by affidavits and be double-checked! I think that'll be the best solution!"

"I'm happy with that, Terry! Debbie? What do you think?"

"Sounds just great! Let's go for it!"

"Good. Now, do you think we should have a meeting with Nick and maybe get him to answer a few questions? I mean at my place, not here of course just in case we are interrupted by Ian!"

"Right Mike ... I'll get on to him now."

"And I'll get onto Karen to organise some food!" Nick was happy with the arrangement, and agreed to drive to the Maynard residence, then take Debbie home after the meeting.

When Maynard arrived home, Nick was parked outside in his car. He pulled into the drive behind Maynard and Debbie then all met and Nick shook hands with the other two.

"Nice place, Mike!"

"Yeah ... it represents years of hard work! Come in and meet the family!" Debbie carried the file and the book with Maynard's notes. They all acknowledged Karen as she led them into lounge, then she retreated to the kitchen to start preparing the meals. Maynard kicked off. Right, Nick, can you please start from the beginning, where you got articles with the firm in question, Cracknell and Williams."

"Yes, of course. I'd had trouble getting articles, so when I was offered a place with C and W, I was pretty pleased, as it was very close to where I had my place in Waylen street, just off the Oxford road. My first few days were memorable for several reasons; firstly when I arrived at the office, there was nobody to receive me, because the partner ... Cracknell, who turned out to be a sole trader had not told anybody in the office that I was coming. Anyway, I was shown into a little office-cum-storeroom, and there was a diary on the small desk in which the previous incumbent, whoever he was and whatever his job was, had noted *'non hic beatus'* indicating some dissatisfaction with his former post, and number of files on the desk which looked like conveyancing jobs. I sat down and was left alone until one of the girls showed me to the little kitchen and asked me to make some coffee for everybody, and added that Roger, Mister Cracknell, would probably be in later in the afternoon. Anyway, I eventually met him the following day, but he didn't actually stay to do any work. I was kept busy I think because the girls seemed sorry for me, so the older lady, Yvonne, took me under her wing and asked me to help her with her divorce cases. In fact, I stayed with her caseload for about a year, attending court with her. Most of the stuff was legal aid, but one obvious problem was that the firm was not making any money. There were no textbooks to speak of. I had settled in and then, one morning, received a 'phone call telling me that there was an outstanding planning dispute relating to the office, and would I please deal with it. A few days later I had to drive my partner to hospital for a minor operation. On my return the next day, I was informed by the girls that Mister Cracknell was 'pissed off' about my taking the day off, and had apparently entered into some diatribe about married men and their family problems. Nobody called me to express their concern for my partner or at all. I just got on with my work. I had stuff to deal with and the work was more important than bothering too much about the call ..."

"Nick, didn't you think by then that you had probably made a mistake by staying there? A relationship, whether it be with a work colleague or a boss, should be rewarding and constructive. So when you first suspected things were not right, didn't you feel that you had to get out?"

"Yes, I did, but other, positive factors kicked in. One, the girls were really helpful, that my place was just round the corner so getting to work was easy, that I had done nearly a year and some guys I was at uni with had still not found articles. I also knew that however bad my articles were, I would still qualify at the end, and when I finally found a position as a solicitor, I would learn a lot on the job, being supervised of course."

"Okay, makes sense I suppose. Anyway, when did things get really bad?"

"Oh, gosh! When my dad died he passed his buy-to-let properties to me, that was where I was then living, I decided to sell because I wanted to go and look after my mum, live with her in her house, as she was not in the best of health, and I asked Roger if his firm would be able to deal with the sale. Of the buy-to-lets, I mean, as I did not want to get stuck with being a landlord what with all the repairing stuff and bad debts and of course, capital gains tax. He agreed, and the sales went through. I left about two hundred and fifty thousand on the client account card so I could draw on the funds to pay the builders who were working on mum's house. No problem with that! Or so I thought! Well, then I started to get strange messages from Roger, about holding onto or controlling money, clients' money. I had no idea what he was talking about, so I ignored it. I was coming up to the end of my articles and I didn't think it was important …"

"So, you had been there for what, nearly three years?"

"Yes, about that … then some accountant guy turned up, apparently sent by Roger, to do a quick audit. The girls were pissed off, had no idea what the hell was going on, and the bloke was there on and off for about two or three days. Then he said everything was all okay, but that I should not have my own account at the office … so I told him that he should move it to the firms other office, which I believed was in Caversham, not far away. Anyway, he took it and as far as I recall, there was then about twenty-five thousand pounds on the card."

"So, quite a lot was spent on your mum's house?"

"Yes. We had the place equipped so she could still have a good degree of independent living, with special showers, access and so on and generally fixing then place up. In fact, it is a very nice property, detached with large gardens … so I had employed a gardener as mum loved her garden. Also had a good-sized vegetable patch ..."

"And I suppose that was when things turned really bad, yes?"

"Yes! I kept getting these messages about me apparently stealing money. Nobody in the office believed it, we had a bookkeeper in every other day, in fact there were never any complaints from any clients while I was there! Then, oddest of all, I had a call from Roger asking me if I had paid fourteen thousand pounds into the office account. I had no idea what he was talking about! It didn't twig then, but subsequently it all made sense, but much later. So, I just told Roger that he was really pissing me off, and I just left the firm. The girls were a bit upset, but they had no idea what was going on. I just drove home. Then I got a county-court summons issued by Roger suing me for eight thousand quid! It was actually a very badly-worded claim, but I sent in a defence and heard no more. As far as I was concerned, Roger owed me twenty-two thousand pounds! Anyway, as I said I heard no more, until that is, I got a visit from the police ..."

"Let me guess, Nick! Detective Sergeant Ronnie Dent and Detective Constable Johnny Forbear?"

"Yes. Then I had absolutely no idea what they wanted to talk to me about ... but it soon became clear that they were acting on instructions from Roger Cracknell." Karen popped her head round the door.

"Come on you lot! Food on the table! Anybody not driving can have some wine as well!"

EIGHT

Not all that far away from where Maynard and company were tucking into a free dinner, Collins' taxi pulled up outside a small parade of shops close to his Green office.

"Thanks, driver. As soon as I need to go back, I'll give you a call, okay?"

"Yeah, Guv, no problem. See yer soon." The cab pulled away, doing a U turn up the road before accelerating away to his next job. Collins waited until he was out of sight, then walked towards his office,. He did not want anybody to see him enter the premises, as he was already on yellow alert, about to embark on what was, in effect, a serious crime. It was not yet dark, so he could not check to see if the office lights were on, which would signify occupancy, but anyway he slipped his key into the lock and mounted the stairs to the offices. There was nobody there. He went into the conference room, a rather grand name for what was in effect just an extra-large office. It had clearly been given a good going-over and seemed clean and tidy, with glasses, napkins and ash-trays stacked at one end. He checked his watch. Half an hour before the two cops were due. He then visited every office, poking about into any files he saw there, then into reception looking at the calls-in log. It had definitely more calls than normal, in fact substantially more, which to the lawyer meant that at least the new guy was doing some marketing. It was encouraging, but his naturally suspicious mind suggested that the bloke was only doing it for his own good. He glanced out of the window to see a white van pull-up in his parking slot. He moved to one side so the occupants could not see they were being observed. To him they looked like coppers. It must be them. He slipped downstairs to let his visitors into the office. Once inside, with the Collins and Goodrich door closed, they introduced themselves. Or rather the bigger man pointed to his mate.

"This 'ere's Johnny, I'm Ron. You must be Ian?"

"Yeah, that's me. Let's go to the meeting room." Once seated, Johnny pulled out a packed of fags and lit one. Ron spoke. Ron was a big man, but dressed in loose-fitting trousers suspended, somewhat incongruously, on wide, stars -and-stripes braces under an over-large jacket, accentuating his size, and which usually held a copy of the Sun newspaper jammed into an inside pocket. Dent had a dislike of tight clothing, and even his shirt hung in gentle folds across his chest, his tie not quite meeting the top button of his shirt, which was anyway undone. His hair was thick and black, looking more like a tight-fitting crash-helmet, and his face was set in a determined grimace, which looked more of an intentional aspect, rather than being natural, as though he was suffering some internal pain. Dent's oppo was a smaller man, looking altogether like a bag stuffed with polystyrene balls, which took up different positions every time he moved. His face wore a look of mild surprise, as though he had fallen asleep in bed and had woken up to find himself somewhere else, like on an escalator in some shopping centre. It would be easy to liken them to Laural and Hardy. But it would be wrong to judge them on their appearance, as they were, apparently, very good at their job which was investigating white-collar crime, but their one failing was that for some sizeable consideration, turned matters to their advantage. Over-confidence would lead to carelessness, but in anticipation of their falling at a fence they had been very careful where they had invested their ill-gotten gains, and even a ten-year stretch would have made it all worthwhile for them. At HQ they were referred to as 'Chip and Pin'; neither of them any good without the other..

"Right, some ground-rules. One. Nothing gets writ down. Two, you and I do as we say we'll do. Three, we get paid once a job's finished. Four We'll always deny we ever met and we tell nobody we've met you, right?" Collins ignored the grammatical errors, if indeed he noticed them, but agreed.

"Yeah. Much as I thought."

"Right, mate wassyer problem?" Collins leaned forward in his chair, elbows on the table, in confidential mode, as though discussing state secrets in a room suspected to be bugged. He looked at the two cops on the other side of the table then spoke.

"I owe my brother some money, to repay him the dosh I used to set up this business. He has set a deadline, which will really get me into the shit unless I pay him, so I want to make it look like one of my employees has stolen a lot of money ..."

"'Ow much?" Collins had an idea that a percentage of the figure he mentioned would be their fee. In his own mind, he knew the amount was going to be half a million pounds.

"He's going to steal three hundred thousand."

"Hey, are you sure you're gonna get it back? I mean if there's no compensation order ..."

"No prob with that! The bloke lives in a house worth over two million, and it ain't mortgaged, either!"

"Bloody hell, mate, he has to be a crook!" The cops also knew that the three-hundred grand quoted by the solicitor would be a lower figure than Collins was going to tell them. The parties were already second-guessing each other. Dent raised his eyes to the ceiling. Whatever he was thinking was pushed out of his mind when he saw the loft-hatch. An idea entered his head. He pointed to the hatch.

"Hey, Ian ... anything in there?"

"No. Shouldn't be, anyway. Why? What's up?" Instead of answering the lawyer's question, he nudged Forbear.

"Hey, Johnny, what about using that place for our you-know-what?"

"Better have a butchers first! Ian, can we have a look up there?"

"Yeah, of course. If you put a chair on the table you might be able to reach it!" Within minutes, Dent's head was poking through the hatch.

"Hey! Looks okay to me! Plenty of room! Er ... can we kinda borrow the place? Just got some stuff to stash away for a few days, will that be okay?"

"Yeah, of course. When do you wanna put it up there?"

"Now! If you organise the take-aways and some beers,

Johnny and I can stash it there … how much of it have we got in the van mate?"

"All of it. I thought it would be best to keep it all together!"

"Good thinking! Let's get started! Then we can finish our meeting, okay Ian?" What else could Collins say but 'Of course'.

"Right, leave the hatch open, we'll stack the stuff on the table, then load it. Ian you wanna go and get the grub and stuff? Come on, Johnny, let's get started!" Collins disappeared to the take away and the off-licence. The two police officers opened the side-door of their van, and started to carry their bundles of whatever up to the first floor. When Collins got back, the last of the packages was being slid onto the floor of the loft. Dent addressed him.

"Hey, Colin, if you can arrange to get this hatch secured it'd be a great help!"

"Yeah, of course … no problem." It was one of the few occasions in his life that Collins did not feel in control. "What is it?"

"Er…it's a load of rather sensitive statements, incriminating police officers … misconduct in public office shit, so we can't really leave it at the station 'cos it'll go missing, like. I'll tell you now, Ian, if that stuff does like disappear we're all in the soup, you an' all, okay?"

"I understand that. I'll get it sealed and nobody will even know it's there! Right, the nosh is in the kitchenette, I'll go and get it!"

"Good. We can talk as we're eating. So, Ian, what now?"

"I need to open a bank account. I've got the details here. The plan is to shift tranches of money into that account, then withdraw it remotely until it's all been secured, then we … I … will blow the whistle. That's when you two move onto the target, 'cos the complaint will end up on your desk, I assume!"

"Yeah, it will. We'll get our solicitor and barrister involved, and the barrister, name of Sowerby-Newton. Noël Sowerby-Newton. Born on Christmas day, see! Lucky he wasn't born at Easter, he'd probably be called Chick!"

"Yeah, Johnny, okay, heard it before! And the solicitor will be Justin Weatherby. They work as a team. The targets usually take our advice, we play the old Mutt and Jeff stuff then we can really stitch them up! I suppose you heard about the railway thefts? That was one of our guys, but he went a bit overboard and got nicked!" Collins handed over the name of the target. There was nothing else written on the paper.

"Right, that's all we'll need. Ron?" Forbear lit another fag.

"Okay. Let's run through the deal again. Number one ...." Dent ran through the deal. "... and looking at a deal of three hundred grand, our cut will be fifty big ones plus expenses, okay?" Collins was not going to argue. Fifty grand? What the hell, wasn't his money anyway, was it?

"Sure. So, if that's all?" He was already getting pissed off with these two. He felt he was being steam-rollered, and he was. When they had left, Collins felt he ought to look in the loft, but he couldn't be bothered. He called for his taxi and made a rather hopeless attempt at clearing up the mess his guests had left with their food wrappers, dirty glasses and cups and fag-ends. He wanted to get back home.

Back at Maynard's house, with the meal over and with the meeting beginning to wrap-up, Mike's mobile rang. It was Terry Thorne from ANWisecurity.

"Yes, Terry ... something happening?"

"Sure is! There was a meeting, three people. The stuff we recorded was pretty bad, I mean bad in content, not quality. Anyway, it'll all be transcribed and certified by Monday, so you can then access it on your PC. Also, two of the people stashed some stuff in the attic above the table. Might be wise to take a look at it before it gets moved again. It's none of my business, Mike, but I think that once you have seen the footage and read the transcript, I would try to arrange some covert police surveillance on this whole deal! There's something else as well. One of the guys there handed over a bit of paper with a name on it. We are trying to have the footage enhanced so we can see what the name was, but that'll have to wait until after the weekend, and if we succeed we'll let you know, okay?"

"Terry, that's absolutely brilliant! Thanks! I feel this is going to be a really big deal!" Maynard put his 'phone down. "Hey, listen to this! Collin's meeting has finished. We now have footage and voice recordings of the whole thing! And according to Terry, it looks pretty good from our point of view! Nick, I think we are on the way to sorting out your problem! I'll let you know as soon as I have the full recording!" Poor Nick was so happy he looked almost close to tears.

"After all this time, I really hope so!" Debbie gave him a hug.

"We all hope so, love. Just you stick with us!"

On Monday morning, Maynard arrived at the Green office to find Debbie already there. She was not in a good mood.

"Mike! Look at the bloody mess Collins has left! Food wrappers, the meeting room stinks of cigarettes! Dirty cups and glasses! I've a good mind to ring Collins and shout at him!"

"Not a very good idea, Debbie, 'cos he'll deny it! Just ask him how the meeting went! See what he says! For the moment, let's see what's been stashed in the loft. Give me a hand please!" Maynard lifted a chair onto the table climbed onto it and eased the loft-hatch down to Debbie. "Don't suppose you have a torch, do you … oh, hang on, there's a switch here!" Maynard pressed the switch and a strip-light flickered into life. For a moment, nothing was said. Then Maynard let out a shout. Bloody hell, Debbie! Looks like slabs of brown … heroin! Can you … here, there are some other packets as well …. here, I'll pass one down open it carefully, just a little to see what's in it!" He passed down one of the several bundles.

"I'll just get a knife from the kitchen!" She was not gone long.

She then passed the bundle back to Maynard. "What do you think that is?" After just a second, he answered.

"It's cash! There must be thousands of pounds up here! It's all drug money! I'll take a picture or two then get the place closed up again! Then you can ask Collins how the meeting went!" A few minutes later, Debbie was on the 'phone. She connected to Collins.

"Mr Collins ... how was the meeting? Anything else you need me to do here?"

"The meeting was cancelled. They both had to cancel. I'll let you know if I need the place again."

"Okay, thanks." Maynard appeared.

"What did he say?"

"That the meeting was cancelled."

It was late afternoon when Terry from ANWisecurity called. He had a result on the name. They were sure it was Mike Maynard.

"Mike, you ought to be really careful! You are being set up. We'll do all we can to ensure that whatever it is for, they won't succeed."

Back in his office, Collins again entered Arnold's office.

"How are we doing on the Fish case, any news?"

"Yeah. We've agreed to hold a retainer against any claims. The sum we're gonna hold on to is a hundred thou. So, I see no reason why you can't put the whole lot into your trust account. But you don't need to do it in the Green office ... you can do it on our client account, surely?"

"Yeah, probably." Collins decided he'd shift it to the Green office once Arnie was happy to use a trust account. After that it was none of Arnold's business. He wasn't a happy bunny as he had also received a court-date for his drink-driving hearing and he knew the press would be there. But he could not risk arrest by failing to turn up. His brother's view was that he should appear contrite, a state of mind he had never before exercised, plead guilty and take what was coming. And he felt that Friday's meeting with Chip and Pin was very much a case of him being bulldozed into the action the cops were advocating, but the only consolation was that they had clearly done that sort of thing before. But with a fair wind, he would be able to walk away with a pay-out from the Law Society indemnity insurance and also have the 'stolen' cash shifted out of the new bank account which Dent and Forbear were confident they could arrange, and into an account to which only he had access. The thought of an estimated million-pound payout was keeping him going. He also thought he ought to see exactly what it was they had put into the loft in the Green office. All in good time.

Maynard was happy. He had managed to increase the workload both for Maggie and himself, thanks to all the hard work put in by his dad, by Karen, Hannah's parents and the golf-club. But he was a bit concerned about the plans Collins seemed to have for the office and also sure that with the support he had mustered and the notes and input from Terry, when the shit hit the fan, he would be okay. As far as Nick was concerned, he reckoned that would also be sorted. They had made a good start. He did however, wonder if he was again walking into a situation he would be better leaving, but he decided to tell Karen what he was planning. He was really concerned about getting things put right for Nick, just as he had, albeit impliedly as opposed to explicitly, promised Sam. However, he was aware as Ed Nelson had said in Professor Slater's lecture, no man is an island … it occurred to him that he maybe ought to recruit the services of Hannah's dad. If he decided to then it should be discussed first with all the other parties involved. He would chuck the idea into the hat when they next met, and keep Sam involved as well. At home, Karen was fully supportive.

"Go for it … Nick seems nice guy, so you can't let him down and with Terry doing his bit, we should be okay. But keep me informed, love, just because I may pick up the danger signals you miss!"

The next day gave Maynard the ideal opportunity to put his plans into operation. Hannah turned up at work to say that Collins had been banned for six months and fined fifteen hundred pounds.
"Excellent, well done Hannah! Now we had a couple of police officers here for a meeting recently … I don't suppose you could ask your dad if he knows them, could you?"
"Yes, of course. If I see him this evening, I'll ask him. Who are they?" Maynard gave her a piece of paper with the names on.
"Keep it to yourself, Hannah, because it might be a bit problematic, I think." The next day, Hannah approached Maynard.
"Dad would like to meet you … it's about those two cops!"

NINE

DCI Mike Ellis, Hannah's dad, sat in the meeting room and leaned back in his chair, his right hand holding the mug of tea his daughter had prepared for him.
"First of all, may I say how grateful I am that you have taken on my daughter's work-experience. She wants to qualify as a legal secretary and then work for the police force, and since she has been with you and your staff she has come on in leaps and bounds. She is not overly-enamoured of your partner, Collins …"
"Well, Mike, he is not my partner, just employer and to be frank, Mike, nor are we enamoured of him! However, to the point … and I must make it clear that what I am about to say has to remain between us because we believe that somewhere along

the line, there is some conspiracy to steal a lot of money from our clients' accounts ..." Maynard went on to explained about Collins' meeting "...and here I have a transcript of what was said." The lawyer pushed a copy across the table to the police-officer. It didn't take him long to grasp exactly what was going on. Then he glanced up at the loft-hatch.

"Can I see what's up there?"

"Of course." Between them, they got the hatch open. Ellis brought two pack down onto the table.

"Straight away, I can tell you this is heroin, and the other pack ..." he peered into the pack through the small incision Debbie had made earlier ... "... is cash. This is serious! But let me be frank with you. Firstly, we have our reservations about the two officers you saw. Secondly, I expect my lab people will want to put trackers on all those packs. They'll look like ordinary metal seals, about the size of a calculator battery, but once activated they are responders. Not a lot of range, but long enough for what we want and the packages are resealed and wrapped so nobody will know that they have been opened. Then we can fix the hatch securely so nobody, unless tooled up, will be able to enter, and of course, any movement like that will be recorded on your surveillance kit."

"That makes sense. I can always deal with Collins on that point, by just telling him that some guy came in and locked it. He'll assume it was our two friends, and they will assume it was Collins!"

"Yeah. And as far as other matters are concerned, you will have my support, and to reassure you, I will not mention this business to anybody at the station, but keep private reports at home. Now, maybe I can get that loft-hatch secured once I have had some trackers fitted to those blocks. Maybe I could get my lab boys in to tag all the packets? And I ought to put a warning out on Dent and Forbear to make sure they do not get any idea that they are marked men! I'll let you know about that of course.

And as it seems to involve you, I will be discrete."

"No problem with that, and thank you for everything." Maynard briefed Debbie.

"Thanks, Mike. Nick would like to have another meeting. He has a lot to tell you so I thought we could show him the footage from the Collins rendezvous with the Dent and Forbear characters. What do you think?"

"Good idea, just let me know when you are both available, then we'll go for it."

Collins was pissed off, as usual. There was always something. Now he was all over the local papers, and there were copies in the office. At least he now had a driver, an ex-con his brother had unearthed. He seemed a decent kind of cove, but unknown to Collins, he had to report to Mark anything that was said about business or personal matters. Mark expected the usual bragging and bullshit his brother was too fond of peddling, but there might be a few gems forthcoming over a period of six months. It was time for Collins to make the next move on his big plan. He dropped in to see Arnold again. The junior partner raised his right arm before Collins had a chance to talk.

"Okay, Ian! Yes, you can transfer the Fisher cash to your trust account, It's a little under half a mill. You can do it now. Just make sure that I have the trustee account details please. I'm sure the bank will be happy to open the account, especially as you have done it before, but they do not usually like …" Collins interrupted him.

"For fuck's sake, tell me something I don't know! I've already spoken about it to the manager. Let's just get on with it!" Then he left Arnold alone. Collins noted; step two of the master-plan was complete. He now had to work on step three.

Back at the Green office, Debbie gave Maynard the message about the next meeting with Nick Forrester. It was two days hence, a Wednesday. Maynard agreed it. Later DCI Ellis turned up to supervise the tagging of the packages, and before the office closed, the job was done and two pretty impressive-looking Abloy PL362 Padlocks and hasps were fitted.

"I have made sure that none of the packs look as though they have been opened, and once our teams lock onto the gear being shifted, they can follow the stuff to all it's different destinations. And the heroin packs have a scorpion logo ..."

"Not delivered by the Royal Air Force's eighty-four squadron, I hope!"

"No! It is a Columbian gang. Probably came in via the Netherlands or by narco-sub." By the time the police officer had finished securing the hatch, it would have been impossible for anybody to enter the loft without smashing the hatch and even then, because of the size of the hasps there would have been very limited access to the loft-space. Maynard declined the offer of keeping one set of keys in the office. However, they did re-arrange the room so that the table was now away from the hatch area, further adding to the problems an ambitious thief might encounter in trying to access the store.

"Right, Mike, I will keep all the keys, and the tracking-device info will be with your Terry bloke. I'm afraid, that even today not all coppers, like lawyers, are entirely devoid of ambition to make a fast buck, illegally or otherwise! If anybody asks for the keys, tell them you'll have to contact your Collins bloke, and to come back later, okay with that?"

"Yes, of course. And I'll ask Terry to keep his motion alert awake after office-hours in case there is a break-in. He'll recognise the Dent end Forbear blokes and of course, Collins. Should he contact you if there's any need?"

"Yes ... on my mobile, please!"

It was the following Thursday evening, that Nick, Debbie and

Maynard had their next meeting. Nick raised two matters.

"Cracknell was calling the office and 'interrogating' the staff about what they were doing and had anybody sent out any bills. There were sometimes two or more calls a day. Nobody was comfortable with that. Further, he had a rather bizarre approach to one of the fee-earner lawyers, Steph, seemingly harbouring an intense dislike of her and suggesting, which was wholly inappropriate, that she was not operating as a lawyer but running some kind of wronged-wives' club. I liken it now to a kind of 'psyops' campaign to wear her down to the point where she would just go. Ultimately, he achieved what he really wanted. Why he could not have just asked nicely for her to leave and perhaps explain reasons for his decision, was beyond me. I was later to be subjected to the same kind of pressure. I believe that the firm was in serious financial difficulties, but that of course was not anything I should have to worry about."

"Again, Nick, didn't that put you on notice that maybe it was a mistake to stick with him?"

"Yes, but as I said, I knew that it would be hard work to go anywhere else, especially if I had jumped ship once …"

"Yes, I understand that. Anyway, carry on."

"Things began to get even more odd. One day we opened a newly-delivered box of headed paper to discover that Steph's name had been added as a partner. She was rightly livid, having received no earlier call or a letter from the head office regarding her 'promotion'. There was absolutely no prior contact, no prior discussion, it just happened. It was obviously a decision made some days if not weeks before Steph found out, as the partners had time to have their headed paper re-printed to show her name. She was later informed by the bookkeeper that the firm's accounts had not been passed by the Law Society for the last financial year, and it immediately occurred to me that this was the reason for her sudden elevation to partner and that they had informed the Law Society that she was a partner long before she ever found out. The alternative was for the partnership to cease trading pending having the accounts signed off. They needed Steph's practicing certificate to continue with their work. We were also informed that an accounts assistant had been sacked or prosecuted because of 'accounts issues'."

"That was very odd, it appears that Cracknell was happy to put at risk Steph's personal assets, including her family home, if the partnership became insolvent as a result of poor performance or a negligence claim that exceeded the professional indemnity insurance. On reflection, there was every reason to believe that the partnership was never a financially sound enterprise anyway. If there were insufficient funds in the partnership to cover liabilities, creditors could pursue individual partners in a traditional unlimited liability partnership, which the firm was, on a joint and several liability basis. That means a creditor could choose to pursue Steph rather than the other partners on the basis that Steph may have had a greater net worth than them other partners. So, did she resign?"

"No. I believe that the boss came to some deal with her, but she did leave some time afterwards."

"So, we seem to have established that Cracknell was dishonest and that the firm was insolvent. That goes a long way to explain what he then did to you!"

"Too right it does! In my ignorance, I shrugged it off because I wanted to make a success of the office, and was working damn hard for no money. In about mid-June I asked if the office would deal with the sale of my Waylen Street property as I could obviously not deal with it myself. He agreed, and was instructed. The sale was, as I said earlier, so I could move to be with mum because we had embarked on some serious building works and I had occasion to sack the first builder through incompetence and was doing some works myself. Then there was this bizarre episode with my account card, which I explained earlier. Then Roger Cracknell would turn up at the office, sometimes rather scruffily dressed, and mooch about then plant himself in a chair just sitting looking at me, saying nothing. It was disconcerting to say the least, and he was also asking questions about my sale and I now believe he was then plotting set me up on the theft deal, and to get his hands on my cash, the twenty-five thousand pounds on my card. I think it was triggered by the accountant's visit. Then as I have already told you, Roger asked if I had paid fourteen thousand pounds into his office account. Of course I hadn't! He just added that he would repay me on a monthly basis, so he was obviously concerned about my asking for the balance of my sale money to be paid to me. Clearly he was a devious bastard!"

"You know, Nick, the guy is an out-and-out criminal! He stole your cash and what he did subsequently was just to cover up his actions! Anyway, continue. What happened then?"

"He suggested that I was holding onto or controlling clients' money! I mean, for God's sake, I was a clerk! Anyway, I got so angry that I just walked out, I realised that the whole business was affecting me badly, and that whatever the consequences, I would be better off without it. So, I left, and the next thing I knew was getting a County-Court summons asking for seven grand, that I apparently owed Roger-bloody-Cracknell! I sent in a defence, and heard nothing more. But I never saw my money back from the guy!"

"And this is where things got really bad?"

"That's an understatement! I was out when I got a call from my mum who told me there were some police officers at the house … wanted to talk to me so I told mum to tell them I'd meet them at the station, which I did on my way back home."

"And those officers were …?"

"Dent and Forbear! They said I had stolen money from Cracknell's clients, about seven thousand pounds, which is the sum the guy had on his county-court summons. Of course it was nonsense! They said I ought to get myself a lawyer, and they recommended Justin Weatherby, and said that they also thought the charge was ridiculous, but that Weatherby would sort it out no problem."

"And you agreed to see the guy?"

"Yes, I did! I went to see him and he and I went to see the barrister bloke, Sowerby-Newton. He looked to me more like a guy you'd see flogging pornography to holiday-makers in some sleazy Spanish resort! Anyway, I had a few more meetings with the solicitor bloke, then it all went quiet for ages, then another visit from the two cops, saying that I had nicked over two hundred and fifty thousand quid, and what had I done with the money. Anyway, again nothing happened, but then I was charged with stealing seven thousand pounds I think, I don't know why exactly, and I had to keep going to the magistrates' court until the case was remanded to the Crown court! By that time I was, quite frankly, unable to even read a newspaper! I had been getting migraines … I was not in a fit state to look after my own interests and I thought I had a couple of good lawyers looking after me!"

"Yeah, Nick … I know it's hard for you even after all this time. But have faith in us please!" Debbie reached out and took Nick's hand.

"Please, Nick … as Mike says, have faith in us. With a bit of luck, we can blow this business wide open, and I can tell you that we've made a good start!"

Somewhere in a pub in reading, Dent and Forbear were enjoying a beer and watching the football on TV when Dent's 'phone rang.

"Yeah!"

"Ron? … Its Stack! Where is all the gear? The shit?" Dent looked at his oppo, mouthing the word 'Stack' "It's safe, we're just waiting for payment, that's all!"

"Payment? You've been bloody paid!"

"Oh no we haven't!"

"I gave the dosh to Toady ... ages ago!"

"You might have done, but he ain't given it to us!"

"Yer windin' me up?"

"No, mate, straight up! We ain't bin paid! You better pay the guy a visit! But I can tell you, when you put it into the van, we went straight away and stored it. It's all ready to go! Just need payment and a drop-off point ... Toady was supposed to give us that as well, but right now we're waiting for the dosh and the address! You promised five grand, and you say you paid Toady? He ain't bin near us, mate! And if we have to hold onto it much longer we'll have to find another customer! You know it's worth more than what you're paying!" Dent ended the call."

In his office, Stack called over his should.

"Ziff! Take Apitz and find Toady. He done one on me. Teach him a lesson. Go blow his fuckin' brains out! No bastard messes with me! Go over his car for anything of value, cash or coke or H, anything, then bring it to me! Right, go now!"

It didn't take long to find Toady. He was just a 'phone call away.

"Toady? ... Ziff. Need a meet. See you at the park in ten minutes, same place. Got a job for yer!" Ziff turned to his boss, a guy who seemed to regard himself as the new Harry Rawlins, a figment of the imagination of Linda le Plant's book, 'Widows' and he was still looking to get into hijacking security vans. "What's the gripe, Boss?"

"Bastard's nicked the five grand I gave him to pass on to bloody Dent, the cop, who won't deliver until they bin paid."

As soon as Toady saw the gangsters walking up to his car, Toady knew it was trouble. Apitz pulled the driver's door open.

"Stack says you ain't paid of the cops for a delivery ... where's the dosh, mate?"

"Ain't paid them? On my life mate, they bin paid! More than a week ago! Them two cops are more bent that a safety pin, I tell yer!" Before the two killers left Toady that evening, they rummaged around in his car and stole all the drugs and cash they could find. It was a worthwhile haul.

At about midnight, Reading police found a body in Prospect Park at Honey End. The police said that the male victim was known to them. Dent remarked to Forebear that they had better shift the shit from the loft at the Green office and deliver it as instructed, as apart from anything else, Toady's death was a warning to them.

TEN

DS Dent was called into his boss's office.

"Hi, Ron … I suppose you know Toady has been given the chop? Are we gonna have a drug war on our hands soon? What's your take on it?"

"Toady! He's bin asking fer it fer ages! Been playing a bit fast an' loose with drug supplies and cash! Was only a matter of time, I reckon!"

"Yeah, maybe so! He was shot through, I mean riddled and nobody heard anything or at least nobody's gonna come forward as a witness! Understandable, I s'pose!"

"Bet it was a Skorpion! Nine-hundred rounds a minute don't give anybody time to argue! I suppose it had to come to Reading's OCGs sooner or later!"

"Yeah, s'pose yer right! Organised crime groups! That's all we bloody need in Reading, armed with Skorpion bloody machine-guns! Just keep yer eyes and ears open, okay?" Dent called Collins.

"Hey, mate … we have some stuff for you and we need to get our gear back now. I assume it has been well secured?" Collins was caught off balance.

"Er ... of course. When to you want it?"

"Tonight, as soon as the office shuts. Say seven?"

"Yeah, I'll be there!" Collins then called Debbie. "Need the meeting room again tonight. Make sure it's free and clean. Need to collect some stuff my visitors left in the office, okay?"

"Of course. Leave it to me." Debbie then dropped in on Maynard. "Mike ... Collins meeting his people again tonight. Talking about picking up some stuff by which I assume they mean all that crap in the loft!"

"Okay. Get into Mike Ellis ... he'd better leave the keys in the office here for the blokes to use, and he'll have to activate the trackers as well!"

"Will do! And Terry ought to be told as well, to watch what happens."

"Good idea!" Ellis was convinced that the Toady killing was drug-related, and frankly with the issues he had with Dent and Forbear, it was not something he had time for. Nevertheless, he had an idea who could give him some information. He called Reading jail to talk to chief warder.

"Hi! ... need a favour. The Toady killing. Have a word with Smudge please ... see if he knows anything? Thanks." Ellis had just finished the call when his mobile rang.

"Mike ... Debbie from the Green. Have some movement on the Dent business. They want to meet here this evening to collect the stuff from the office. Collins is meeting them here at about seven, so thought you ought to know. Need the keys and of course get all the surveillance kit running. And your little trackers will need to be activated!"

"Yeah, good thinking! I'll be there myself shortly!" Ellis was well aware of the connection between Mark and the lawyer Collins, and that sooner or later the brother would go a bit too far and finish up in the dock. He knew too that Mark was getting regular updates from the lawyer's driver, Doug. That was just how the system worked. Knowledge was power. He collected his bits and pieces and told his secretary he was away for the rest of the day. That was all he needed to tell her. Too much information spilled over to the wrong people, either intentionally or otherwise. His secretary knew that, and she never asked questions, and was adept at avoiding passing on information to anybody. Ellis arrived at the Green office and took the stairs two at a time. Hannah was pleased to see her dad, and made him a NATO standard coffee, milk and two sugars, a throw-back to his earlier RAF career. He entered Debbie's office as her door was open.

"Hi, Debbie. Got some keys here and a device to switch on the trackers. Hopefully, we'll see where each package is delivered, then ruin this particular caravan of supplies. And may I thank you for involving me in this. Hopefully we can see an early demise of quite a few illegal enterprises including the one Collins is working on involving your Mike!" The man in question entered the office.

"Mike! Nice to see you! I expect you'll have a team of officers ready to pick up all the people who receive bulk deliveries of the brown?"

"That's the idea! In fact, we plan to set up a surveillance op using our spec telecom teams, to see exactly who visits, record it, then at some opportune moment drop in on them!
We do not want to in any way impede the progress of the drugs as we need to know all the drop-off points, as well as keeping Dent and Forbear unaware of what we are doing as we need to find their supplier or otherwise how they are getting hold of, or managed to get hold of, the drugs here. It is just possible they are being paid to hide then to deliver. We'll soon know. How does that sound?"

"But why the bundles of cash?"

"It's for laundering. The cash is taken to people like market traders, bureaux de change, estate agents who collect cash for their buy-to-let clients, from tenants every month ... look at the figures! Say twenty or thirty properties, fifteen hundred quid per month per property, tenants who are below the radar working for cash, no bank accounts. So, say they collect twenty-five times fifteen hundred say thirty-seven thousand quid, they get to keep ten percent of that, pay their staff in cash, put the rest into their bank accounts and suddenly you've got clean money! In fact, of course, there are no rent collections, it's all a fiction! The cash is all drug money!"

"Bloody hell! Anyway, what about our little game with Dent?"

"I was coming to that. We don't want to interfere with that because we believe that they are or will be working with other dishonest professionals, perverting the course of justice. We want them all at the same time! And currently, I am making an application to the CCU to ..."

"CCU? What is that exactly?"

"Counter Corruption Unit ... an application for them, Dent and Forbear, to be put under scrutiny. Anyway, it's time I cleared off. And remember, we will be watching over the whole operation, so there is no chance of any of you getting involved in anything unpleasant!" In Maynard's mind. He assumed that Ellis was talking about some kind of altercation with the baddies.

"Well, Mike, that's of some comfort!"

"Right! Get Terry on standby, and I'll take my leave now, and perhaps, Hannah, we can go home together. The meeting will be in about an hour, so we'll make sure we're well away before seven. And good luck!"

Shortly after Ellis left the office, warder Mark Collins called for Smudge. By habit, the con spent time in the library, so it would never be odd to see him talking with certain of the screws at any time of day. It had to be that way; his cover story was that he was doing an open university degree in social sciences, in fact he was. The protocol was easy. Smudge would be standing looking through a book, and close to him but facing the door in what was normally an empty room, the screw, generally the head warder or other senior rank, would ask the questions, but with his head down so it seemed as though he was not talking. This time, it was Smudge who initiated the conversation.

"Toady?"

"Yes. Tell me."

"I tell you, Boss, the idiot was tied up with your two, Dent and Forbear. They're working with some lawyer bloke, your brother I reckon. They're a couple just asking to get whacked if they're not careful! And they're making' loadsa dosh! You wanna crack down on 'em unless you bro is getting on your nerves!"

"Thanks fer the warning, mate! D'you know who greased Toady?" It was easy for the warders to fall in with the porridge slang. Mark Collins tried to avoid doing so, but sometimes it just happened.

"Yeah, but right now, it wouldn't be too 'elfy to tell yer!" Smudge moved along the rows of books so it appeared to any casual observer that there was nothing going on between the two. Occasionally, another screw would walk in and appear to separate the two or even tell him time was up, and to get back to his cell. It was all very carefully planned. Making a mistake and being seen by the other cons would not make for a comfortable life. "He apparently kept some dosh meant to go to some couriers. He had paid it, but the couriers were being a bit too clever!"

"And the couriers?"

"My lips are sealed ... there's a time and a place for everything, and here and now isn't it!"

Dent and Forbear were early, but by that time Ellis had his men in place, and fully briefed. None of his men knew either Dent or Forbear, as they were operating from another police HQ a good few miles away, but they were not under any circumstances to stop the white van, which was registered to a Jane Dawson, at an address in Aylesbury, and it was taxed, MOT'd and insured. From his studio and the camera monitors, Terry saw the men enter the offices, and with Collins, who was already there, enter the interview room, slide the table back to its position under the loft-hatch.

"Impressive looking locks, Ian! The keys had been on the table when Collins came in and they were now in his pocket.

"Yeah ... here, the keys." Dent took them and using the chair again reached up and opened the padlocks, then declared that all the gear was there.

"Good. Right, Ian, we've got some stuff for yer." Dent reached into his pocket and produced some documents. First, a passport, name of Mike Samuel Maynard. Driver's licence, same name. Address is a flat in High Wycombe, and he also has a police officer's warrant card, 'cos he's a copper now!" Dent laughed. "All communication with the bank will be by e-mail only, and here is the e-mail address. 'Ave a butchers and let me know if it's okay!" Collins took the paperwork and shuffled through it.

"Yeah ... looks kosher to me! Now what?"

"The guy in the picture will be delivering the stuff to the bank, it's in Aylesbury. He'll have your blokes real national insurance number. Story is, he's going through a divorce and needs a new account without his wife's name on it. Anyway, we have briefed the bank contact and as soon as the account's opened the copy docs will disappear so there'll be no probs, okay? Give it a week to set-up the account and you'll get an email, so give me your e-address and when you receive confirmation, get a few quid into the account via on-line banking and use the password and card-reader you'll get to make sure everything is working. And the fee for all this is five grand. We'll put it on the bill. Right, that's it." Dent shoved the information back into his pocket, leaving only the email address for Collins. "Now let's get the shit into the van." By seven forty-five pm, the van was loaded and it quietly slipped out of the parking slot. The sat-nav had been programmed for the drop, an Amersham address, just a hop, skip and a jump away. The cops who had attached a tracker to the van, watched it until it was out of sight, then started to follow. They checked in with HQ. Terry from ANWisecurity passed the meeting audio to the admin pool for transcribing.

Once everything had been sorted in the office, Collins chucked the padlocks and keys onto the reception desk, then did a quick sweep of the other offices and was pleased to note that the file of conveyancing jobs on Maynard's desk looked very healthy. Oddly, the fact that the cops thought it was he who had fitted the locks to the loft-hatch did not disturb him. Then he called for his driver Doug to come and pick him up. Tomorrow, he would check with Arnold that the Lady Fisher cash was paid into the Green office client account. On his journey back to his house, he drank the two bottles of beer he had bought from the Bottle and Basket whilst waiting for Doug, and in his mind ran through his next actions regarding the clients' cash. He smiled to himself, pleased that as far as he was concerned, the job was as good as done. All he had to do now was execute the transfers say a hundred thousand a time, then declare the money stolen after doing the transfers from the new Maynard account to the nominated donee account, and the cash was as good as in his pocket. Then once a conviction is secured, claim the cash from his professional indemnity insurance. Simple! Then he pays off his brother, and when his mum is found dead at the bottom of the stairs, he will inherit her estate, and with a house worth in excess of a cool million, he can retire. The only fly in the ointment was his brother, so he'd have to think of a way to get rid of him or otherwise put him off for good. He might have to enlist the help of Dent and Forbear, see if they were into the killing business, or knew somebody who was. As the beer got to his brain, it crossed his mind that he might have to do it himself. Then he fell asleep.

When the white van pulled up all the packages were off-loaded at the Amersham address. At least that made it easy for the following cops. All they had to do was watch and secretly video it all then take-off and let the Open Reach Covert Ops guys do their stuff. In the meantime, DCI Ellis had to decide what to do with Dent and co. It was going to be awkward as he didn't want to blow his cover, as he explained to Maynard.

"And the lawyers?"

"Well, Mike, this is a lot more than the nineteen fifty-nine case of Wintle versus Nye, solicitors putting a bit on their clients' wills for themselves, it's …"

"Hey, you sure keep up to date on these cases !"

"It's Hannah … keeping me in the picture!"

ELEVEN

Maynard wanted to finish debriefing Nick, so he asked Debbie if she could make the arrangements, and again meet at Maynard's house. Nick was only too happy. He collected Debbie from her house that evening and made his way to the Maynard residence. The group soon settled in, and Mike started questioning Nick.

"Right, last time we got as far as your meeting with the lawyers."

"Yeah, that's right. But there was very little going on. I mean, over the years they or somebody took to get the matter to court, we had only four meetings. And even when we got to court, I still didn't know what I had been charged with. Then the lawyer bloke told me to plead guilty!"

"Did you?"

"Did I 'eck! I refused point-blank! But every time he got me to court, he said the same thing!"

"So?"

"The trial took I think about three weeks, and I honestly only recalled the first few days of the case, and when the prosecution finish it's presentation, I just told my barrister that I could not give evidence, after all, I heard very little of it. His response was that the prosecution would tear me to pieces ... so obviously, I was found guilty."

"Were you on any drugs for your migraines? For example, amitriptyline?"

"Yes, I was, why?"

"Amitriptyline is a Tricyclic antidepressant, an older class of antidepressant drug prescribed used less often these days, but some people still use tricyclics for depression, anxiety disorders, obsessive-compulsive disorder and nerve-related pain. The drug blocks the action of serotonin, norepinephrine and other chemical messengers in the brain which can lead to a number of side effects, including lapses in memory."

"But my lawyers knew I was on the stuff!"

"Was it prescribed for you?"

"Yes, it was! And this is the first time I have ever heard about those side-effects!"

"Well, that's positive news! Now, we know what happened immediately after the verdict, but what did you do after your release?"

"I found that my lawyers had appealed, but I did not know that they had done so through the Criminal Cases Review Commission."

"The CCRC ..." Here, Maynard recalled Professor Slaters views on them. He thought Nick ought to know. He repeated her views word for word.

"Nick, may I quote Professor Slater's views on the CCRC? She was concerned about the corruption in the UK criminal justice system failing to perform the roles for which it was established, evidenced by incompetence, laziness, ignorance stupidity and prejudice inter alia. But worst of all is the appalling performance of the appeal system, and in particular the Criminal Cases Review Commission, and she concluded that the criminal justice system is not fit for purpose; the appeal process including the justifiably much-maligned Criminal Cases Review Commission has long been on its knees'."

"You know, Mike, that was my experience exactly! The appeals were more on procedural and capacity issues than evidential, and I tend to believe that counsel's opinion on taking up this case was that the prosecution had the case 'sewn up'; hence, perhaps, the pressure on me to enter a guilty plea. I was now unemployed, probably unemployable and suffering with migraines ... debilitating headaches. Nausea. No fun at all. Anyway, as I said, I had no feedback from my lawyers, no contact after the case, no idea that the CCRC were involved, but when I mentioned my reservations about the case, somebody suggested that I contact them to see if they could help, but I was doubtful. Anyway, I did and much to my surprise, they had been involved and they also said that they had written to me years ago setting out their views, but if I had received anything from them, I would have responded immediately! It's possible they wrote to my lawyers, but they certainly did not write to me! Also, their communication set out the charge, something I had never seen before, basically, that I had been in financial difficulties and that over a period of thirty months, I had extracted the sum of one hundred and eighty thousand pounds from the clients' accounts ... that works out to be six thousand pounds per month ...!"

"Hey, Nick! That's ridiculous! Even half or a quarter of that would just be impossible!"

"That was exactly what I told the CCRC! But they said that because they could not get hold of any case-files, they just could not deal with any application I might make! Apparently, neither the cops nor the CPS had any file! Then I discovered that all the other so-called offences were only issues which concerned the

Law Society, and which were not in fact criminal offences per se! And the CCRC's own files just mentioned, understandably, the alleged cash losses, so they had no need to see the files! The sum allegedly stolen was already in their own files, and all they had to do was establish that it would have been impossible for me or anybody else to steal that amount of cash over the period stated!" Maynard was stunned. He was lost for words. He looked at the lad, then to Debbie. Eventually he recovered enough to respond.

"I ... I ...! Bloody hell, Nick, that is just ... words fail me! It bears out all I understood the CCRC to be ... Oh, God! A survey of lawyers suggested the CCRC was not fit for purpose, with one of them describing the watchdog as an office-bound, moribund organisation that does not actually investigate, that it suffers cultural, structural and financial problems. The director of the charity, Appeals, when commenting on the appalling case of Andy Malkinson, said Andy's case highlights institutional failings at the CCRC, including its lack of an investigative mindset and deference to the courts and police. These problems have festered because the CCRC is not accountable. Poor Andy spent seventeen years in prison for a rape he did not commit, and he says the CCRC has an attitude problem and it had still not contacted him since he was cleared by the court of appeal. The CCRC was set up in 1997 as an experiment as an extra-judicial body that could give another chance to cases that had reached the end of the legal road."

"Well, Mike, it has bloody well failed! "

"You are so right, Debbie! The time has now come to acknowledge that it was an experiment that failed. It may have led to the quashing of over three hundred convictions but that is not quite the real situation. Firstly, the CCRC refer some cases to the court of appeal on the basis of sentence alone, and if the sentence is subsequently varied, then the CCRC, inaccurately, marks this down as a success! It also counts as successes

cases where alternative convictions are substituted, the most common example being manslaughter
of the prisoner."

"Mike, your knowledge of the CCRC is impressive ..."

"Not exactly, Nick, I just looked into it when Professor Slater mentioned it at a conference I attended not all that long ago. How many times did you contact the CCRC?"

"Many times, Mike. Over several years. I even sent them a booklet, paperback, to make it easier for them read, and they just ignored it!"

"Okay; Let's have a break!"

"Mike, In my communications with the CCRC, they mentioned a 'schedule of offences' about which I knew nothing at the time, apparently presented by an auditor called by the prosecution, and later that *there was no dispute that the defendant had carried out the transactions alleged'* this is absolute nonsense as I never saw the schedule, but if it represented an unadulterated copy of my own client account card, then indeed I could have agreed it, but I do not recall any agreed facts between prosecution and defence, the CCRC note added and that I had used client accounts, I don't know how that was supposed to work, in order to pay the builder who was working on my mum's house. In fact, I had my own account, containing the sale proceeds of my property as I have already said. The land registry documents I have confirm the sale transaction as well. This is important; the only payment into my account which was opened simply and only for my sale transaction, was the proceeds of my house sale, being £260,000 less disbursements. There were no other 'payments' as stated above, and this would be borne out by my client account card which Roger Cracknell had in his constructive possession over the whole period of this business, and which would clearly show that all and any payments out were made from my own funds. I have no doubt that the 'schedule' above was made up of payments I had quite legitimately made from my own funds. However, this is an assumption, firstly, as I never saw the 'schedule', and secondly, it must have been doctored somehow as it clearly would not show that the payments were made up from my own funds. For that I blame either a conspiracy between Roger and the forensic accountant, or just Roger having made up his own draft to give to the guy."

"Quite honestly, Nick, there must have been something funny going on ... and I would suspect that Dent and co were involved ..."

"Well, I assume that Roger made a claim on the indemnity insurance for the cash allegedly lost ..."

"That, Nick, was the whole point of the exercise, and I suspect, is exactly what the two coppers are discussing now with Collins in my case! In fact, I expect that pretty soon we're going to see payments made out of the account here in the Green office, all down to my stealing it ... he knows that even if the insurance does not pay out, he could obtain a charging order and have my house sold to repay all the cash, so he's in a win-win situation!"

"But Mike how will that help me? I mean ..."

"Because if the matter ever gets to court, and as far as I'm concerned it will, and once we have blown the case wide open, we point to your case and we'll have the key players all lined up in court already ... and it is possible that the judge will have them taken into custody immediately. All of them!

"Another issue, Mike. My case was being handled by a solicitors' clerk and with all due respect for the guy, I don't believe he should have had conduct of my case, and incidentally, he was the one telling me that I should plead guilty to the charges, but I refused to agree to do so. Consider why was he was asking; was it because he took it upon himself to push the point? I doubt it. More realistically that bloody barrister had his own agenda to push. And as soon as I saw the info from the CCRC I realised exactly what Cracknell was up to, that he had used my own sale monies ... you know it already!"

"Nick!" Debbie chipped in... "...the main point is, how could you steal that kind of cash from the clients without at least one of them working out that he was short! As soon as he did he would have been in touch with your office or Roger Cracknell to query the account!"

"And if anybody did, and got no satisfactory response, the next step in the protocol is to approach the Law Society, and they would most definitely have done something about it! I mean, for Christ's sake, even if half of that sum or even a quarter of the sum went missing, that's still one hell of a lot of money!"

"It sure is! Six thousand per month, three thousand per month or even fifteen hundred per month! It don't add up!"

"Yes, and do you know what? I actually spoke to about five firms and all of them said that with the bookkeepers, partners, banks and the annual accounts there is just no way that such a load of money could be stolen. In fact, one of the firms mentioned Cracknell and Williams, and asked if they were involved. Of course, I avoided answering, but that said a lot, doesn't it!"

"It does, now all we have to do is somehow get onto those two ... I mean the barrister and clerk or solicitor who represented you and trip them up. That, Nick, is my next task! But right now, let's have a break."

TWELVE

"Nick, it's clear to me that the lack of documents was a major issue ... didn't you at any time ask about them?"

"No, I didn't, because it was not until I saw the information from the CCRC that I learned about the amount of cash allegedly stolen and it was only then that I realised what they had been up to ... bearing in mind their sub-text in supposedly representing my interests, it would not have been to their advantage to produce them. I always thought it was about Roger's seven thousand or so quid that he initially sued me for ...! Nobody asked! I did a lot of research on this afterwards. But the other issue is the time delay. I think it was engineered to enable the prosecution, by which I mean Roger of course, to deny their existence if at any time I asked for them. Looking at just the delay, I did a lot of research into prejudice caused by the delay in bringing the matter to trial. Delay is not a dead-cert get out of jail ticket to overturning a conviction. Where there has been substantial delay in bringing a prosecution, the court may stay the case as an abuse of process but a stay of proceedings on the ground of unjustifiable delay will only be granted by the courts in exceptional circumstances. It will be very rare for a case to be stayed where there is no fault on the part of the prosecution. A period of forty-two weeks is an extraordinary period and as I have said a few times, every piece of paper relating to my time at the firm was readily available. However, to establish abuse of process based on delay, I would need to prove that, because of the delay, I suffered such serious prejudice that a fair trial could not be held. Even where delay was unjustifiable, a permanent stay should be the exception rather than the rule. For God's sake, the prosecution must have thought something was odd with the time delay, so why didn't they make an application to see who was standing on the hose-pipe? The European Court of Human Rights Article six-one gives a defendant the right to be tried 'within a reasonable time'. This right flows from charge or summons!"

"Yes, that's true! When a court considers whether there has been a breach of the right to a trial within a reasonable time, they will consider the length of the delay, the reasons, whether asserted, whether there were complaints and whether there has been any prejudice. In your case an earlier trial date may have made the discovery of documents easier to achieve. But the stress of waiting for all that time may have seriously affected your ability to look after your interests".

"Yeah, exactly! But the House of Lords held that a breach of the reasonable time requirement should not automatically lead to a stay of proceedings ... I was entitled to a hearing. There is no support in the Convention or case law that there should be no hearing of a criminal charge once a reasonable time has passed. Clearly, there was no application made, and that must surely be down to the ulterior motives of my so-called defence team! Well, that deals with the delay issue. Or does it? This legal maxim is surrounded by caveats but whatever the reasons apart from the defence deliberately delaying, account should be taken of the effect on me. Ergo, it should be considered applying the known effects of delay on the ordinary man and decisions as to whether the delay did or was likely to impair my ability to give a good account of myself then becomes a matter of applying humanitarian issues and common sense. Legal get-outs are just not acceptable!"

"Justice delayed is justice denied? Apparently not!"

"Thanks, Debbie, that about sums it up!"

As the little party settled down for a quick bite, a point occurred to Maynard.

"Nick, apart from Roger Cracknell and his money problems, were there any clients you met who would for some reason have it in for you? I mean someone you may have upset?"

"Well, not as far as I know ... there was one guy whose case I worked on, but I doubt he would want to screw me for any reason."

"Tell me about it!"

"Well, we had, like every law firm, good clients but a few bad ones, the ones who just - or appear to just - stay within the law regarding their business and personal affairs. My two worst were

Stan, who ran a small manufacturing business, and a property developer, George whom I recall was thoroughly unpleasant to his wife when they both visited the office and he wanted everything done yesterday. Things came to a head one day when we were supposed to complete on a mortgage-funded purchase of a business premises as a re-development deal but as the day of completion loomed I discovered that the property was still occupied by the vendor and he was still hard at work. I have no idea whether this was some kind of deal George had arranged with the vendor. Anyway, on completion day the place was still being used as a workshop, with no sign of anyone moving out. I obviously asked my principal what we would do about it, and he told me simply to tell George that we could not spend mortgage cash when we were supposed to have vacant possession. Even after all the usual notices, the vendor refused to leave so I was told to return the mortgage funds. I told the client we had a cause of action for, inter alia, loss of bargain, but he seemed so wary about it, asking if I would deal with it 'personally' and not through my employer. Obviously I could not do that and I told him so. I discovered later that Roger and George were good friends ... and I believe I was supposed to have completed anyway with my taking the blame if it all went pear-shaped."

"Well going by Cracknell's history, that sounded about right! Clearly he was due to have made a lot of dosh out of his mate George! I expect you were pretty stressed-out by this time!"

"Nothing unusual about that in this profession! In a report by Staci Zaretsky, quoting American Bar Association Commission on Lawyer Assistance Programme, she noted that people in the legal profession struggle with mental-health and wellness issues thanks to the nature of the job! Twenty-one percent attorneys qualify as problem drinkers, nearly a third struggle with depression, and twenty percent with anxiety. And in the UK? Yes. The Law Society interviewed over two thousand solicitors about stress at work and, shockingly, more than ninety-five per cent said their stress was extreme or severe, and about forty percent cent of stressed-out calls to the charity LawCare were from solicitors below five years PQE. Not much of a succession plan!"

Collins was on a high. Everything was working out just fine. He had transferred five hundred pounds into the new Maynard account, and later the same day done another transfer to what he referred to as his 'secret' account. It had worked perfectly. He dropped in on Arnold.

"Right, can we do the trust monies from the Fisher account now? How much can you transfer?"

"We can if you insist. Five hundred and seventy thousand plus or minus a few quid. You'll have to get the bank to put it into a high-interest account, 'cos I'm gonna have to show all the interest it makes when I do the estate account for the beneficiaries ... when we find them!"

"Yeah, I'll deal with that. Let's get the transfer done!" Arnold decided that Collins was up to no good, and anyway, Arnie surmised, Ian Collins would have no more idea about drafting an estate account than he would of building s moon-rocket. He would talk to Goodrich as soon as Collins went home.

"Okay. Give me the account details and I'll do it today. Maybe you should put it straight into a trustee account, in case it gets tangled up with Mike's own clients ..."

"Look, Arnold, I don't give a shit about Maynard's accounts, after all ..."

"Ian, I cannot do a transfer ... get a trust account sorted out please, I do not want to have to trawl through a load of different accounts when the time comes ..."

"Okay! I'll do it now!"

"Then let me have the details and I'll do the transfer immediately!" Collins reached into his pocket and pulled out a piece of paper and slapped it down on the table in front of Arnold.

"There!" The succession partner slid the paper across so he could read it, called up his clients' account and commenced the transfer. It did not take long to do. In the minutes he had, he took a quick photo of the slip of paper, certain that Collins did not see him do that. The sum transferred from the Fisher to the Green trust account was five hundred and seventy thousand and seventy eight pounds. Arnold called after his boss.

"Okay, Ian, job done"

"Thanks." Collins snatched back the slip of paper and left the office. Arnold decided that he had to talk to Chris about the deal. Something was seriously wrong. He also thought it essential that he involved Maynard, as there was something definitely fishy about the deal and the guy ought to know. It was only an hour or so later that he heard Collins calling for his driver, Doug, asking for him to pick him up at a specified time, which meant thet he and Chris would then still be in the office. In the meantime, he scribbled a few notes of what Collins had done, and also the reservations he had about the whole deal. Looking at it in the worst possible light, it appeared to him that Collins was about to mis-appropriate a lot of cash, but somehow he did not believe his instincts. Nevertheless, it needed some action. It was not all that later that he heard Chris asking Collins when he would be back in the morning. The reply was indistinct, but it did indicate that Collins was on the way out. Then Chris strolled into the office.

"Arnie, what the fuck is Ian doing with the Fisher money? Whatever it is, I don't like it!"

"Me neither, mate! Something is up! Look, I've got the account details here, so I am gonna keep a check on it, after all, Lady Fisher is my client. Anyway, why did she choose you? I mean, this bloody firm?"

"'Cos Pauline used to treat her. They got talking …"

"Now Ian wants to rob her, right? that'll be a bloody good advert for the business!"

"But why did Ian choose the Green office? Do you think that … I hate to say it, but do you think that Mike is in on the deal? I mean to rob the Fisher cash?"

"No, I don't, but I do think that Ian is going to blame him!" Arnie put the accent on the 'do'.

"Then why don't we drop in on Mike and have a chat?"

"Better still, why don't we get him over here, preferably when we know that Dick 'Ed is gonna be away!"

"Good idea! Let's work on that!"

Shortly after Doug dropped Collins off at his house, another vehicle pulled up in the drive. Two men emerged from the vehicle and approached the front door. They called out.

"Mister Collins! Sir?" Ever cautious of strangers, Collins eyed them from a side window. They looked respectable, in fact he correctly concluded they were police officers. One of them held his mother's jewellery box. The lawyer went to the open door.

"Yeah, can I help you?"

"Er … we think you left this in your vehicle when we arrested you recently. I suppose it belongs to you?"

"No. It belongs to my mother. Here … let me take it and I'll give it to her."

"Well, hang on. Why was it in your car?"

"For safe-keeping."

"Surely, it would have been safer to keep it in the house?"

"I was concerned about burglars."

"Burglars?" The officer conducting the dialogue just knew that Collins was never going to tell them the real reason, and in fact Collins' brother had already told the police that he believed his brother was going to sell the stuff. As he knew, honesty and Collins were very distant acquaintances. "I didn't know that burglars were operating around here, did you, Mac?" The guy turned to address his mate.

"Na, not burglars. Other incidents of law-breaking, yes, but not burglars!"

"Well, Sir, maybe you ought to put the lot into a safe-deposit box or something. Anyway, we've done our duty. Here, take it!" The officers returned to their car. Back on the road, the two conversed.

"Hell, Spud, imagine flogging yer mum's jewellery! What an arsehole!"

"Mac, me old mate, you don't know half of it! The guy may be a lawyer, I mean, that alone is bad enough, but that Collins bloke is a total fuckin' shit! Maybe I'll tell you about it sometime!"

"Chris, you gonna talk to Mark about his brother?"

"I don't think so … maybe chat with Mike first 'cos I think he's in the line of fire. If we get any really bad vibes about this deal, then maybe rope Mark in … I think he is probably the only guy Ian listens to!"

"Okay. I'll let you arrange something with Mike, and we'll go together. I just hope that when he sees us, he doesn't just walk out like Sam did, but I certainly wouldn't blame him! Anyway, I think that with Debbie there, she's a damn good secretary, she could apply some pressure on him to stay!"

"Yeah, Arnie, but if he does go, then I am certainly not gonna fill in for Ian at that office, no way!"

"Er … I reckon if we are right about Ian, then as far as I can see that will be the end of the firm! Imagine trying to work with a total arsehole!"

"An arsehole and a thief. Bloody hell, mate, I didn't think I would ever find myself in a position like this, ever!"

"Let's just hope we're wrong! Anyway, get onto Mike, like now, Chris!"

"Righto!" Goodrich dialled the number on his mobile and got through immediately. It was Hannah who answered. "Hi, Hannah! I trust you are well! Is Mike Maynard there please? I need a quick word!"

"Yes, he is. I'll put you through now!"

"Chris! Mike! How's things?"

"Good, thanks. We, that is you, me and Arnie need to have a chat. When will you be free for about an hour? We think it better that you maybe come over to us, but we do not want Ian to be in on the conversation, so we'll have to see what his programme is before we make any hard and fast plans, okay?"

"Of course ...or maybe you could drop in and see me here? I can always arrange a lunch deal as well?"

"Yeah ... maybe that's a better idea! We'll let you know!"

THIRTEEN

Emma Collins paused as she was about to pop a slice of pizza into her mouth, and turned to address her husband.

"You know, darling, when you told that brother of yours that you wouldn't be surprised if he wasn't even your half-brother, well, I've been thinking about that. Why ..." Mark Collins stopped chewing for a second, then swallowed so he could reply without spitting food all over the table.

"So have I funnily enough ... "

"So, why don't we do one of those DNA jobs?"

"What exactly do you mean by a 'DNA' job?"

"It's easy. Go onto one of those websites, like My Heritage, and get a kit. Then you simply follow the instructions, and then they will tell you if there are any connections! All you have to do is exactly as the instructions say."

"So, we ask my mum for a sample of blood, some from Ian and some from me and send it away, right?"

"Well, I'm not sure about blood, but maybe anything that contains DNA …"

"Like what?"

"Like blood, of course, but also semen, skin, muscle, brain cells, bone, teeth, hair, saliva, mucus, perspiration, fingernails, urine, faeces …"

"Hey, you've been thinking about this for ages, haven't you?"

"Yeah, I suppose … most DNA is found in the cell nucleus, but a small amount can also be found in the mitochondria, the structures within cells that convert food into a form that cells can use."

"Okay, smart-arse, I'll give you fifty quid if you can tell me what DNA stands for?"

"Deoxyribonucleic acid."

"You bugger! You knew damn well that I'd ask you that! Okay, now what do we do?"

"What you do is pay me fifty quid. What we do is get a kit, first thing, then you do a sample, we get a sample from mum and then from Ian. Easy!"

"Easy? Getting a sample from Ian?"

"Possibly … I reckoned that if we went to the house, we'd find some DNA from him."

"Yeah, right! Just ask those kids who look after your mum if they can find some of his DNA!"

"Oh, Jesus, no! Are you suggesting that he has sex with them or something?"

"No … maybe they clean the house a bit and you never know, he might leave a lot of hair or something lying around!"

"Or something?"

"Or we get a cup he has used … lets get the kit anyway. I think you have a good idea. Then we just hope that the Heritage folk come up with a match?"

"*Exactement!*"

"*Tu es un génie!* Let's go for it. But I cannot imagine there are any buggers knocking about who are anything like your brother! And of course, let's ask your mum if there was any funny business with other men!"

"It's here, Mark! The DNA kit. Now we'll have to drop in on your mum!"

"Okay, love, give her a call. I'm free next Monday, Tuesday and Wednesday!" Emma made a call. The visit did not take long to organise, and the couple were going to go whether or not Ian Collins was going to be there.

"Your mum said she is having her hair cut on Monday, but it's being cut by one of the carers … I wonder is she also cuts Ian's hair?"

"Hey, hopefully they keep the clippings! It'd save an awful lot of messin' about if she did!"

"Right, Monday it is! And I don't care if Ian is there or not!"

Ian Collins was not at home when Emma and Mark Collins rolled up. There were three young ladies at home though attending to their various chores, one for cleaning, one caring for Mrs Collins' personal care and one who was looking after the meals. She was the one who met with the visitors when they entered the kitchen.

"*Cześć dzień dobry!* Sorry. I'm Petyra ...you don spik Polish, no?"

"No. How's mum?"

"Mum okay. I cut her hair now. You go up and see her. She tell us you come." Emma and Mark climbed the stairs to the master bedroom. It seemed that the girls had been doing a good job. Everything seemed in good order and clean. 'Mum' was seated in a chair, a sheet round her shoulders, obviously ready for her haircut.

"Hello! What you poking around for?"

"Hi, Mum! Feisty as ever! How's Ian looking after you?"

"Ian? I don't see him from one day's end to the next! He might as well live elsewhere! Anyway, as I said, what do you two want?" Emma took up the challenge.

"Well, we really want to do some family history stuff. We want to get some samples from you and Ian. We are going to do one of those DNA jobs …"

"What? You mean like those murderers getting caught out fifty years after they thought they got away with it! Then a DNA job comes up and the police pounce on them! Don't suppose there are any murderers in our family! Don't know about Ian's though!"

"What? What about Ian's?"

"Nothing really … I suppose you'd find out about it sooner or later!"

"Mum, there has to be something … I mean, he doesn't look anything like Mark or his dad …"

"Well, he wouldn't, would he? I mean … it's obvious. When I was in hospital giving birth to my second child, he didn't survive, so I left hospital empty-handed. Then a very strange thing happened …"

"Mum, do you really want to tell us? You don't have to!"

"You want to hear it or not? … A girl came up to me in the carpark and thrust a bundle into my arms. Said she didn't want it, nor did the dad 'cos his family was well-known and it would bring shame on them having a child by his dad's secretary … during her pregnancy she was packed off to be out of the way, returned to Reading to have the baby when the dad thought she had had an abortion, so it was mine to keep! She also gave me about two thousand pounds in cash for expenses … she never told me who the father was. Obviously, I did not refuse. There, I've told you!"

"Does Ian know?"

"No, of course not! You are the first people I've told! Not even my husband knew! As far as he was aware, the kid was his. Now I suppose you'll go and find out who his dad was?"

"Mum we have to … Ian is going to get himself into a lot of trouble, I mean with his business and the law!"

"Mark, I know! He has taken a lot of my money, without my consent, by the way, but I doubt I'll get it back. It was to keep his business afloat, but he has no head for business. He is a boozer and a gambler and doesn't give a fig for anybody else. He has been a lot of trouble, between you and me, being chucked out of schools, and I know it isn't in your or my genes, and dad was sometimes driven to distraction! He could never hold down any job, and dad packed him off to the army, and even then he didn't do well, until you helped him. There, now you know! Do your worst, find out who his dad was. I'd like to know!"

"Bloody hell, mum! That's quite a story! We definitely need some of his DNA!"

"What do you need for DNA?" Emma ran through the list again, leaving out semen.

"Hair you say! Ask Petra if she kept the stuff she cut off him yesterday! If she didn't, I can always ask her to keep some next time!" Mark Collins stood up and went over to his mum and kissed her. He was clearly upset by the story.

"Thanks, Mum. We will not say a thing but we will do all we can to find out who the father was. With all criminals having to give DNA samples, somewhere it is very possible that we'll get a result!"

"Good luck, son, but do be aware that it could turn out good as well as bad, or you might not get a result at all. Anyway, why the sudden interest?"

"Because we had occasion to take Ian to task about his business dealings, and the money we knew he was taking from you but neither I nor Emma recognise me or you or dad in his make-up, I mean, he seems to be utterly devoid of any interest in anybody but himself, and now we know he has made himself the sole beneficiary of your estate, 'cos he forged your will, now he is about to try and scam a lot of money from god knows where to repay the money he took from you to support his business, his boozing and his gambling!"

"Well, you be careful! He can get very nasty!"

"I know! Mark let's go and find Petra but go easy on the hair issue! Where does she normally cut Ian's hair?"

"Emma, we both get it cut in the ensuite! Then as far as I recall, it gets swept up and dropped into the little pedal bin there. Go and have a look, you never know, his might still be in there. And if you take my nail scissors, you can cut off a bit of mine, though I do not think it will be of any use to you in your mission now I've told you the truth!"

"Mum, our only aim is to make sure you don't lose everything you own because Ian is cheating you! We'll leave now, and let you know as soon as we get any results from the DNA people!" Emma went into the large en-suite and found the small pedal-bin. She opened the lid and looked inside at the contents, then put her hand in and pulled out some chunks of hair. Then she called to her husband.

"Mark … ask mum if anybody else has their hair done in here!" The answer came. No. Emma lifted out the hair in the bin and wrapped it in some kitchen-wipe that was sitting on top of the toilet cistern. Job done. She returned to the bedroom. "Okay, I've got what I need. Thank you Mum for being so honest and understanding."

"No, thank you. I should have told you long ago, but at least dad died still believing Ian was his son. I think it would have broken his heart to learn the truth and as I said earlier, he gave Dad a lot of trouble, but it's all over now!"

"Okay, but if you ever need to deal with Ian, I mean, if he gets too demanding or anything, for God's sake call us!"

On the way back home, Emma raised the subject of the next move.

"I think, Emm, that we get onto the DNA people and send the hair. How it all works from there, I don't know, but maybe you can call them and get some idea of how it all works. I mean, if there is a match, who tells whom? Does somebody tell the other person and leave it to them to call us? Do they give away our names and addresses …?"

"There might be legal implications … what if they do not want to be exposed?"

"Can't imagine that'll be the case! Obviously they will have approached the DNA lot voluntarily? Then I suppose they will also have signed some disclaimer? I don't know, love, but I am damn sure they will have figured out all the angles!"

"Right, but Ian won't have any idea …"

"No, he won't, but as we have legitimate grounds for doing what we are doing, and as we'll be the people dealing with it, then really, he doesn't have to know! And anyway, I doubt that he'll give a toss anyway!"

"I think you're right! But as you say, he doesn't have to know, nor will he ever know what we know, and I doubt he would do anything about it anyway. So, lets get the stuff send off and get the ball rolling!"

Ian Collins punched the air.

"Yes! Yes! Yeees!" He looked at the screen, which confirmed that one hundred thousand pounds had been paid from the Fisher trust account to the new Maynard account. All he had to do now was wait for a decent period before he switched the sum to his own 'safe' account, which he would do from his home computer. He slipped out of the Green office and walked round the block to where he had asked his taxi to wait. The reason was that he didn't want the driver to know that he had been anywhere the office, and with his baseball cap pulled down to a ridiculously low angle, he doubted anybody would recognise him anyway. He asked to be dropped at a spot near Reading station, from where he would take another cab home. It was fifteen minutes past ten when he got to his first cab. Nobody would be any the wiser about his trip to the office. Tomorrow, he would call Chris and Arnie to tell then he had a bit of food poisoning, and would not be in.

At nine-fifteen the following morning, Chris took the call from Collins, then he dropped in to see Arnie.

"Hey, mate, Ian's sick. Unfortunately, he'll probably live but it clears us to go and see Mike about our suspicions. You okay with that? I'll drive!"

"Yeah, let's go for it! We can get a takeaway for lunch. I assume you've cleared it with him? Mike I mean, not the arsehole!"

"Yeah. I'll call to give him an arrival time!"

FOURTEEN

Cedric Willoughby-Clarke stood outside the porticoed entrance to his property and watched the autumn leaves chasing each other round the generous car parking area. He was waiting for his aide, Bethany, to bring his car from the garage. Referred to as WC by his associates, he was having a bad day. It was nothing to do with the business or with his personal financial situation, it was just depression. The cause of his depression was his Azoospermia and he knew that ten percent of infertile men and one percent of all men have the problem, and, as he had heard time and time again from the medics he had consulted, of every fifty thousand men, around fifteen percent will be infertile, and five hundred of those men will be azoospermic. He knew a lot about the condition, and of many potential causes; genetic, such as Klinefelter's syndrome, chemotherapy, radiation, anatomical abnormalities like varicoceles or absence of the vas deferens on each side, poor testicular development or environmental toxins. And recreational drugs such as narcotics. Yes, he knew he had been a wild kid, and had come close to OD'ing many times when with his mates. Yes, he had the money and the place, his late father's huge mansion, to do what the fuck he wanted with nobody to tell him to stop. Yes, it was probably his own fault that he was impotent. And it pissed him off. He looked a bit like Putin, not a great advantage, maybe a bit taller, a bit fatter in the face, but, he thought, not nearly so bloody stupid. He was pushing seventy, too old for marriage, too old to have kids, and anyway unable to have kids, and pissed off with dealing with his dad's business, which he had done since his dad died, or so he thought, but in reality he neither knew nor cared what the business was all about and it was run by a team of trustees who had to apply all the conditions set out in the management document, a legally-binding instrument, of which he knew nothing. In fact, his merely being alive was the only condition he had to fulfil and his ideal retirement was to go to his property in Gran Canaria, soak up the sun and when bored and too old to enjoy himself, just die quietly of an intentional OD. His immediate problem was simple and now he thought about it every day; who could he leave the business to? He had some vague notion that he could not sell the business, and anyway. What he did not know was that his father appointed trustees were doing a damn good job and on excellent salaries, and he was also well looked after and knew that his cash was all his so-called friends wanted, and they got a lot of it. He knew that on his death, his will would deal with the business, and believed that if he wanted to he could appoint new trustees or let them work for the beneficiaries as they worked for him. He looked at his watch, a Chopard Alpine Eagle, now worth north of seventy thousand quid. It remined him just how stupid he was with his exceedingly generous allowance, but as always, he never listened to anybody, he just wanted to show off. Well, he was past that stage now. He was instead obsessed with his own bodily comforts, not finding someone to take over his business, a hugely successful enterprise supplying consumer goods to Unilever and to AstraZeneca et al, growing markets which his father and grandfather established when they escaped from Russia nearly two generations ago and changed their names from Jaworski to a more English-sounding Willoughby-Clarke. Technically, they were an importer, storage and distribution network, with suppliers scattered world-wide, and which took from end-users the strain of sourcing stock away. Basically, a hugely successful administration organisation, never actually seeing any of the stuff they sold. For all his wealth, Cedric led an unutterably pointless, boring life. He had no ambition, no drive and his everything was managed by his kind of personal assistant, Bethany, a frighteningly efficient individual who arranged his life for him. She had been employed initially by Cedric's father, and before he died he doubled her salary, moved her into her own suite of rooms in the mansion home near Oxford, her brief being to keep the boy occupied, out of trouble and away from his so-called friends. Beth knew of the incident which motivated old Mr W-C to take this action; it was when Cedric, aged just seventeen, had a sexual encounter with his father's secretary, Angelica, an incident which amounted to nothing, as the girl concerned was paid off handsomely and basically told to disappear, which she did. Old man W-C was known to be a hard negotiator, and although all his staff were frightened of him, he was at least fair but expected a great deal of people he paid. Ultimately, his secretary contacted her ex-employer to tell him that the child was still-born. W-C asked her to drop in to receive a final pay-off for not making a big issue of the baby. Angelica then moved on with the pay-off money to pastures new. The old man was happy; he gave the news to his son. The Angelica incident was game over. However, he reckoned that the girl was or seemed to be, too happy about the death, and being a double-belt and braces guy who wanted any reassurance he could get, and not certain Angelica was telling the truth about the baby, and with the advent of paternity DNA profiling in the early twenties, he and his son supplied a DNA sample. Even at his death, there had been no match. The issue of who could take over the business was one which became of greater importance every day, as the trustees were obliged by their terms of reference that the hand-over, such as it was supposed to be, had to be to the founder's blood-issue, subject to a few caveats all fairly complicated. And to his dying day, he had no idea that his son was now impotent.

Bethany pulled up outside the front door, and Cedrick climbed into the car as usual into the back seat. On the front seat was the day's mail, unopened. It was Beth's job to deal with post, as Cedric had no interest in mail, and rarely ever sent postcards to the house when he was away on holiday. Again, that was a duty Beth managed. In fact, the boy, even though he was now in his late sixties, still referred to by all the business staff as 'The Boy', was rarely if ever consulted on any company matters, and such was the way the old man had organised things, that fortunately, referrals were never necessary. Rather ingeniously, 'The Boy' managed to fill his day with the business which most other people seemed to do as second nature; eating, sleeping, reading, ablutions and looking at holiday brochures. It was a process which Bethany had the good sense not to interrupt, but in a way managed The Boy's life by steering him in ways he was unaware of. Today's excursion was to a travel agents, as, with the winter approaching, Boy was going to be pushed out to the Canary Islands again, period end November to end February. Beth always went with him, as, on his own the Boy would not even be able to pack or negotiate his way through customs and immigration, organise meals or even arrange a sauna at the resort. It was also a period for the mansion, Woodspen House, to be given it's annual deep-clean, a chance to refresh The Boy's wardrobe by disposing of his old clothes. That was the house-under managers job, which gave her the chance to make a bit of cash by selling quite a lot of hardly-ever, or never worn, clothing via her eBay network. So everybody gained.

The visit to the travel-bureau was a well-trodden path, and fortunately there were no complications with the latest booking. Their villa was permanently manned by some young ladies who managed to mix work with play and making money on the side. As long as they knew the owner's holiday dates, and those of his hangers-on, they were very much left to get on with things. It was a win-win situation all round, and although Bethany knew what went on, and carried on with The Boy when he was there, she never interfered. All she was surprised about was how any of the staff could find playing with an old-man's parts interesting or satisfying for them, but correctly concluded that it was all to do with the Euros they were getting for the 'interactions' or, more likely, an exchange of body-fluids.

Back at Woodspen House, Cedric let Bethany garage the car while he went to the kitchen to raid the fridge and gather a handful of chocolate biscuits which he took to the TV suite to watch, again, a few of his favourite films. Cowboy films generally. Back in her small office, Beth slit open the mail. They were still getting mail addressed to old man W-C, and today there were two for him. One was about life insurance, a bit late now, the other from the DNA profilers. It took seconds before Beth realised it was of great importance. They had a recent match with the sample which had been sent to them years ago. That was interesting, but she did not feel she ought to tell The Boy until she was able to be certain that it would lead to something positive, even though she knew that her charge had no living, close relatives. She therefore decided to reach out to the match by contacting the testing company's message system. She was actually quite excited but determined that, until she had the go-ahead from the company that the match, whoever it was, wanted to make contact, she would tell no-one. But would concentrate of finalising the details of the imminent move to Spain for the over-winter break. She scribbled out the essential actions which she needed to attend to for the holiday, and on the assumption that it would take certainly weeks if not months to hear from the DNA people, drafted a contact note and emailed it within the hour. She then dug out the holiday brief to inform the girls at the villa of the dates with a note of what they must do before the WC party arrived; she then dug out the suitcases and started to fill with summer wear; transferred the twenty thousand Euros to the GC bank account; check passports, holiday insurance, required inoculations if any; get travel itinerary from the travel agents. It kept her mind off the DNA news, but she had to admit that she was actually quite excited about it all.

FIFTEEN

It was nudging ten past ten when Chris Goldrich and Arnie pulled up outside the Green office. Within minutes, they, Debbie and Maynard were seated in the meeting room. Hannah greeted the visitors then nipped into the kitchenette to make the coffees.

"Welcome, gentlemen! To what do I owe the pleasure?"

"Er ... well, Mike this is a bit sensitive, but we are here to alert you to something er ... we think Ian is up to something..."
Maynard knew exactly what they were referring to. He played ignorant, as he didn't want to take the wind out of their sails, and anyway, maybe they had something else in mind.

"I'm all ears, Chris! Shoot!"

"Well, first thing, can we get onto your accounts to check something?"

"Of course, we can. Debbie can fire up the PC for that. Debbie?" Debs looked at Maynard, a look that said she knew damn well what was coming.

"No prob. Do you have any particular account in mind?"

"Oh ... yes! Here!" Chris pulled a slip of paper out of his pocket. "Here ... call it up then we'll have a butchers at it, okay?" Maynard glanced at the information. He didn't recognise the details, but that was not unexpected. Debbie took the slip and disappeared. Chris leaned towards Maynard, arms on the table, and in a low, conspiratorial tone, started talking.

"Mike ... as I said, this is a bit sensitive, but we believe that Ian is trying to nick about half a million quid from one of our clients, and er ... blame you for it!" Chris expected a reaction but was surprised when Maynard just smiled. "You don't seem surprised!"

"I'm not! In fact, I'm way ahead of you ...!" Then Debbie came back into the office. She had printed off the details of the new trust account. Three sets of eyes looked at her. The girl looked a bit flustered.

"Hey, you ain't gonna believe this, but ..." She looked at the paper. "...according to this account, just over half a million quid was paid into a newly opened account, and ... here's the punch-line ... according to the statement, a few days ago a hundred thousand pounds was transferred to another account. Guess who that account holder is, Mike?"

"One Mike Maynard?" Chris and Arnie looked at each other then at Maynard. Arnie got the question in first.
"How the fuck ... excuse my language ... how do you know
 that?" Debbie was grinning.

"Well, guys, it was not exactly a guess! Let me explain. Do you by any chance know a guy called Roger Cracknell, he is or was ..."

"Cracknell! Of Cracknell and Williams!" Chris interjected. "Do we know him! He is probably the weirdest bastard ever to draw breath! He had a bit of trouble not all that long ago with a clerk, I believe!"

"That's right, Nick Forrester. He was stuffed by the cops and his lawyers, did time on what was trumped-up charges".

"Wouldn't surprise me! What else do you know about this Cracknell guy?" Maynard answered.

"Nothing except that his practice is and has been for ages on the verge of closing down. I understand that he used Nick's money to keep it going. And I believe that Ian's going to try the same trick on me. Same cops, no doubt the same so-called defence team, Messrs Noël Sowerby-Newton, barrister, Solicitor Justin Weatherby …" This time, it was Arnold who spoke up.

"Well, of them let's just say that they don't move in the best circles! In fact, I'm surprised they are still alive! Anyway, Mike, carry on, this is getting interesting!"

"Okay. Now, when I took over from Sam, he left a note to ask if I would look after his nephew, Nick, who had been stuffed by Cracknell accused of stealing around two hundred thousand quid of clients cash over a period of just under three years, I think it was Debbie, is that about right?"

"Yes, as near as makes no difference."

"Well, Nick gave us the names of the cops who investigated the case, a couple of real tossers, Dent and Forbear, and lo and behold, a few days later, Ian asked us to prepare the meeting room, this room you are in now, for a meeting … with guess who?"

"Not Dent and Forbear?"

"The very same! So, we had the place wired for sound and video, and then Ian turns up for the meeting, after hours, I would add, and they outlined a plan similar to the one that Ian is apparently, involving me now! And now you tell me that Ian has already transferred that money to the bogus account fixed up by Dent and Forbear's dodgy mates! And for which they are getting a pretty big slice of the cake for doing it!"

"Bloody hell! This is just not on!"

"That's putting in mildly! Tell them about the drug job, Mike!"

"What! There's more?"

"Yeah, listen to this! When the cops were here, they noticed the loft-hatch, and asked Ian if they could stash some papers up there, and of course Ian said yes, and it turned out that it wasn't files, but packages of drugs and cash! So, we got Hannah's dad, a cop by the way, a senior cop to boot, to look at it then he put a tracker on every bundle so his men could follow each package to its destination!"

"Hey, what if the dealers find the trackers and then want the cops to explain!"

"Not our problem, but anyway they were designed to be reactive devices, and looked like ordinary security fixings to indicate if there had been any tampering with the stuff. I assume the guys who did the job knew what they were doing!"

"Well, the drug stuff is all very well, but what about Ian's dodgy dealings, how is that going to help you, Mike?"

"The idea is this; once Ian accuses me of nicking all the Fisher cash, I have no doubt that the cops who interview me will be Messrs Dent and Forbear, and also they will very probably convince me to use their lawyers, the aforementioned Sowerby-Newton and Weatherby by suggesting that as the cops do not believe that I stole the cash, their guys are very good at what they do, have done it before and have a close-on one hundred percent success rate. Let me tell you, I have heard all that crap from many barristers and solicitors when they know bloody well, that the accused hasn't got a snowball in hells chance ... all based like a lot of legal work, based on bullshit, total bollocks which is what poor old Nick was told, and his team didn't even bother to look at his private bank accounts or even ask for the conveyancing files on his own sale, and to boot he was not a well guy at the time, was he Mike?"

"No, you're right there, Debbie, thanks for mentioning it. So, what I plan to do ..." Chris cut in.

"Mike, I fail to understand how Nick's experiences will help you if and when Messrs Dent and co jump on you!"

"I'm coming to that. As I told you, we have video evidence and sound recordings of Ian and the cops actually plotting the case against me, and once in court, and the prosecution have finished their case, and it is then that I will feel the surprise and no doubt shock that my defence team will have totally and deliberately fucked up ... excuse the language again, Debs, totally fucked-up the defence, leading to a certain conviction, and into the bargain, subsequently make a claim on their various insurances which would cover the claim, and who will, as mentioned in the recordings, attach my house to repay them, or in the alternative, have the prosecution seek compensation, then a sale-order nisi, then a sale of my house, but we will also be able to point out later in the proceedings, that Ian bloody Collins actually removed the sum allegedly stolen, into an account of his own. Honestly, if we do that I see the cops and certainly Ian going down for a minimum stretch of what, ten years before parole? And into the bargain, by the time I have finished with them, the lawyers will have to pay compensation to me and to Nick! All in all, it should be a good day's work."

"Mike, it seems all a bit iffy to me ..."

"It is, Arnie, but the clincher will be the tapes and the videos, and the tapes have been transcribed and certified as accurate, and even if the other side question them, we have obviously kept the original recordings. And into the bargain, Dent and co removing the drugs and cash from the loft makes interesting listening, including something about some Toady guy having paid them, but they wanted to double up by pretending to some guy called ... who was it Debs, can you remember?"

"Yeah, some dealer, goes by the name of Stack!"

"So, Mike, I'll buy this one, this idea of yours, and maybe we can finally get a business without a bloody great hole in the bucket! What do you want us to do?"

"Right. You have the account details. I think we need to find out where Ian is sending the money once he takes it out of my 'new' account ... I assume it will be into an account he controls, but I doubt it will be in his name, then somehow get the passwords and stuff we'll need to access the account."

"I suppose we can work on that, yes. But what worries me, Mike, is that if we stuff Ian, where the hell do we go? By that I mean, you, me and Arnie and all our staff go to? We'll be jobless!"

"No you won't! If it all works out, I have spoken to Karen, my wife, and she's agreed that I can buy out Ian's interest and start a new business, same offices, same staff, different name!"

"Well, I think Ian's brother Mark will like that! He's always whinging about Ian spending their mum's money, and with the boozing and gambling as well, it never works ... can't chase gambling debts by betting more every time! Anyway, maybe we ought to get Mark involved?"

"I would say no! Blood is thicker than water!"

"True! Maybe we ought to leave him out."

"Yes, Mike, I think that would be sensible, and as far as Arnie and I are concerned, we ought to keep what we have learned today under our hats!"

"I'm happy with that. And thanks for coming in today. I don't suppose you expected to hear about all this, did you!"

"No we damn well didn't!"

In the car on the way back to their office, Goodrich addressed his oppo.

"Well, mate, I certainly did not expect that! I hope Mike knows what he is doing, but I will agree with him on one thing, possible the most important thing to come of it, and that is getting to court on his case so he can blow the whistle on the case of young Nick! I don't think that he has any option, bearing in mind what a load of crap the appeals process is!"

"Yeah! Exposing it in open court will probably be the only way of doing it! I'd love to be there when it happens, to see the reaction of those cops and of Ian!"

"Priceless! Anyway, we ought to be able to get hold of the details the account Ian is using to move the dosh. Won't be easy, but I'm sure we can do it!"

"I think we have to, Chris, in fact in view of what Mike said, I think we have a duty to see for ourselves exactly what's going on! If Mike is wrong, then of course we have to tell him but I feel in my bones that he is right!"

"I feel the same way. And if he is right, that that'll be the end of Ian and the firm, so the offer Mike made to take over the firm is a good one. I think we should both make life as uncomfortable for Ian as possible, until he breaks cover by making a mistake."

"Any ideas?"

"Yes, actually, I have a good idea … why don't you tell him that the Fisher case is close to being wrapped up, and that the beneficiary wants his money!"

"Can do! I can say that I have had a 'phone call, and the documents are on the way. There'll be no evidence that Ian could ask to see …"

"Hey, that's a bloody good idea! Let's go for it!"

"That'll give the guy a few sleepless nights, if nothing else, and I expect we'll have a bit of a laugh at his expense!"

"Or … Ian might suddenly transfer the lot and get the fuzz in to investigate! Start the ball rolling immediately!"

Shortly after the meeting broke up, Terry Thorne from ANWisecurity called Maynard.

"Mike … got all that. Do want it transcribed?"

"No thanks Terry, just file it in case we need it later."

In the office the next day, Arnie intercepted Collins as he strode past in reception.

"Ian!... We have some movement on the Lady Fisher case." Collins stopped dead in his tracks.

"What exactly?"

"All issues sorted out and the beneficiaries want their money. I told them it would take a couple of days, maybe a week, then if we get their account details we can pay them out. I added there will be a small extra charge ..."

"Well, I want to see exactly what and who, we can't just..."

"It's okay, Ian, it was only a 'phone call, and I also said that we'll need something in writing agreeing to their pay-out proposals. We could delay matters, but I don't see that we need to really!"

"Maybe you don't, but I do! It's a lot of money, and we can't afford to make any mistakes! Delay things for as long as you can, until I give you the go-ahead!" Colins then slipped into his office. Under his breath he was swearing. And he was worried. There was nothing for it but to transfer the cash out of the trust account into the new Maynard account then on to his own overseas bank.

SIXTEEN

"Mark! There's a letter here for you!"

"Open it love"! Any idea who it's from?"

"Just a mo." Emma ripped open the envelope. "Er ... it's the DNA people ... looks like they have found a match!"

"Wow! When I've finished my shower, I'll come down!"

"Okay ... see you in about an hour?"

"You bloody comedian." It was not an hour, but more like ten minutes, when Mark Collins appeared in the kitchen. He held out his hand for the letter. "Just the one contact? Well, that makes it easy! What's the next step?"

"Read the blurb, and it'll tell you!" Collins cradled his lemon drink as he read the letter.

"It seems we have to agree to a contact! Well, let's do it!"

"That seems to be the right thing to do, Mark, but I see the letter was addressed to you, but you ain't your brother …"

"I know that love, but can you honestly imagine that Ian would want anything to do with this? I mean …"

"No, I can't … but how do you intend to impersonate him! You are two years older than he is, and your birth certificate says so, so …"

"We just use Ian's if indeed he ever had one! Anyway, they are not interested in birth certificates, only DNA!"

"So, talk your way out of that problem then!"

"Don't have to … we'll make contact, say nothing we don't know about Ian and depending on what they need …"

"At least we get to see Ian's family, and I assume they only want what we want, a peek into Ian's blood-relatives, to see if they are as stupid, psychopathic self-centred alcoholic gamblers as Ian is! Maybe we could then confront Ian and give him the good news, that he is not the only total fuckin' idiot on the planet, but he has maybe a few dozen blood-relatives who are exactly like him!"

"Well, I suppose that would make it all worthwhile?"

"Yeah, I suppose so!"

"Mark that was a question, not a statement!"

"Whatever! … at least it will give us something do keep us occupied over the winter!"

"Look, mate stop pissing around … send off the request for contact!"

"Okay. I'll do it before I go to work. I'm on late shift!"

Ten days later, after a reply from the DNA people, it was

Bethany who took the 'phone call from Mark Collins. She had agreed with the DNA people that the contact from Reading could call her, as 'Cedric's secretary and PA', as she called herself more for convenience than anything else, rather than 'The idiot who does every bloody thing for The Boy except perhaps wipe his arse', and added that she looked forward to the call and agreed to scribble a quick note on how the DNA company had performed, one of those now all-too common and intensely annoying 'How did we do today' stars out of five. She was hoping that the contact was the blood-issue of her charge, and not some distant relative, perhaps someone from Russia and then very old. Beth did not see fit to inform The Boy, but did inform the business trustees that there might soon be some good news as regards the future ownership of the business; JaworInt. Ltd. The trustees would be elated, as they knew that in the event of a sale, as per the conditions under which the business would be operated if there were no blood-line issue to carry it on, they would be out of a job. Beth knew in any event, that all Cedric would want to know, was that the match, whoever it happened to be, might be an occasion for celebration. After all, he had little else to look forward to. But whatever happened, and although the meeting would be important, it must not clash with the upcoming holiday in November. It even crossed her mind that the meeting could take place in Gran Canaria, with the contacts staying at the villa to give everybody a bit of time to get to know each other. She made the call.

"Mister Collins?"

"Yes, can I help?"

"I am Bethany Knight, the PA to the DNA match, Cedric. I suppose the next step will be to meet. I don't know what if any restrictions may limit your available time, but Cedric and I will be flying out to the Canary Islands at the end of November. It had crossed my mind that as we will have an awful lot to say and that we all ought to get to know each other it will certainly take more than an hour over a cup of coffee in some dingy restaurant! So, if you are minded, we could meet out there! We have a fully-staffed villa, and with spare accommodation, so if you could make it between the beginning of December and the last week in February? It's Cedric's birthday on the seventeenth of December ... he'll be sixty-seven" Collins was a bit taken aback. It was a fast ball, but it was certainly possible. And with the guy that old, the maths meant that Ian would only be seventeen years younger, fifty.

"Er ... yes, I think that's possible. Could I bring my wife as well?"

"Of course! And of course, your children. I suppose they'll be on holiday then?" Another fast ball for the prison warder.

"I doubt they will be able to come with us as they have already arranged to visit the in-laws, who are more Christmassy types than us!"

"Okay ... anyway, let me know the most suitable dates, then we can move on from there. Accommodation and meals will of course be on us. The callers exchanged a few more pleasantries, then rang off. Mark Collins breathed a sigh of relief. At least, he concluded, it was all going to be pretty informal. Or so he hoped. He turned to his wife, who had been listening on speakerphone.

"Looks like you had better take some leave! I suppose a week will do?"

"Yes ... and maybe you could look up the name, Willoughby-Clarke to see what, if anything comes up! I'll book some leave and unless you have any preferences, I'll take say ten days off over Christmas, say fly out to Spain on fourteenth of December, back twenty-first or so?"

"Sounds good to me! What about the kids?"

"Emma, I don't want to upset them and have them kicking their heels in Spain when they really want to be spoilt rotten by the in-laws! ... if we need kids we can always borrow Mike's two!"

"Yeah why not? I mean even easier, why don't you just kidnap a couple from the nearest playschool group? Nobody'll notice, and when you've finished with them just dump them in some supermarket carpark!"

"Now, that's an idea!"

"Right, I'll work out a plan! Bugger off to work and book that holiday!"

SEVENTEEN

Ian Collins decided he had to make a move. He did a quick check on the Fisher trust account. He had about four hundred thousand to shift, and on the assumption that it would take at least ten days for the written instructions to arrive from the Fisher beneficiaries, he could safely shift a hundred thousand every two days, starting from today, and every day after making a payment he would transfer the sum to his overseas account. He clicked onto the account site, then the 'Move Money' link, and did a transfer. He had agreed with Dent and Forbear that as soon as he reported the 'theft' they would descend on the Green office and arrest Maynard. Once he had been charged with the theft, he would pay off the cops then draft a statement about his relationship with the 'new lawyer', his shock at his behaviour and how he would do everything he could to assist in getting the matter 'sorted out'. He grinned. It would be great to see the rich bastard in jail and his kids' lives and that of his no doubt smarty-pants wife disrupted. He would also teach his brother a lesson by paying him off in full, and deal with the other points he had raised, something about a trust. He could always discuss the way ahead. He did though know full well that his business was not producing enough cash for him to carry on with his gambling and boozing, which he never regarded as an issue, just the way he chose to live his life, and it was nobody's business but his. Chris walked into Ian's office.

"Heard any more about the Fisher people? Arnie reckons it is on the very edge of being settled. Be glad to ..."

"Oh, for fuck's sake, Chris, don't bother me with trivia! I've got more important things to deal with. I'm on the brink of a really good deal with a major construction firm, building a huge new estate near Abingdon! They want me to do all the sales stuff for all the new-builds. ..."

"Oh, really? Which builders?"

"I can't remember who they are ... I had a meeting with them the other day. You remember when I was out? Look, give me a break, okay?"

"Okay!" Goodrich backed out of Ian Collins' office. "Sorry to have bothered you!" Chris knew damn well the bloke was lying. He called Maynard, and when he got through, he told the guy to check the trust account, and to call him back. It took no time for the call.

"Well so far, Chris, the bugger has taken two hundred thousand. I don't suppose he'll call the cops in until the whole bloody lot has been syphoned off. Then the fun will start!"

"Mike, I hope you know what you're doing ... but I assure you that Arnie and I are behind you all the way! And I am going to stick to Ian like a leech until I find out where he's parking the money from your new account! I have a notion it will be overseas somewhere, maybe the Cayman Islands. He used to talk about then place a lot when he had a load of dodgy clients a few years ago. Thank God, they just took off one day and we ever heard from them again. Anyway, Mike leave it with us!"

"Okay, you've got it!"

Over the next six days, Collins emptied the Fisher trust account, and one day after that he moved the final tranche of cash to his own private overseas account. All he had to do now was wait until the money had to be paid to the Fisher estate beneficiaries, and he would then 'discover' the loss and call in the police. He grinned at the thought of totally screwing-up the Maynard's family Christmas. He thought about paying off his brother, but then decided he could also wait. As far as stage two of the plan was concerned, he would brief the cops, get Maynard interviewed and hopefully arrested and charged, and he could already see himself spending the half million in his overseas account. Chris Goodrich had learned when his boss was up to no-good. Whether is was drinking or juggling with the accounts. He always closed the door on the pretext of making important 'phone calls, and he had followed this habit at roughly the same time over a six-day period. Maynard confirmed that every other day, another hundred thousand pounds was removed from the trust account. Goodrich knew neither he nor Ernie could ask about the account, as neither of them were supposed to have the account details, but he was determined to see just where the stolen money was going. As soon as Ian had left for the day, he called Arnie.

"Hey, mate, Mike says that all the Fisher cash has now been moved … maybe we can go over Ian's PC and see if the history file will tell us where he's sent all the dosh. What do you reckon?"

"Let's go for it. Nowt to lose! Wanna coffee?"

"Yeah. See you in a minute." Chris slipped into Ian's chair, and moved the mouse. The PC screen lit up. After all, it was only a very short time since Collins had used it. And thank God, Chris thought, Collins had not bothered to switch it off. He opened the screen, and clicked onto 'History' and up came the RBC bank. Ian had a notion that Ian had very probably just used the account his former clients had used, and he knew it cannot have been all that long ago. He wracked his brains to remember the clients' names. He called out to Arnie.

"Bugden, I think it was! He's in jail now, and I don't think Ian ever told the cops that he had an overseas account … probably empty at the time of the trial! If you can find the file, the account details are probably in it somewhere!" Ian's filing cabinet contained only a few files, but was mostly taken up by overload from the other offices. There was no Bugden file, or anything like it.

"There's no file!"

"Look in the desk drawers! Or under the table or something, I don't suppose Ian will have memorised the details!" Chris opened every drawer, and lo and behold, the file was there, open at the page with the account details, and severely straining the green treasury tags holding the file together.

"Arnie! Got it ... come here!" It was clear that Ian had used the details to make payments into the account, otherwise, why was that file in his desk drawer. The two men entered the details; account name; password. It took seconds for the details to show up. There had been several recent deposits, one being a very small amount, only forty pounds. That was followed up by five further payments of one-hundred thousand pounds. "Bloody hell, Arnie, the Fisher cash! Do you have on you details of the trust account?"

"No. First thing tomorrow, call Mike!"

"Yeah. And don't talk to Ian about the account, let's see what his next move will be! And print off the statements as well. I'll turn the printer on. Then delete the history. We'll have all the info we need!"

The following day, Ian Collins did not appear in the office, and when Chris Goodrich called Mike in the Green office, the message was that the Fisher account was virtually empty.

"Thing is, Chris, when will I get a visit from the cops? I imagine Ian will get onto it as soon as the Fisher beneficiaries ask for their money!"

"Yeah, but neither I nor Arnie are going to press the issue ... fact is, we have no idea what's happening with the estate, and until we hear from the various people concerned, we have nothing to go on! We do not want Ian to get any idea that we are onto him 'cos there's no telling what he'll do if he finds out!"

"Makes sense, I suppose. I expect the next thing is, I'll get a visit from the cops then it'll all kick-off! At least, we've kept DCI Ellis informed, so obviously we will also keep him informed about what Dent and Forbear are up to. What we do not want to do is blow the whole thing wide-open 'cos that'll screw-up Nick's chances of getting cleared. That little charade will be done in open-court!"

"Yeah! I'd like to be there when that happens! And to see the faces of Dent and co, and of course, the two lawyers, Noël Sowerby-Newton and Justin Weatherby. I have no doubt that the revenue will also find out that their income exceeds anything they have been grossing honestly, if any!"

"Well, five grand to the cops for some false IDs is some indication of what they'll be charging Ian for the whole show! It'll be in the tens of thousands! Anyway, let's leave it there, and keep each other of any developments, okay with that?"

"Yeah, of course Chris. Regards to Arnie!"

Ian Collins was on a high; everything was falling into place nicely. He would pay off his brother and the insurance pay-out would settle the Fisher beneficiaries claims. He would leave the police contact as close to Christmas as possible to really bugger-up the Maynard's' holiday. The rich bastard could sweat it out when he was in jail. He reached for another bottle of brandy, then popped up to see mum to chat about repaying some money, but for some reason, she seemed to be on a bit of a high as well and was not interested in talking money, but wanted to watch her programme on TV. He was well over the drink-drive limit, and he knew it, but aware of his own infallibility, he carried on with his nefarious business. He called his brother. Emma answered the 'phone.

"Yes, Ian. How can I help" She was in the process of packing her kids stuff for their in-laws visit, and her and her husband's bags for the flight to Spain. She was not exactly over the moon about any 'phone call interrupting her and especially not from Ian Collins.

"Yeah, just thought I'd tell you that I will pay Mark's money soon. Possible early next year if that's okay!"

"I suppose so. Is that all?"

"Yes."

"Okay, I'm packing right now … we're off to Spain for a while. I'll tell Mark when I see him. Bye." Then she chucked the 'phone onto the bed. "What a tit! I wonder who he stole that money from!" She returned to her packing.

Mark and Emma had agreed that they would fly out of Bristol with Tui at about nine-thirty on Tuesday twelfth December.

"Darling, how romantic! That is National Ambrosia day and Ding-a-Ling day, and Poinsettia Day in America! And International Day of Neutrality."

"Why the hell is that romantic?"

"Oh, never mind!"

It was a four and a half hour flight, and Bethany had arranged for a car to meet the Collins at the airport to take them to the villa. There would be a driver holding a board with their names on. It seemed to be well organised. Mark had arranged the time off on the basis that the break was not a jolly, but more of a personal, family issue which could not be put off. He would be able to return to work on Saturday the twenty-first of December to cover Christmas. Both Emma and Mark were looking forward to the first real break in a long time, and being short-staffed at the prison, as always, made family-life pretty hard, especially on Emma and the kids, and overtime payments barely made up for it. Forty-one hour weeks on less that forty thousand per annum was barely enough for all the hassle of the job especially the commute to

Winchester and back every day or night depending on the shifts. All Emma and Mark had to do now, was get their story right. It was, inter alia the subject of the conversation at the dinner table.

"Ian called today. Said he had the money you wanted and he reckoned he could pay you in the new year."

"Oh, really? I wonder where he nicked that from!"

"Exactly what I thought … maybe he stole it from Mum's account? maybe we ought to ask her to check it! Perhaps we could call on her again and ask her to look at her balances. I'll be really pissed off if he has nicked it from Mum!"

"Or maybe this 'big deal' he was working on has come to fruition!"

"Bollocks! Anyway, about our Spain trip! We need to get all our ducks in a line. Exactly what are you going to say about this?" Between mouthfuls, the pair discussed the issue.

"Right, Emm. I was born on the same day as Ian, and then when we wanted to do some serious family history stuff, you spoke to Mum and she came up with the story of me being handed over by a girl who knew that Mum had had a still-birth, and she also handed over some cash as well. Then basically disappeared! I don't for one minute believe she was fibbing, I mean, why would she it if it weren't true?"

"Are you absolutely determined to pretend that you are your brother?"

"Emm, I do not have a brother! Just some arsehole mum and dad looked after for years with no thanks or respect, he just gave them both a hard time! So what if at least one of us can get something out of it?"

"Well, that's about it I suppose. What else is there to say? Everything else you say can be true, about you being a prison officer at Winchester after Reading prison closed, that at least gives you a degree of respectability, albeit very small, …"

"Hey, watch it!"

"… And I don't suppose for a minute that there's gonna be any question of fraud or anything is there?"

"I dunno. It all depends on how Bethany reacts, what she tells us, why they went onto the DNA site in the first place, and anything else she has to say. Anyway, would you turn down a free holiday? Apart of course from the air-fares which came to about five hundred quid! And how's the packing going?"

"All done. And the kids' stuff. We can drop them off at the in-laws, who by the way, have volunteered to take us to the airport."

"Have to be there by seven-thirty latest!"

"Yeah, that's why they have suggested that we stay over Monday night, then leave at about six-thirty latest on Tuesday. We're doing hand luggage only, so you'll have to wear a few spare clothes and that vest thing with all the zip-up pockets to carry our tickets, passports, bank-cards, cash… any anything else we can't afford to have nicked!"

"Yeah, good idea … maybe I should wear my prison uniform?"

"No, love … somebody might try to kill you!"

"Wouldn't be the first time!"

"Yes, and that's another thing! As soon as you get the cash from Ian, we'll move house. And for God's sake try and find another job! Being a prison officer is a shit job…"

EIGHTEEN

When Mark and Emma landed at Las Palmas, they went straight to the arrivals lounge with their cabin baggage, to be met by their driver, a young lady holding a very prominent sign above her head, and smiling broadly as the arrivals approached her.

"Mr and Mrs Collins? Welcome to Spain! My name is Sophie. Follow me please! As they followed the girl, she dumped the board into a waste-paper bin!"

"Cor, Emm ... I'd follow her anywhere!"

"Behave, mate, or so help me, I'll cut your balls off!" The drive took just under an hour in the small mini-bus, and all the way the scenery was beautiful. The driver was talking most of the time.

"Temperature today is about twenty degrees. Weather dry and it will be like this most days. I think you people in England are daft living there! Mister Cedric and Miss Bethany very sensible people! Have nice villa, can walk down the garden to the beach. Can swim every day but make sure you leave no valuables on beach otherwise bad men steal it all! All immigrants!" The chat was incessant, but interesting and neither Emma nor Mark thought it appropriate to ask questions about their hosts. "I work all time for Bethany ... my friends also we stay in the villa and look after all the guests when Miss Bethany and Mister Cedric not here ..." Well, that told the visitors something. In what seemed like no time at all, the little mini-bus drove through some wrought-iron gates and pulled up in front of a very impressive villa. The front was white, fronted by three arches, the centre one leading into the property, and above and set back was the first-floor again with an arched façade, and a large dome to the left. Just inside the property, stood a lady, whom Sophie introduced as Bethany.

"I get your bags from the 'bus. Miss Bethany here will look after you now!" Miss Bethany advanced and shook hands with the guests. "Emma, Mark ... welcome to *Casa Aurora*!"

"Bethany ... this is beautiful ...!"

"You ain't seen nothing yet! Let's go to the back ... follow me!" The small party walked through the house out to a large circular pool, surrounded by grass, and beyond that a sweeping garden at the end of which was a private thirty-foot path to the beach. The lawn was bounded by beautiful bushes and flower-beds. "You might want to get into a change of clothing ... it's a bit warm here! And later, we'll meet Cedric ... he's sleeping at the moment, the heat makes him a bit tired." In fact, Beth was not being totally honest; the man was sleeping off a hangover, after all, he had very little else to do apart from drink and take the drugs some of the female staff obtained for him at a substantially inflated price. All he was interested in what came out of a bottle, a dress and Columbia; ergo, what went into his stomach, his bed and up his nose. Even he could not recall when he last read a newspaper or watched the news. As the group stood and gazed out to sea, Bethany addressed the visitors again. "I think we should leave the business matters until the day after tomorrow, as there is plenty to occupy you until then And hopefully, Cedric will have some input as well … come on, I'll show you to your rooms. Then you might like some light refreshment … it's all available in your room then maybe a stroll down to the beach. There's a bar, café and souvenir shop there, so please just do whatever you want. In case you don't have any Euros, we have some down here for our guests!" Emma and Mark were shown to their room. In fact it was a suite of rooms, looking over the front of the villa, the cool side, where the sun only peeked into their rooms in the morning.

"Wow, Beth, this is beautiful! You are very lucky having all this!" Beth smiled.

"Maybe, but I do enjoy it while I can! Anyway, your cases are here, so I'll leave you to do whatever you want, and we'll be serving the evening meal at about seven. I'll see you then." The hostess left them, closing the door behind her.

"Mark, this is something else!" Mark put his finger to his lips, and Emma got the message immediately. "Lets unpack, put on the summer stuff and go for a stroll!"

Within half an hour, the couple were on the promenade, taking in the views, the yachts, bars, souvenir shops. They talked as they walked.

"Emm, I don't know enough about these people … it may be that they have listening gear in the bedrooms, hence my being cautious! Anyway, there's some money there, love. I wonder if they own it or have just rented it? Either way, it really is beautiful. Imagine spending three months of every year here!"

"Oh, don't!"

"Love to. Imagine having the kids out here with us! They would love it too!"

"And imagine how the school would love to fine us for keeping them off school for three months!"

"Yeah, just imagine! They'd get full marks for the Spanish exams! Let's buy some postcards! Gonna send one to Ian?"

"No I am not!"

"Okay. We can probably get some stamps as well. We'll write the cards tomorrow."

When the guests had left for their walk, Bethany tapped on Cedric's door. He was awake watching, yet again, the cowboy film, 'The Man who Killed Liberty Valance'. The Boy did not even acknowledge her presence.

"Cedric … your guests are here!"

"Which guests?" Oh dear, thought Bethany, this is not going to be a good start to what's left of the day.

"Maybe I forgot to tell you!" On the side-table, Beth could se the drug paraphernalia from last night's fix. She knew that to let The Boy out on his own would mean he'd probably buy some adulterated shit which could mean his death, but the girls knew what to buy and what to avoid. She could not risk having The Boy die before all the business issues were sorted with the trustees. She also knew that the young ladies and he had some kind of weird sex programme which they rehearsed from time to time but which kept him away from the street-prostitutes. She turned a blind eye to the whole deal, whatever that was. "Anyway, never mind. You will see them at dinner this evening."

"Don't want dinner. Just a pizza and a couple of beers. I'm tired!"

"You must be love after the hard day yesterday!" The 'hard day' was him walking round town with a couple of the villa's female staff for a few hours buying a load of new clothes for them and for himself. In a way, Bethany was glad that she and the guests could just talk about everything and anything without having to entertain Cedric.

As was expected, Cedric did not appear at the dinner table. Beth and her crew laid on a standard Spanish fare, comprising a Gambas al ajillo starter, followed by Paella with seafood then olive oil lemon cake. To drink, Tinto de Verano. Apart from Beth and the gusts, the four villa girls sat with them and also served the food. The girls spoke pretty good English, and when Mark started talking about his job in the prisons, he had the whole table in stitches.

"Mister Collins, you have very many people on your prisons, yes? How is that?"

"Because my dear," he replied to their driver, "because the justice system in the UK is utter rubbish! It is on its last legs, and the appeal system is about as useful as tits on a bull!"

"Mark! That's rude!" But everyone laughed just the same.

After their busy day, Emma and Mark slept well, but before they nodded off, they talked about their programme.

"I suggest we leave here well after breakfast, then just spend a good few hours walking around. I see that we can walk for miles on the promenade, so maybe we could get lunch out and pick up some brochures from the various hotels in case we want to come back here. The only prob is the four-hour flight!"

"Yes, that is a bit of a pain but at least you get decent weather guaranteed! Look how annoyingly healthy the locals are!" Next morning, they showered then moved downstairs for breakfast. Helpfully, there was as note setting out mealtimes and in which room each meal was served. The air was already warm, and both were keen not to overdress and finish up having to carry some of the clothes if they got too warm.

Once the visitors had gone, Bethany put in a call to the senior trustee of the business. She had already primed him about what was going on, so he only needed an update.

"Hi, Ted …. so far so good. The guy is married and they have two kids. He is a prison warder so moderately respectable. Not overly enamoured of the job, so all looks good. Not in the least bit like The Boy, glad to say, and unless you have anything you want to add to the notes re the meeting tomorrow, I assume you are happy for me to proceed as agreed?"

"Of course, Beth. And to be frank, unless we can stop The Boy from all this drug-use, it may be that we need to inject a degree of urgency into the process, if you'll excuse the pun, before the bloke kills himself!"

"Frankly, Ted, I don't think the guy has a clue about his situation, either about how dangerous the drug-use is, or about exactly what he is sitting on, about the business I mean!"

"Yeah, and none of us here want to lose our jobs which will happen if the business gets taken over on Cedric's death, so we have to make bloody sure that the Mark bloke is the right guy …"

"Ted, he's the only one! It damn well has to work, and the same goes for me as well!"

"Well, Beth, if you encounter any problems, like if we have to make the package look more attractive, for God's sake, call me and I'll find a way, okay with that?"

"Yeah, of course!!"

"And I'll email a note of issues I'd like you to raise as well. One more thing, Beth, all this is highly confidential!"

"Got it!" As Beth ended the call, Cedric entered the room

"Who was that, Mum?"

"Ted from the office. I was just talking about …" Cedric interrupted her.

"Have I got to meet these guests? Who are they? Friends of yours?"

"No, Cedric, I've already told you, they are here on business! You should meet them …"

"I don't want to meet them. I don't know anything about business, either. Business bores me!"

"Okay, of course you do not have to meet them." Beth did not feel that she ought to remind him that the business was paying all the bills in the house in Oxford, and for the villa, and to boot his bank account was being credited with several hundred thousand pounds per annum, the minimum the trustees felt he should receive. The trustees' argument for that was that there were business owners far more useless than Cedric but who were paid a hell of a lot more.

On their walk around the coastline, Emma and Mark were having a similar conversation.

"Right, Mark, let me ask you some awkward questions."

"Okay, go ahead,. But remember, we can always back out of this business, if, that is, it isn't going to do either of us any good."

"And Ian?"

"Don't give a toss about him. Anyway, fire away with the questions!"

"When were you born?"

"Same day as Ian … fourteenth February seventy three. And I'll be fifty-two next February."

"Schools?"

"Same as Ian. Last school was in Lower Early, Reading. Then I applied to become a youth justice worker before I joined the prison service. I know all about that because I actually did it!"

"Do you have any siblings?"

"Yes, one. Ian. He is two years older than I am and he joined the army."

"Kids?"

"Yes, two ... I know all that! Ask about why we did the DNA thing!"

"You know that! And do you plan to stay in the prison service?"

"No. I might stay in the training role, but am really fed-up with the job at the moment. Abuse, crap pay, long hours ... not ideal for a family man at all! How am I doing?"

"Pass – so far. Lets stop at a café and get a drink and some lunch!"

After their lunch break, Emma and Mark took a slow stroll back to *Casa Aurora*. Beth intercepted them as they crossed the lawn towards the villa.

"Had a good day?"

"Yeah, great! Lovely little place, this island. Must visit more often!" It occurred to Beth that if they played their cards right, they could spend one hell of a lot of time here.

"Glad you like it! I'm trying to get you a meeting with Cedric ... he's being a little bit difficult to track down at the moment. And of course, tomorrow we have our day going through a lot of stuff. We don't need to have Cedric present for that, but I'm sure he'd like to meet his son. I have not yet told him who you are ... it might be a bit of a shock to him, if indeed we tell him at all. He does have problems, as I'm sure you'll understand!" neither Emma nor Mark really had to be told that, bearing in mind that Ian had issues like nobody would believe.

NINETEEN

The following morning, after breakfast, Beth ushered her guests into what was a rather impressive office.

"Please take a seat ... this is where the business employees can take instructions and are generally updated when here on holiday. It also means that in the event of any issues arising, the staff can have a full-attendance conference. Not bad, eh?"

"Very nice!" Emma and Mark settled in. Beth took control.

"Right, I'm hoping Cedric will pop in. He doesn't like to involve himself in business issues. I think his policy is that as lots of people are paid to run the business, he does not need to bother with it!" Emma picked up the point.

"Beth, what is this business thing? We had no idea ..."

"Sorry, maybe I should have mentioned it before ...the business is called JaworInt. It imports, stores and distributes to purchasers stuff like food product ingredients and biochemicals for the pharmaceutical industry. We have a network of suppliers scattered world-wide, and which takes off manufacturers the strain of sourcing stock ingredients. Basically, a huge successful administration organisation, never actually handling any products. We also ..." Mark interrupted.

"Sorry, Beth, what is this to do with us?" Beth smiled. She had noticed the quizzical expression on the guests faces as she outlined the business set-up.

"I'll come to that ..." Then the office door opened. Cedric popped his head round to look at the three people seated round the table.

"Mum ... I'm going out now. With Angie and Sophie in the car." Beth waved in acknowledgement. Cedric's eyes just swept over the guests, no acknowledgement at all, as though they were just not there, then he was gone. Beth got up and closed the door.

"He calls you Mum?"

"Yes ... I am a bit like his mum, but all will become clear during this meeting. Er ... break for coffee and biscuits?" Beth pushed the button on a little bell fixed onto the table, one of four. "Okay ... same as you had yesterday?"

"Oh, yes please!" Within five minutes, the door opened again and a tray with coffees and biscuits was slipped onto the table. "Hey, that looks very efficient!"

"Glad you like it! The whole JaworInt ethos is based on

efficiency! The old man was almost fanatical about it. I think you would have loved to meet him. He passed away only a few years ago. He was cremated. I'm sure that is not important to you, but he made a big hoo-ha about it! Anyway, where was I?"

"The business!"

"Ah, yes. The business. It was set up by Cedric's grandfather and great uncle, when they moved to the UK from Russia and it was set-up so it could only be owned by the family and run by trustees who would between them decide on replacement trustees, and if the business were sold then all the trustees would be redundant, and if no blood-issue family was available to take over ownership then on the death of the last surviving member the business would have to be sold. Clear so far? Can you see where I am going?"

"Er … yes … Cedric …"

"Cedric is currently the last surviving member, that is, apart from you, Mark! We know that all the Russian side of the family died off mainly because of purges in Russia … mainly the Great Terror of thirty seven, the Great Purge, the brutal political move by Stalin to eliminate anyone he considered a threat. Cedric's family just avoided it, which was lucky as nearly a million people were executed and roughly the same number were sent to the Gulags. Cedric's dad and I used to discuss this a lot. It hardened him and also made him very distrustful of anybody … except family!"

"What are you saying?"

"I'm saying that you and your issue … children … could inherit the business!" Emma looked at Mark, and he at her. Both were initially speechless. Mark broke the silence.

"But what about Cedric's mum? I mean, real mum? I know she's not real blood, but …?"

"Ah, yes! Old man Jaworski, Aleksandr or Alex as he preferred, became Willoughby-Clarke. Anyway, his secretary Angelica and Cedric managed to get together and the result was that she became pregnant. Alex was incensed! He bought her off and he was then told that the child was still-born, which we obviously know was incorrect. When were you born, Mark?"

"Fourteenth February seventy three. And I'll be fifty-two in February next year!" Emma looked distinctly relieved that he got it right.

"That checks. So, your mum, by that I mean the lady to whom you were given, just used you … why? I mean didn't she have any issues with it?"

"No, because her own baby was still-born, or died soon after he was born, I don't know which, and mum told me that when she went to the carpark to go home, this girl she had seen in the maternity ward came up to her and just handed over her baby. She also gave mum some cash. As far as the birth registration was concerned, I have no idea, as I did not ask, but I expect dad and she managed to deal with it alright, as far as I know, anyway! And where is the girl now?"

"Well, we have no idea! I mean, it was just over half a century ago … could be anywhere, but I do know that when Alex was told of the still-birth, he was relieved and gave her a bag full of cash. In fact, bearing in mind that Cedric is now impotent, which he put down to his excessive drug use as a teenager, some of the trustees think that it could have been Alex's baby anyway, ergo, his keenness to get rid of the girl!"

"Hey, Beth, this is looking like turning into some nineteenth plot involving illegitimate heirs and princes in the tower!"

"Eh, what was that then?" Mark knew Beth should not have asked. History was Emma's forte, but to give her her due, Beth did not stop the flow.

"Oh, Beth, you should not have asked!" Emme continued, nevertheless.

"The Princes in the Tower! Glad you mentioned that! It refers to the fate of King Edward fifth and his brother Prince Richard, heirs to the throne of Edward the fourth. Edward and Richard were the only sons of the king by his queen, Elizabeth, living at the time of their father's death in the late fifteenth century. They were aged twelve and nine, and were imprisoned in the Tower of London by their uncle Richard Duke of Gloucester, in preparation for Edward fifths coronation, but before he was crowned, he and Richard were declared illegitimate. So Gloucester ascended the throne as Richard the third. It is believed that the two princes were murdered by Gloucester to secure his position on the throne!"

"Well, I'll be! I can assure you that as far as I know there were no murders in this case! But, I must say, Emma, you certainly know your history!"

"I tried to warn you, Beth!" The door opened again. It was Millie taking luncheon orders.

Luncheon was served under an awning on the rear patio area. It was very warm, and with the sun reflecting off the sea, a most enjoyable situation.

"Well, if you are both happy to continue after lunch, we can go into more detail. I am happy to put you forward to the trustees for serious consideration. And the other issue is..." she lowered her voice so none of the villa staff would hear, "...that the way Cedric is behaving, with his over-fondness for drugs and the wrong kind of food, we have no idea how long he'll last. We need to get this business sorted once and for all!"

"Well, Beth, Mark and I will do all we can to help. I don't know how much time off work Mark can get once back in the UK, but certainly, kids permitting, I can make myself available twenty-four seven!"

"That would be good! At least, there's nobody else in the running, and Ted is pushing me to get some closure on all this before some of the other trustees jump ship on the basis that the business will be sold on. Then I expect, the buyers will float it on the London or New York markets and walk off with a big pile of dough!"

Back on the promenade, Emma and Mark found a café and bagged as table under the awning where they sat with their drinks.

"Bloody hell, Emm, this thing is massively bigger than I ever thought! I reckoned we were going to meet some idiotic, self-centred plonker who looked a bit like Ian ..."

"Well we certainly saw a self-centred, plonker and probably idiot as well, but he's not a bit like Ian to look at, but do you know what? I don't think Beth or this bloke Ed - Ted - in the UK gives a toss! It appeared to me that they want us to be who we want them to think we, or rather you, are because their futures depend on it. I think Beth's job is on the line if they fail, as well." Mark took a long pull on his beer then put his glass back on the table.

"You know what as well? I imagine that the villa and the place where Cedric and co live is ... are ... probably owned by the business, so if this weird deal goes through, I reckon that we ..."

"Hey, hang on a minute! Are you saying that we might, just might, have use of them? I mean if we don't actually get to own them? Bloody hell, Mark ...!"

"Bloody hell does not even begin to sum it all up! I ...I just cannot believe what we have got ourselves into, love!"

Back at the villa, Beth watched the guests walk down the path to the beach and promenade. Cedric was still not back, and she just wondered what he managed to get up to all the time apart from the obvious drinking and buying drugs and spending money on his female escorts. Whatever else he did, it was bound to be unhealthy. Anyway, he had very little else in his life, but at least after meeting Emma and Mark she was pretty sure that she had found the answer to all the business worries which had for probably years now so engaged the trustees. She was also relieved that her place in the mansion was secure, and she'd probably have a slightly easier life than hitherto when, and if, The Boy just woke up dead one day. She looked at her watch, then went back to the office and called Ted again.

"Well, Beth, what's the verdict?"

"Very, very positive. He is intelligent, not overly enamoured of his current job, she is also intelligent, they look respectable have two children, one boy and one girl …"

"How did they take to the business idea?"

"Well, it all came as a bit of a surprise to them, but they are by no means averse to the idea, or at least, as much of it as I was able to tell them. It will be up to you guys to go into it in any depth buy I'm positive they will not by any means baulk at the idea."

"And are you positive that they are who they say they are? Not that I really give a toss! If they otherwise fit the bill, I'm happy! In fact all of us will be ecstatic!"

"You know the DNA check came back positive, and they explained to me exactly what happened with Angelica's baby, and nobody but Mark would know that, and he got it straight from the woman who was given the baby … in the Royal Berks hospital, in Reading!"

"I don't suppose any better CV is possible! So, bearing in mind your feelings about the guy, I'm happy to endorse the deal. I'll tell the board! And thanks, Beth, we owe you one!"

In the Oxford office, Ted Willetts slammed the 'phone down.

"Yes!" He called to his secretary. "Cis! Can you arrange a meeting with the crew … I want them all there by …" He looked at his watch. "… by three, okay? No need for any notes, and it will only last about ten to fifteen minutes! Everybody must attend! Don't even bother with coffee and stickies! Thanks!"

"Got it! I'll do it now!" Cis made it to the conference room. Everything was in order. Then she went back to her desk and called every one of the other six trustees' secretaries and made it clear; attendance was compulsory. Ted Willetts smiled to himself. He was going to give them a tough introduction. He looked at his watch. It was five past three, so he stood up, put on the grimmest expression he could, then made his way to the meeting. As he entered the room, all faces turned towards him. They could see that the Boss was looking distinctly pissed off. It was intentional. The six seated trustees were each thinking, 'Oh shit! What the fuck's gone wrong?'

"Gentlemen, I have some news about the business's future. As you know, we have tried to ensure that the sale clauses in the founder's trust documents will not be invoked. You, all of you … your futures depended on our finding blood-issue to enable the company to carry on without interruption for the next God-knows how many years, probably beyond the death of every one of us here." Willetts stopped for effect. He saw six long faces looking at him. He was relishing their discomfort. "As you probably know, old man Alex had managed to - or rather tried - find a DNA match after the appalling episode involving his son and the then secretary, Angelica. Of course, none of you were here then, but are nominees of those who were, just as the appointments and resignations rules allowed. Even I was not here, but the baby thing was not all hearsay, I know it actually happened. Indeed, there was some rumour that the father, Alex was the father, not the son. Well, be that as it may, we have to live with it." The room was deathly quiet, with six people and their families livelihoods hanging in the balance. Each reflected on their generous salaries, the respect they engendered as a result of their positions in one of the most successful private companies in the UK; their children's private education, their impressive properties, holiday lodges, ski trips to St Anton, holidays in Gran Canaria, their albeit modest motor launches. Willetts could see some of the six now with their heads down, elbows on the table, foreheads resting on their open hands. He was actually enjoying their misery. He continued to rub it in. "As you know, Bethany and Cedric are currently in Spain and apparently Beth was due to have a meeting there. She called me probably an hour ago, now." He effected a slow, flamboyant look at his watch, his left arm stretched out straight in front of him, then slowly curving round so he could read the dial. A movement engineered to give the impression that everything was utterly hopeless. He was masochistically deriving satisfaction from his apparent, and their actual, pain. "The news from Spain. We have a prison warder and some history buff … who …" Another painful hesitation … "Fit the bill perfectly!" The relief on the faces was palpably, they all looked at their boss as if to say. 'You bastard! Their bodies slumped in their chairs as if they had just been told by their doctors that the cancer diagnosis was incorrect! That they were gonna live! Willetts grinned. "So we're saved! Provided that you all agree! So, once Beth gets back and fills me in on all the details, we can have a full board meeting to either agree or decline their engagement, and by the way, they have two children. So why so down-in-the-mouth? Is there no pleasing you lot?"

"Bloody hell, Ted, we were all gonna jump out of the bloody window!" Then that all applauded, turned and hugged each other. As far as Willetts was concerned, it was job done. Even he managed a very broad smile. He knew they would offer the new people a package they could not refuse.

TWENTY

"Arnie! Chris! Get here now!" both partners heard the shout no more than fifteen seconds after having just seen Ian Collins walk into his office. And they knew their senior partner was about to tell them that half a million pounds had been stolen from the Fisher trust account. Ian Collins attempted to look mortified, pummelled by the news he had just discovered, to feign shock, all a show to rope his partners into the big fiction he was peddling. Arnie and Chris were way ahead of him, but even so, tried to look concerned about the news Ian Collins was about to impart. They waited.

"What, Ian ... what has happened?"

"That bastard Maynard has stolen all the money in the Fisher trust account ... half a million bloody quid!" Chris again.

"How do you know?"

"'Cos I just checked the account!" Chris was having none of it. He was determined to make his boss feel uncomfortable.

"No you didn't. You have only just arrived, and your computer's off!"

"No, I mean when I was at home! Then I checked it!"

"Okay, show us! Do a check now for us! There must be a mistake!" Chris was deliberately leading Ian into a cul-de-sac. Ian sat down at his desk and opened the drawer where he had kept the Bugden file, then opened the computer. Another question this time from Arnie, who knew straight away what Chris was up to.

"Hey, Ian ... what was that file doing in your desk drawer? He was my client! What's in there that has anything to do with my Fisher client?"

"Er ... it's where I hid the account details!"

"What account? The only account he had, if I recall correctly, was in some off-shore place like ... er ... where was it, somewhere in the Caribbean?" Ian Collins knew he was cornered, and Arnie and Chris both saw it. "You know, Ian, you'd better stop pissing about and call the cops. Are you sure you didn't move the money? I mean, really positive? And surely you have the trust account details for the Green office, and not tucked away in my old file? Call the cops, Ian, and for fuck's sake, get organised before they turn up and start taking statements!" Then Chris and Arnie walked out. Over his shoulder, Chris called out.

"Maybe we, or better still you, ought to get your arse over to see Mike before you do anything else!"

Alone, Ian Collins sat down knowing immediately that he had already messed up. He decided to make some notes before he called Dent and Forbear. He pulled out a counsels' notebook, and started scribbling. As soon as Chris got back to his office, he called Maynard. Debbie answered.

"Hi, Debbie. Is Mike in? Its Chris."

"Yeah, he's right here ... handing you over now."

"Hi, Chris! What's up?"

"Mike! I think the bubble is about to burst! That idiot Ian dragged us into his office to tell us that he has er ... just discovered that the Fisher trust account has been emptied, and when we asked him to check he inadvertently tried to open the old account one of our criminal clients used, the account in the Cayman Islands. In fact, he really screwed up! Anyway, we told him to contact the cops, 'cos we know his story is so full of holes, that it ain't going anywhere. Just thought I'd warn you. Maybe have a look at the account."

"Thanks, Chris, I will do. And I'll also get ready for a visit from the cops! What's the betting on it being Messrs Dent and Forbear?" Maynard finished the call and spoke to Debbie who was standing next to him. "Debbie, can you open that Fisher account and do a print-off for me? From day one please. Thanks." He then called DCI Ellis on his mobile. "Hi, Mike. Looks like Ian Collins has just discovered that the Fisher account has been emptied. Chris reckons that its all been transferred to a Cayman account, so no doubt your Chip and Pin cops, Dent and Forbear, will soon be briefed to drop in and see Ian, then me later, no doubt!"

"Thanks, Mike. I'll have a watch put on those two now. There's already some backlash about the drugs packages, some dealers reckoning that the packets were tagged, but as far as we are concerned, they have served their purpose and they look like blaming those two, so in my view, life is gonna get pretty rough for them. I just hope that they don't get silly and start blaming your lot, I mean, Ian! I'll keep you informed and please let me know what happens. Maybe Debbie can open a file to record events? Have you still got those ANWisecurity guys on board?"

"Yeah, we have. And the idea of Debbie keeping a record of events is a good one."

Ian Collins' day was turning out to be bad. Never any good at imaginative writing, he even had trouble writing a postcard when on holiday, but trying to make up a convincing story about someone nicking half a million quid, was a nightmare. He decided to rope in Arnie, whom he considered to be the weaker partner. He walked into Arnie's office.

"I know you're busy, mate, but I need help with this statement thing. Can you spare an hour or so sometime before lunch? I want to call the cops in as soon as possible, okay?"

"Yeah, Ian, I suppose. I'll pop in at about one? Can you order a pizza for lunch, save me having to go out!"

"Yeah, okay!"

Arnie wandered into Ian's office and sat facing the guy.

"Right, Ian, what do you want me to do?"

"Help me get this story right! I can't seem to set it out on paper. I've been wrestling with it for hours!" Arnie noted the word 'story'. It was, he thought, appropriate. He also noted that the waste-paper bin had a lot of scrunched-up balls of paper, and he thought he ought to get hold of them before they were chucked into the bins outside for the refuse-collectors.

"Okay, Ian, it might help if you told me the story first, then maybe we can get something down on paper, okay?"

"Yeah. Right." Arnie knew he had to be pretty harsh with the statement, but was also determined not to say anything which would put off any police investigation into Mike at the Green office, bearing in mind his ultimate objective regarding the lad Nick Forrester. It had to get to court to expose Ian's grossly corrupt behaviour and his underlying intentions as regards the account. Both he and Chris were fully aware of exactly what Ian had done and what his further intentions were, and he would not escape the consequences of his actions.

"Okay, start." The senior partner glanced at his notes.

"Right. Er ... during the course of my work, we were obliged to secure the funds realised on our client, Lady Fisher whose estate we were instructed to handle. We subsequently managed to obtain the sum of around half-a-million pounds, which for safe-keeping my junior partner Arnold Medland asked ..."

"Woah! ... I asked nothing of the kind! You insisted for some reason, and frankly, I wondered why. Was it just a set-up for Mike to have access to it? What was the reason, Ian?"

"Well, I said that because it was your client ..."

"I know that, and I also know that it was you who insisted on transferring the money to the Green office ... can you explain that? And what was the idea of resurrecting the Bugden account, if indeed you did?"

"Arnie, as the senior partner, I do not have to explain anything to anybody!"

"Yes you do! For one, Mike Maynard's defence team! Do you not think that they will ask why you did it? Don't you think that they will not see that as the first move on some master-plan to facilitate ..."

"Arnie! If you are not going to co-operate with me how do you think that looks? Don't you think that maybe you are part of some scam, set up between you and Maynard? And maybe Chris as well?" Arnie stood up.

"Well, Ian, if that's what you think, you obviously do not need me here anymore do you? I've got work to do and a pizza to eat! Maybe Chris can help you, but I'm damn sure that he'll say the same as me!" Arnie closed the door behind him, grabbed his

Pizza from the kitchenette and walked into Chris's office. "He's in the shit, Chris!"

"Ian? I already know that! He has just not thought things through, has he!"

Back in his office, Ian Collins swore under his breath. He knew that if he didn't sort out the details of his complaint, and indeed if the cops were to ask Arnie and Chris about the alleged theft, it would finish up coming back at him and smacking him in the face. He needed help. And he was clearly not thinking straight. He picked up his 'phone and buzzed Pam.

"Pam! Can you please get me the number of the Reading police station…? Thanks." Within minutes, he had the number on a yellow post-it note. He dialled.

Reading police. Is this an emergency!"

"Yes … er.. no. I'm trying to contact DS Dent please. Or Forbear."

"Who's calling?"

"I am … Ian Collins, senior partner of my firm Collins and Goodrich, lawyers."

"Thank you. And the matter?"

"I want to report the theft of clients cash."

"Thank you. I'll pass the message on. What is the best number to get you on?"

"This one … Reading two eight six six eight two."

"Thank you. I'm sure the officers will be in touch soon." Collins breathed a sigh of relief. Well, there was no going back now.

At Reading police station, the message re. Dent and Forbear was passed up the line. DCI Ellis had been authorised by the Chief Constable, to deal with and be informed of, all calls and movements of the two officers. The excuse was that their lives may be in danger due to some issue with a drugs deal. And neither Dent nor Forbear were to know that they were being 'looked after'. Ellis picked the note off his desk, and dialled Mike Maynard's number.

"Hi, Mike, Ellis here. Looks like we have some activity on the Collins case!"

"Had to start sooner or later! I expect Chip and Pin, Dent and Forbear, will soon be knocking on my door. I'd just love to be a fly on the wall when Collins briefs them, but I suppose Ian will meet them in his office ... unless we can somehow get the meeting to be held here, in the Green office!"

"It's an idea, and if we can arrange it with you and them somehow, we will!"

It was about two hours later, that Ian had a call from Dent.
"You called. How can we help?"

"Yeah, I did. I want to report the theft of about half a million pounds from my client account."

"That's easy. Why did you call for me and John Forbear?"

"Because I know you, of course!"

"Er ... Mister Collins, don't you mean you know of me and Johhny? Maybe we have a known reputation for dealing with white-collar crime? I admit we have a few solicitors on our books!" This was said by Dent as other people were listening to the man speak, after all, it was in a busy operation room. And he had to give the impression that neither Collins nor Chip and Pin had ever met before. Dent reminded himself that he should have made that very clear when they met. Maybe he did, but it was perhaps a case of just Collins being stupid. Dent upped the volume, specifically so the others in the room could hear. "Now, Mister Collins, when and where do you want to meet? Where is your office?" Before Collins had time to answer, Dent just blurted out, "The Green office? Where is that actually?... Oh, I get it. I think I know the place. Date and time?" ... again, Dent beat him to it. "Tomorrow evening, at seven. Yeah, I know you're a busy guy, Mister Collins. See you there then. Bye." Then, again for the benefit of the earwigging in the room, and after the phone was replaced, he blurted out, "Odd bugger! How the hell can anybody just nick half a million quid from a solicitors accounts! Must be bloody mad!" He sidled up to his oppo, Forbear, and told him quietly, that they were in the Green office again, and that he had fixed up their evening meal at Collins expense.

Collins also put his 'phone down, then called out to his secretary.

"Pam, can you please tell Maynard that I'm having a meeting in their office, tomorrow evening at about seven. If anybody there had any plans to work late, then they can't. And ask that Debbie girl to make sure the place is clean and tidy."

"Yes, I'll get onto it immediately!" Collins then made for the exit.

"I'm off now, working from home, okay? And I may not be in tomorrow!" As soon Doug had picked up the lawyer, and driven off, Arnie went into Ian's office and emptied the waste-paper bin into a small plastic bag. He was planning to take it home and sift through all the different scenarios his boss had dreamed up regarding the alleged theft of his client's money. He was actually on a high.

In the Green office, Mike Maynard got the message. He knew damn well what it was all about. First he called Terry Thorne, at ANWisecurity to make sure that the surveillance would be up and running over the period in question. He got the reassurance he wanted. Then he called DCI Mike Ellis, and told him what had been agreed between Dent and Collins.

"Thanks. And be aware, we'll be watching those two, and if they give you any nonsense, we'll be onto it immediately!"

TWENTY ONE

It was well after seven pm when the cops climbed the stairs to the lawyers office. Collins had been sitting in the meeting room revising his story for the cops. He had told his driver that he had to finish some important jobs upstairs, and didn't know how long he'd be, but to park at the back of the offices as he did not want his driver to see the police officers arrive, but Doug knew damn well what was going on anyway. Then Collins heard the visitors climbing the stairs, so he got up to meet them at the office door.

"Hi, mate! Got the pizzas sorted yet?" It was Dent.

"No. I'll go and get them now. Drink? What do you fancy?"

"Milk shakes." Collins scuttled off to the nearby takeaway. When he'd gone, Forbear raised the issue of payment.

"Is he gonna pay us today?"

"Na. We'll tell him when he's gonna pay. Yer can't just magic fifty thousand quid out of thin air! The blokes a dick 'ed anyway, so the first thing we do mate, is get that Maynard bloke charged and off to his first appearance in the Magistrates' court! They won't deal with it there, of course, but at least we'll get him on bail." Then Collins appeared in the room with three pizza boxes and three milk-shakes. He also fed his driver, Doug, telling him he wouldn't be long. Doug didn't give a shit anyway, but he just wondered what his boss was going to do with the other three pizzas and milk shakes. He concluded that Collins was not very bright.

Upstairs, the three ripped open their meals and Dent, between mouthfuls, asked Collins what story he had come up with.

"All sorted! When I engaged Maynard, I thought he was a bit iffy, but nevertheless Chris and Arnie seemed keen on him, so I agreed to sign him up. Anyway, then we had this client Lady

Fisher, she died and we dealt with her estate and finished up with a lot of her money in our clients' account, which I thought was a bit dangerous, so I …" "Why was it dangerous?"

"Cos I did not want it to get mixed up with the other money in the clients' account!"

"Ian, that is just daft. Explain!"

"Well, with all the other money going in and out on property sales and purchases …"

"No, Ian, that won't wash! Look, we ain't stupid, you know we probably know more about solicitors' accounts that you do, so why don't you just say that you accidently transferred the dosh into the Green office account …"

"Yeah, could do …"

"And rather than get it back, you just told the Maynard bloke about it."

"Yeah, that sounds okay …"

"And when did you notice that the money was being taken out?"

"Er …"

"Let us help you." Dent seemed to have taken over the whole deal. "You did your monthly check on the accounts, then you realised that all the Fisher money had gone, yes? And according to your computer it had been transferred to an account in the name of, surprise surprise, Michael Maynard perhaps?"

"Yeah, that's right!"

"So, did you talk to the guy? Or do anything about it?"

"No, because I had to be sure!"

"Ian, for fuck's sake …" Dent finished his pizza and then wiped his fingers on his handkerchief. "… be sure of what? I mean …"

"Well, it might have been a mistake!" Now, even Forbear saw the problems, and was grinning, something which not many people knew he was capable of. Dent stood up.

"Look, Ian, may I suggest that you write down the whole story, and make it realistic. Also, we'll want a print-out of each movement of the cash away from the Fisher account, where it went to and I assume that it is still all in the new Maynard account?"

"No, Ron, it isn't. I moved it to another account, to my ... to the account in the Cayman Islands!"

"So, is it still there?"

"Yes!"

"Right ..." Dent rummaged around in his pocket and drew out a piece of paper. "Right, Ian. Transfer the sum of fifty thousand pounds into this account. Write down the details ..."

Collins did as he was asked. "We want that done within the next forty-eight hours, and at the same time we want your revised statement, one that is at least half-believable, okay? Once we have that, we'll go through it together, then we'll get onto this Maynard bloke!" Then the cops were gone. Outside, Doug saw them go. He recognised them, the two best-known cop-caricatures in Reading, or probably in the business. Then he went back to sit in the car.

The next day, after Maynard and Debbie had cleared away the pizza boxes and milk-shake, cardboard mugs, Mike called ANWisecurity.

"Hi, Terry, any results?"

"Cor, yes, I'll say! Your mate Collins is as thick as pigshit, and the two cops aren't all that bright either! I'll send you the full transcribed brief for your file. I think you'll enjoy reading it!"

At the same time as this conversation finished, Ian Collins called his office to say he wouldn't be in as he had some important drafting to do. Everybody there knew damn well it was a black lie, except in so far as it related to the Maynard case, which now everybody in the office knew about.

Overnight, Arnie had spread out the balled-up paper he had

recovered from the bosses waste-paper basket, and he managed to come up with five different scenarios regarding the stolen money. He had copied the original notes, all conveniently hand-written by his boss, and on the copies had highlighted the different stories Ian Collins had noted down. If he and Chris were seriously doubting Ian's sanity, there was no reason to doubt any longer. The scribblings made it pretty certain that he was seriously deranged; psychopathically so. He now walked into Chris's office, and laid out his efforts from the night before.

"Chris, look at this lot! The bloke's a total nutter if anybody believes this crap! I don't think the bloke's very far off being sectioned!" Chris Goodrich took the papers and scanned them.

"Bloody hell, Arnie, you're right! I'm gonna call Mike and ask what happened at the meeting!" He dialled and Debbie answered.

"Debs! How are you?... Good. Mike in please?"

"Mike … how was the meeting! Any feedback yet?" For a while, Chris listened. Then; "I don't believe it! The cops asking for fifty thousand, and offering to do Ian's statement for him, whatever next! And it's all recorded? Absolutely brilliant! Now, it's just occurred to me … we surely have enough to finish the cops and Ian so why don't we just call it a day?"

"We can't. Chris … we need to rope in those bent lawyers as well, Sowerby-Newton and Justin Weatherby, because we need to show the court just how bloody corrupt they were in Nick's case!"

"Yeah, of course. Good thinking! And it seems Ian is on the back-foot as he does not seem to be able to make up a realistic scenario about why he put the money into the Green account, how it was transferred to another Maynard account which we know was arranged by Dent and co!"

"Now, bearing in mind the cops wanting their money into their own account, and as it is to be paid from the overseas bank, why don't you just keep an eye on him …"

"Even better! We can hide the file in which he has the bank details with passwords and account name! If he can't find it, he can't pay off the cops, so they ain't gonna play ball with him!"

"Yeah, but don't forget the aim of our exercise … to get to a court to achieve the aim of getting Nick cleared of the charges which the CCRC are very reluctant to do!"

"It might otherwise be a very risky strategy, but with Ian being so daft, and all the recordings new have of him and the cops, I think it is a goer!"

Ian Collins was a worried man. He knew he was practically incapable of drafting a convincing statement for the cops, one that they could not pick to pieces. Maybe he would have to rely on just the fact that a new Maynard account had received all the money, and wherever Maynard chose to put it afterwards was not his concern, and not within his knowledge. The cops now knew otherwise, but for fifty thousand quid they could or rather would have to be creative. He spent the rest of the day mooching about the house, getting on his mum's nerves, and drinking. He retired to bed, and decided to get to the office early and do a transfer into the account the cops had nominated.

Doug was not happy about the early start, but the feeling that he was onto something made him less annoyed than he would otherwise be. He was determined to find out what was going on. He picked up his boss at seven in the morning, and dropped him off and was then told that he would make the return journey at no later than two in the afternoon. Collins let himself into the office and fired-up his PC. He then made himself a coffee, sat at his desk and opened the drawer looking for the Bugden file. It was not there. He almost sprinted to Arnie's office and went through every drawer, every bookshelf every corner of the office. No luck. Then he tried Chris's office. Still no luck. Without the file, he could not access then account. Basically, he admitted to himself, he was stuffed. He spent nearly an hour and a half searching every room int his offices. Still no luck. Then Pan appeared.

"Pam, where's the Bugden file?"

"Who? Did you say Bugden? Never heard of him …!"

"You remember, Pam, the guy who's now in jail? Sent down a couple of years ago?"

"Oh, him! Wasn't that one of Arnold's files?" Hope looked on the horizon for a brief moment.

"Yes!"

"Where's the file?"

"Absolutely no idea! Haven't seen it since the trial, sorry!" Hope was snatched away.

"Shit! It must be somewhere, Pam!"

"You're right there! But I don't know where that is! Anyway, I've got work to do! How was the meeting the other day? Okay?"

"No it was not okay! It was cancelled!" Pam thought it would not be too wise to ask her boss who then apparently, ate three pizzas, drank two large milkshakes and left fag-ends on a saucer in the meeting room, just as Debbie had reported to her. But she did not ask, she just knew Collins was in for a bad day, and she was not going to make it worse for him, as she was sure Arnie and Chris would make good job of doing that.

Not long before Chris turned up, there was a special delivery envelope marked 'Private and Confidential. FAO Mr Ian Collins'. Pam took it straight to Ian's office. It looked very official, but whatever it said, Pam instinctively knew that sooner or later, she would see it. She walked into Ian's office and dropped the envelope onto his desk.

"Special delivery."

"What is it?"

"I don't know … its marked for your attention only. Do you want me to open it and read it to you?"

"No! … No. Just leave it on the desk." Pam obliged, then left the room. She saw Chris come into the office, and Pam signalled to him to follow her, which he did.

"Wassermatter, Pam?"

"It's Ian. He is acting very strangely today, something's not right with him!"

"Pam, nothing is ever right with him! What's he been doing?"

"He's going ballistic 'cos he can't find an old client's file, Bugden or somebody. He's got a right strop on!"

"Really? It's because it's got some bank details in that file, which I think is the bank account where he has diverted all of the Fisher client dosh! Hear what I say, Pam, and don't let this information ever pass your lips, okay? But just bear it in mind whenever you are dealing with him. He has shot himself in the foot, really bad!"

"Chris, he's been doing that ever since I started working here, and a long time before I think! Anyway, where is that file, do you know?"

"Yeah. Arnie's got it. No doubt Ian will ask him when he arrives!" As if on cue, Ian barged into Pam's office.

"Ah, Chris! Where the bloody hell is the Bugden file?"

"Bugden? No idea. Isn't it one of Arnie's files|?"

"No … I mean as the senior partner, all files are in essence, my bloody files!"

"Hey what's al the noise about?" It was Arnold. Ian turned on him.

"Arnie! The Bugden file? Where is it?"

"Bugden? It's with all then other expired files, in the basement ready to be collected and shredded …"

"What!"

" … in accordance with standard Law Society protocols!"

"Jesus! For God's sake go and get it! There's some info I need …!"

"Was it by any chance the Cayman Islands bank account

details?"

"Yes! I mean no! For God's sake go and get it! Somebody go down and get it!" Just to cause further distress to his boss, Arnie could not help but add that the collection was yesterday, he thought, so it was all long gone. "Oh no!" Ian left the office like his pants were on fire, and all the others could hear was the slamming of doors as Ian exited the building to get into the basement. Arnie had not finished by a long chalk

"Pity. I was about to add that I copied the account information. It ... or at least a copy of it ... is on his desk, under the table lamp! He'll be gone for hours if the stuff is still down there!" Pam slipped into Ian's office. On his desk was the opened letter delivered that morning. She called Arnie.

"Arnie! Please go down and see what Ian is doing ... I need five minutes to copy something!"

"What?"

"Tell you later, promise! Just hold him down there!"

"Okay. Going now." Pam slipped back into Ian's office collected the seven-page A4 sized report. It looked to her like a police statement regarding the theft of monies from the Fisher client account. Now this was interesting!

In the basement, Arnie found Ian trying to open bags of discarded documents, frantically pulling, pushing like a demented soul Arnie called out to him.

"Ian! For God's sake what the hell are you doing?" Ian for a brief moment stopped, looked up, then started again.

"Help me!" Arnie went up to his senior partner, and held onto one of his arms.

"Stop! What are you looking for?"

"The Bugden file!"

"I know that! What in the file?"

"I need the account details ..."

"You mean the Cayman account?"

"Yes!" Ian Collins froze and looked straight at Arnie. "Yes, the fuckin' Cayman account!"

"Okay ... I've got all the details! I knew it was important to you, so I copied it! Here. Take it and don't lose it 'cos I do not have another one." By the time the two lawyers returned from the basement, Pam had made three copies of the morning's hand-delivered letter. She would take one copy home. Read it then decide on her next move. Arnie had the whole Bugden file, including Ian's own writing showing the account details, and he intended to pass it to Mike Maynard. It was the least he could do for the guy who was putting his career on the line for the benefit of the firm.

Doug the driver, engaged through the services of Mark Collins, tapped on their front door. Mark opened. He noticed his brother's truck parked in the road.

"Sorry to trouble you, Boss ... there's something you should know! Hell, you look healthy! Where'd get the tan?"

"Holiday. Okay, Doug ... come in ..." Mark called over his shoulder. "Emma ... put the kettle on! ... What's up, Doug? Ian giving you a hard time?"

"Er ...no, but It is about Ian. There's something going on an' I think you ought to know about it!"

TWENTY TWO

After Ian got his Cayman bank details, he shut himself away in his office for about half an hour. Then he just walked out of the office having just transferred fifty thousand pounds into the cop account. He had also picked up the hand-delivered letter, determined to read it at home. He already knew what it was, and hoped he was in a position to agree it and get the show on the road. Pam watched him go, and saw the truck pull into the light traffic, then away down the hill towards High Wycombe. She walked into Chris's office. Arnie was there. She shut the door behind her, and the two lawyers looked up.

"Hi Pam ... what's the problem?"

"The problem, my friends, is Ian!" Feigning ignorance, Chris answered.

"What about him that we don't already know?"

"Okay. No beating about the bush, he's a bloody crook!" Chris held up a hand.

"Pam, tell us something we do not already know!"

"Right. Firstly, he has been having a series of meetings in the Green office, then he says the Fisher trust account has been emptied, then he starts transferring cash to the Cayman Islands, now he is working with the police to prepare a statement accusing Mike Maynard of nicking half a million pounds! And is that's not enough, he ..."

"Pam, we are already on to it!"

"Yeah, maybe, but he has just transferred fifty grand into a UK account, name of Jane Dawson! So, we have dosh going from Arnie's clients to the Green office, being transferred into an account in the name Maynard, from there to the Caymans which seems to be controlled by Ian, then from the Caymans to a Jane Dawson in what is an Aylesbury bank account, going by the sort code! So, maybe you know what's happening ... and maybe you don't! Now, look at this! It seems to be from the police, actually drafting his statement!" She handed out the copies. After a brief glance at his, Arnie looked up.

"Well, this certainly differs from the other five or so he scribbled out the other day! Anyway, Pam, can we assure you that we do know what he's up to. And let me add, that Mike Maynard has not touched a penny, it's all been engineered by Ian. We cannot do anything about blowing it open, 'cos the people who matter are already in the picture, but there is a sub-text, and that is, Mike is going to be dealing with cops, a barrister and a solicitor who are all in on the job, but Mike has to have the whole deal aired in court because there was a very similar case a few years ago, same people, where a young chap was jailed for something he did not do. I know it sounds a bit kind of fictional, but bear with us, and thanks Pam for telling us what you know!"

"But, Chris, this will mean the firm shutting down! We are all going to lose our jobs, and who the hell will employ us after we have been working for a bloody crook?"

"Pam, that aspect has also been approached. We have an individual who has agreed to buy the firm and keep on all the staff. And I can tell you, that he is fully aware of what is going on now behind the scenes!"

"Well, thanks for the reassurances. But can we agree that we share any further information just in case something crops up which needs handling?"

"Of course we will. And thanks."

Back at home, Ian Collins called the number noted on the draft statement. DS Dent answered.

"Ron ... I'm happy with the statement. Can we get going with it please?"

"Yeah. Done the transfer yet?"

"Yes."

"Okay. We'll drop in to see Maynard tomorrow. We won't give him any notice just in case he chooses not to be in!"

"Good! The sooner he's charged, the better! Keep me informed!" Across the office, Forbear looked up from struggling with The Sun newspaper.

"That bloody Collins?"

"Yeah. He's paid the dosh, so I'll get onto Jane and ask her to send it to our account."

"Okay. How much does she get to keep?"

"Ten percent! That's er ... what, five, six thousand?"

"Something like that, yes! Apart from Maynard, what are we doing tomorrow?"

"Dunno. Maybe we'll just cruise, yeah?"

"Doing a cat job?"

"Looking for prossies?"

"Yeah, mate, I believe that's what it means!"

"So, what time do you wanna drop in on Maynard?"

"Say four. Then we can get another take-away for supper, then log off duty."

At approximately four the following day, detectives Dent and Forbear climbed the stairs to Mike Maynard's office. They paused at Hannah's desk.

"'Ullo, darlin'. Looking for Mister Maynard."

"Thank you. Who's asking please?"

"Dent. Reading police." Hannah knew exactly who he was, and the other man who was about to light a cigarette. Hannah leaned forward and removed the cigarette from Forbear's mouth.

"Sorry, Sir. This is a no-smoking area, the workplace regulations apply!" She handed the fag back to the officer.

"That's odd, cos last time …" Dent trod on his foot.

"Thank you. I'll go and see if Mister Maynard is in." She knew very well he was in. As she moved towards his office, she heard one of the officers say that 'he wouldn't mind giving her one'. She surmised that the visiting officers were not exactly the cream of the bunch. Hannah entered Mike Maynard's office and closed the door behind her.

"Mike … Dent and Forbear are here to see you … are we ready?"

"Yeah … give me a minute to speak to Terry to make sure we're live! Then when I give you the nod, show them into the meeting room and I'll join them shortly afterwards. Need to know what they say when they get in there!" Hannah returned to reception. Terry confirmed that all was up and running. It only took the flip of a switch.

"Mister Maynard will see you in the meeting room …it's …" But the two were already on their way. Hannah followed. "He will be with you shortly." She closed the door behind them. The first thing Dent did was to point to the loft hatch.

"Hey, mate, I hope there ain't any brown still up there!"

"Or maybe a bundle of cash!" The two laughed. Then the sat down. A minute later, Maynard entered and sat down opposite them.

"Gentlemen, how can I help you?" Dent pulled a sheaf of papers from his pocket.

"Mike Maynard?"

"Yeah, that's me."

"We have had a complaint regarding some money missing from the clients' account." Maynard said nothing. "Er … don't you have anything to say?"

"Well, no. Tell me more!" Dent unfolded the sheaf of papers and smoothed them out on the desk.

"Mister Maynard … we have had a complaint from Ian Collins, we believe you know him, that over a period of approximately two to three months, you extracted the sum of, or in the region of, five hundred thousand pounds. Is that true?" Forbear was playing a kind of game with a toothpick and his fingernails and he looked wholly disinterested.

"Half a million quid? No, most certainly not!" Maynard had rehearsed this interview many times over. Least said, soonest mended, and the more frustrated his interrogators would become..

"How much then?" Maynard was struggling to keep a straight face.

"Nothing."

"Are you sure?"

"Positive."

"Well, according to our information, you have been regularly transferring monies to your bank account in Aylesbury!"

"I do not have an account in Aylesbury."

"Yes you have. We have all the details."

"There? Can I see them?"

"No, not at the moment. That's evidence!"

"When was it opened ... and when did I apparently, start paying money into it?"

"Again, that's evidence, so we cannot tell you. But you were paying in about a hundred thousand each time, weren't you?"

"Are you asking me? Or telling me?"

"How much were you paying in then?"

"I can tell you that. Zilch. Nowt. Nothing. And I do not have a bank account ...!"

"Mister Maynard, you are not being very helpful. I expected you, as an intelligent man, to be more co-operative!"

"Well, I am just a little surprised that you have not already produced a statement, a confession or something, for me to sign!" Now it was Forbear's turn in the 'Mutt and Jeff' partnership.

"Look, Mike, we are not totally convinced by your boss's allegations, but we want to help you. But you'll have to give a little ..."

"Can it, Johnny! Look why don't we get you a couple of really good lawyers. A couple who have helped in the past with situations such as you are facing now. Frankly, in all my time as a cop, I have never met any lawyers as good as these, a solicitor and a barrister, who can represent you. Let me give you their details ..." Maynard knew exactly who they were talking about, Messrs Noël Sowerby-Newton and Justin Weatherby. "... Johnny, give him ...!"

"No, why don't you two just brief them with all the rubbish you appear to have, then they can interview me and get on with the job. I assume you'll get the solicitor bloke to meet me first, then he and I can brief the barrister, whichever one that is! Obviously, I'm gonna have a hard time dealing with all these lies! I mean, I do not think Ian has a particularly good relationship with the truth, so I'll need all the help I can get!"

"Okay, let's do that then. The solicitor is Weatherby."

"And can I have a copy of that statement you've got there?"

"Don't see why not!" In fact, you can have this one. I've got copies in the office."

"Okay, thanks." It was nearly five when the two cops left the office and went round the corner to the take-away, where they were already fairly well known.

"The usual, gents?"

"Yes please!" Then to Forbear. "Don't forget to write-up the notes on the meeting, and let me see them before you file them. Don't want to give anything away, do we!"

"I reckon that he's gonna be a tough nut to crack!"

"Maybe, maybe not. Anyway, I reckon if he's facing maybe a ten-year stretch, he'll come round if Noël can convince him to plead guilty for a shorter term!"

"He'll bloody have to if he wants his five grand fee!"

"Yeah, as per usual!" The food counter guy picked up every word.

Back in the office, Mike Maynard called Terry at ANWisecurity.

"You get all that?"

"Yeah! By golly, Mike, those guys are digging one hell of a hole for themselves, aren't they?"

"They sure are! Anyway, if you can get it all transcribed, and get a copy to me as per usual, I'll file it. One problem; if I have to meet the lawyers in their offices, I'll need to record everything ... can you help on that?"

"Sure can! I'll drop in as soon as I can get away from the studio and bring a couple of little devices for you."

"Great. Look forward to it!" Maynard was beginning to consider the admissibility of secret recordings in criminal cases. He was aware that the courts have power to exclude illegally obtained evidence under section seventy-eight of the Police and Criminal Evidence Act if, having regard to all the circumstances, the court considers the admission of the evidence would have such an adverse effect on the fairness of proceedings that the court ought not to admit it. However, covert recordings have been admitted in evidence even when there has been a breach of PACE. He continued with his research, looking at firms Frenso, et al, and concluded that in his circumstances, it would all be admissible. He would run it past Terry when he dropped in. His conclusions were based on the fact that dishonesty by the police and members of the legal profession, especially on the scale envisaged in his case, would be in the public interest to admit it. He tidied his desk, and left for home.

TWENTY THREE

"Right, Doug, what's the issue with Ian?" Doug swallowed the well-masticated chockie biscuit, took a swig of his coffee, and spoke.

"He's keeping bad company, namely Chip and Pin, a couple of bent cops. He's ..."

"Sorry, Doug, who are Chip and Pin?"

"DS Dent, Ronnie Dent, and detective constable John Forbear .... Bent as arseholes! Been holding meetings in the Green office, after hours, when there is no reason for him to do that unless what he is up to is a little bit illegal. And he has sneaky 'phone conversations in the car, thinks I can't hear him, and it doesn't sound too good to me. Talking about a lot of dough, like hundreds of thousands, and if it was all kosher, why not talk normal? I think, Mark, that you ought to pop in an' talk to the guys in the Green office, and I am sure they will have a far better idea of what he's up to than I do, and that they'll be honest with you.

Also, as I'm sure you know, the whole Collins law business is on the bones of it's arse, always had been, so I have no idea where Ian gets all his money to keep it afloat ... Summat's going on, Mark, and I think you ought to do a bit of research before the whole thing goes belly up!"

"Doug, I'm of the same mind as you ... I think he's been running it on Mum's money, and that's gonna stop! I've already told him to repay her, and maybe that's what he's worried about, but hundreds of thousands ... that ain't legit, can't be!
Keep your ear to the ground, and if any more info comes your way, let me know, okay? Here ..." Mark Collins fished out his Wallet. "Here, that's for your troubles!" Collins proffered a fifty-pound note.

"No, Mark ... I didn't ..."

"Take it. It's for your troubles. I really appreciate it! Maybe I'll drop in and speak to Chris and Arnie, Ian's partners. Thanks."

"Oh! Okay, if you insist! Thanks!" Then Doug was gone. Mark called out to Emma.

"Emm? Did you get all that?"

"Yes I did ... I reckon you ought to drop into Ian's office like asap!" Mark thought it would be a better idea if Arnie and Chris dropped round to see him.

The next day, Maynard received two 'phone calls. The first was from Terry at ANWisecurity, who said he could be there by lunchtime, and the other from Justin Weatherby.

"Mister Maynard? Weatherby. Had a call from Reading police who say that you have appointed me or want to appoint me as your solicitor. Gather you are having a bit of bother which needs sorting out. Have to meet sometime."

"Yes. Bother does not even begin to describe it! I have been accused ..."

"Yeah, it's okay, I have read the police statement. Looks like you could be in a bit of a pickle! When are you free?"

"No idea .. where are you based?"

"Not that close to Reading, but I do pop down there from time to time ... in fact, I'm due there er... I think the day after tomorrow er ... yes, that's right!" Maynard was supposed to believe that the solicitor was thumbing through a pretty full work diary, but in essence had no other appointments, and perhaps not even an office, a WFH cowboy. "So, let's say the day after tomorrow ... what's the best time for you?"

"For me ... anytime after nine. Perhaps you could call me when you are an hour away?"

"Fine. I have your address!" On finishing the call, Weatherby dialled another number.

"Justin here. I'm meeting Maynard the day after tomorrow. Make sure you get that money to me by end of today, okay?... Yes, five grand. I'll get more from the Maynard bloke when we finish the case ... I don't know about Noël, you'll have to talk to him! ... And yes, of course he's going down, guaranteed! I mean for half a mill, it will probably be a good stretch inside. Anyway, I'll report back after the meeting." Justin stood up and looked out of his office window, to the bustling crowds in the Sainsburys carpark, in Wantage. Business was equally good for him. He re-read the information he had from Dent and noted down his line of attack. Give the defendant the idea that it was a weak case against him; get him into court; then allow the Crown Prosecution Service barrister to knock down every one of the defence arguments, delivering a knock-out blow to the accused.

Maynard heard Hannah greet Terry from the security firm, asking his if he'd like a coffee. Soon, both the visitor and Maynard were seated in the meeting room. Terry was burdened with an impressive looking bundle of kit. After the usual niceties, the guy got down to business.

"I assume, Mike, that you are expecting to meet someone out of this office ... so I have here a few well-worn briefcases each of which is fitted with a seriously modified bit of kit, basically, a Domisk micro HD video camera with audio capability. You see these little metal studs holding the handles on ... each is a small camera, with all the gubbins stored below the leather base inside the bag. To switch it all on, you just twist the lock, the bit fixed here and you'll feel it lock on ... try it! ... That's right! And off again, anti-clockwise. You can do both on and off fairly discreetly, and the batteries last from full load for about two hours. If you for some reason are going to run over, you can turn on another two hours by turning the lock, as before, onto a second click. You will appreciate that for video you will have to have the handle facing the target, but it will pick up audio from quite a range. If you need more video coverage, get the bag a suitable distance away from, for example, a table. If you are sitting in a chair, not at a table, hold the bag sideways on your lap, a fairly normal thing to do, okay? It is a usefully wide cover anyway, and the mic is pretty sensitive." As usual, Terry and his company had come up with a pretty impressive solution. The technician was soon gone. Maynard then opened his PC to try and find Weatherby in the Law Society register. He was there, but it showed him working for a Leicester firm, Below and Bauer Law, but that was probably out of date.

Weatherby in his bedroom-cum-office, checked his account for the third time that day. Once paid, he would engage Noël. It was strange, he mused, that two well qualified lawyers were now involved in the business of deceiving the clients they should be properly defending. It was, too, a coincidence, that the cops had come into information which had both of them expelled from their chambers. The situation involving him was, as he had continued to tell his employer, just a mistake, and maybe it was but his boss wanted him gone. Now, working from home, or the home of his deceased mother, and not having to lodge annual accounts as he never touched any clients' cash, was proving lucrative. A job like Maynard's could easily net him ten thousand, but he knew the cops were getting fifty thousand each so he and Noël, he believed, should get at lease twenty-five each. No tax, as he had not registered for self-assessment, and he was still using his dead mother's HSBC account. She had no assets, the flat had been transferred into his name ages ago, and there was no need to even do a will and apart from the very useful 'tell us once' facility, and with no assets it was done and dusted very quickly. He picked up the 'phone and speed-dialled Noël's number. The guy looked the part. Silver hair, tall, well dressed, he looked more like a guy who worked in a men's' outfitter, and he had a somewhat off-putting manner of over-confidence, hated being questioned or contradicted. A lot of what he did was for show, which he supposed was what any barrister was about; he was a showman, loved being the centre of attention in a court, everybody hanging onto his every word. He loved himself.

"Yo … Justin! I suppose you're calling about that solicitor bloke?"

"Yeah! I've seen him already, and I told him about you and he's okay with the deal. When can we pop along and see you?"

"Any time mate. Just pitch up. Have you had anything from the cops?"

"Money?"

"Yes, and papers?"

"I've had five thou so far. Hey, as this guy has by all accounts nicked half a million, I was thinking we ought to get at least twenty-five thou each!"

"Yeah, go for it. Papers?"

"Only the police statement. You?"

"Yes, just that. Anyway, get your arse along here when you can, okay?"

Mark Collins called Chris Goodrich at his office.
"Hello!"

"Chris ... Mark. Mark Collins. Is Ian in?"

"No, Mark. Has not been in for at least for a whole day, for a while now. What's up!"

"I have heard a few disturbing rumours about Ian ... look, I don't want to bother you with them now, but I think maybe you and Arnie could drop in and see me sometime? The sooner the better. Would that be okay?"

"Yes, it would. And there have been a few rather strange goings-on and I'd be delighted to share them with you."

"Right, speak to Arnie, try and fix a date and let me know. I'll even get Emma to feed you both!"

"You got it! I'll be in touch!" Chris slipped out of his chair and dropped into Arnie's office. "Arnie ... we haver a problem! Mark has picked up on this business with Ian and Mike. Wants a meeting, and I think we should go!"

"Me too! Get it organised. I'll fit in with anything you arrange, okay?" Mark went into the kitchen to see his wife.

"Emma, I have a nasty feeling that Ian is stealing money, but not from Mum this time but from his clients."

"No surprise there! So, I do not think you should take the money he says he is going to pay you next year!"

"Right, love, but should I approach him on it? I mean, what do you think he'll say if I tell him that I think he's stealing clients' money? He'll go ape-shit!"

Just ignore him for now. And if he offers you any money, just refuse it. Now, I've had a call from Bethany. She wants us to nip up to Oxford to talk to the trustees ... when do you have some time off?"

"I'll check the roster when I'm next in. When does she want us up there?"

"Not until March, when she gets back to the UK. She said to leave the details up to you. I've got an address in Oxford, so I looked it up and work out how to get there. It's a big white building, loads of parking. If we allow an hour to get there should be plenty. Are you actually sure you want to go through with this?"

"Yes, I am sure! And I got the impression that Beth does too, and looking at the state of that bloke, Cedric, I think the sooner they get somebody, the better!"

"But what about Ian? I mean if …"

"Don't even go there, love! Ian can damn well look after himself! Anyway, we have not been offered anything yet, so at least we can take it as far as we can before making a final decision!"

"Okay … lets see just how far we get!"

"Right, maybe we should concentrate on getting Christmas out of the way!"

"And the meeting with Chris and Arnie!"

Ian Collins was having a bad day. He had been constantly ringing Dent asking what was happening on the case, and was being told very little except that the solicitor had seen Maynard, and he now would be having a meeting with the barrister as well.

"Once that's all done, Ian, we will get Maynard to the police station and charge him. He'll then be out on bail, have to attend the magistrates' court before the case is remanded to the Crown Court for trial. The CPS will have all the statements and they'll decide if it is a goer, which of course it is. That's all we can do for now. And by the way, the lawyers want fifty thousand!"

"Bloody hell! …"

"Ian, you're getting off with four hundred thousand plus any insurance monies! You know the deal … no payment, no deal!"

"Yes but … Oh, never mind!" Collins was in no position to argue.

TWENTY FOUR

Chris Goodrich and Arnold Medland pulled up outside Mark Collins' house.

"I reckon Mark is in for a shock! I mean, how would you feel if your brother was operating a massive scam, perverting the course of justice, stealing half a million quid …"

"Well, Chris, let's go in and find out!" Emma let the two men into the house, and led them through to the conservatory where Mark was just bringing in some extra chairs.

"Hi, you two! I hope I have not got you here on a wild-goose chase … have a seat. Emma's gonna deal withy the food. "

Hi, Mark. It's okay, we know damn well Ian is overseeing a potential disaster."

"Okay, be seated. I have some notes here. Let's see … the prison warder shuffled through his few papers. "Yes, by all accounts Ian has recruited a couple of dodgy cops, the ones I supposed were going to help him straighten out his business. What do you know about them?"

"Well, Mark, I'm afraid its bad news!" Chris explained what he and Arnie had discovered. "So, Mike has been suspended from his job, obviously, and Arnie and I are trying to deal with his workload. Then there's a trial set for I think March, and I've just been informed that there are two dodgy lawyers involved as well. They are going to make sure that they get a guilty verdict, which means that Ian can claim on the professional indemnity insurance, as well as keep what's left of the cash he took from the clients' account, which is rapidly being diminished due to the payments made to the cops and the lawyers, around a hundred thousand so far, I believe!"

"What! Emma!" He called his wife. "Did you hear that?"

"Yes! So why is Mike not just blowing the whistle on Ian?" Arnie explained the complication of Nick Forrester.

"So in court, Mike is going to play the audio and video stuff which I assure you, is a bloody nuclear bomb! I reckon those cops and the lawyers will be arrested on the orders of the judge!" The evening meal arrived, but both Emma and Mark were still trying to get over what they had heard.

"Right, Chris, Arnie, can you please make sure that whatever you have on this bloody awful business, you make available to Mike? He seems a decent kind of guy. Now, a surprise for you." Mark and Emma had agreed beforehand how much they were going to release on the JaworInt business. "We might be moving. I have got the possibility of a new job, kind of anyway, which means I will have more free time and hopefully extra cash, so I might be able to ensure that neither you two nor the firm will go down if, and indeed I hope, Mike does manage to sort out the business with Ian. I have some plans of my own ..."

"Mark, Mike has already told us that he would be very happy to pay for the business to allow it to continue under another name ... he does not expect Ian to be allowed to practice nor does he believe that Ian has the ability to practice so that would ..."

"I will be able to look after Ian ..." He was thinking of Bethany. "And I will look after mum as well." There was no mention of the DNA business. There was no need for anybody else to know.

In the car after leaving Mark's house, Chris made things clear to Arnie.

"We must give Mike everything we have on this business, including the Bugden file, a print-out of the office account showing we are in the shit financially, the statement Pam copied and every other bloody thing!"

"I'm with you on that!"

Back in the office next day, Chris again called everyone to a meeting. He explained to them that he had a meeting with Mark, and as a result, they had all agreed to give as much information to Mike as they could find, so the conspiracy with Ian, the police and the lawyers would be dramatically exposed in court. There were no dissenters.

Now at home, Mike Maynard had the time to organise his evidence. It was substantial. His only appointment that day was to attend the cop shop to be charged. It was Dent who did the business and the formal caution.

"Mister Maynard, you do not have to say anything but it may harm your defence if you do not mention when questioned something which you later rely on in court. Anything you do say may be given in evidence." Maynard wondered what they would say if he asked them whether they had been paid yet, that they were a couple of crooked cops and he would be delighted when they were both sentenced to a long stretch in jail. But he said nothing then he was released. The next step was to attend the local magistrates' court to be formally remanded to the Crown court for trial. It was all very embarrassing but it was nothing like the embarrassment the police and the lawyers will face. With all the prelims over, at least he had all the time to himself. He was in almost constant contact with Arnie, Chris and Debbie was watching out for him. He retired to his office, and went through the pile of documents and the CDs from ANWisecurity. The transcribed audios were all neatly labelled and in order. Then the doorbell rang. Maynard popped his head out of the window. Nick Forrester's car was inn the drive. He rushed downstairs to the front door, and Debbie and Nick were both there.

"Hi, you two! How's things!"

"Okay with us ...how about you?"

"Busy sorting out this stuff. Come in and have something to drink ...Debbie, rummage around in the fridge to see what's there! You know, I am really looking forward to the trial, and as long as I have all the documents I need everything should be okay!"

"Ah, yes! Documents! Chris and Arnie gave us a load of stuff for you. It's all stuff they think you should have. Also, they are planning to run the business without Ian, and we believe that you could do a good job in setting up your own law business from the bones of this one once all this is done and dusted!"

"Well, that's very kind of you. That is exactly what I had in mind, and Nick, when that happens we'll all be seeing a lot more of you!"

"I really hope so! And Uncle Sam is planning a big campaign to advertise the practice once everything is sorted!"

"You know, Mike we all miss you. Chris is doing his best to keep up with the work, but ..."

"Debbie, I am positive that with your help, he will manage. And I've told Chris and Arnie that once all this is over, I will be very happy to take on the practice, with some obvious changes!"

"Oh, Mike! That makes us so happy! And if we find out any more information we will pass it to you immediately!"

"I am very grateful for what you have done so far, and anything else you think is useful will be gratefully received." Maynard waved then goodbye, then returned to his files. Then his 'phone rang. It was Justin Weatherby.

"Mister Maynard ... I have an appointment with the barrister, Noël. It's tomorrow an eleven am. Can you make it?"

"Yes ... where do I go for that meeting?"

"It is in his office ... the old court building in the high street, opposite side to the Butts centre, walking away from the old Ramada hotel ... he's on the first floor. Have you been charged yet?"

"Yeah. We are hoping for a trial in I think March. The sooner the better!"

"Yeah, I agree." Weatherby put the 'phone down then turned to the barrister. "He's okay with the meeting. Have you had your dosh yet?"

"No, but I gather that the funds have been transferred to the Aylesbury account, the one in the name of the Dawson girl,

The one who works in the bank!"

"What has Dent got on the girl?"

"Dunno, but it must be something pretty heavy, if she's been co-opted to work for them! maybe I'll ask them next time I see those two, Dent and Forbear!"

"All set for tomorrow?"

"Yeah, you?"

"Of course. I'll tell you when the dosh comes through!"

The following morning, Maynard checked his special bag and that he had sufficient papers to indicate that a bag was essential to carry them all. He would leave it on the table during the meeting and find an excuse to leave the room for a lengthy-enough period so the two lawyers would start to chat about things they would most certainly not want Maynard to hear. He just hoped that whatever they said would be enough to pin them down when it was relayed to the court. He and Karen decided to both go, and Karen would stay at the Butts café until they met up again after Mike's meeting, then do a big shop. Despite all the trauma Karen was probably more eager to get the show on the road, knowing full well thet her husband never did things by halves. The pair left home and parked in the multi-story car park then got to the café at ten-fifteen for a coffee, then Mike walked to the office for the meeting. He arrived at ten to eleven, found the lawyer's office and entered. There was no one in reception, but through an open door he sighted the two lawyers, so walked in to see them. His audio device was switched on. When Maynard entered, neither lawyer stood up, but just pointed to an empty chair. Maynard sat and placed his bag on the label.

"Morning, Mike ..." It was Justin who greeted him. "This is Noël Sowerby-Newton." The barrister just lifted his hand off the table in acknowledgement. "You know why you are here, of course, and I want to reassure you that we will do all we can to get a not-guilty verdict. However, we must first of all run over a few facts..." Justin Weatherby turned to look at the barrister.

"Noël ...?"

"Right, first thing, the evidence against you is pretty substantial. You had the trust account on your office PC. Yes?"

"True, I did."

"Why?"

"Because Ian Collins put it there."

"When did you know it was there?"

"When my Debbie noticed it."

"And when did you open your Aylesbury account?"

"I didn't open an Aylesbury account."

"Mike, we have a witness who saw you when you opened the account." This was a new one on him.

"Impossible. As far as I know, I have never been to Aylesbury! And who was this witness?" He had a damn good idea it would be the same woman who was forwarding cash to the cops and the lawyers, the one who apparently worked at the bank. But he said nothing.

"We cannot tell you at the moment, but it will come out in court. Now, when did you start moving money out of Ian's account to your new account?" Maynard knew this kind of question was supposed to catch him out, and the expected answer was something like, 'as soon as I opened ...'. But Maynard was not caught out.

"I have never moved cash from any of Collins' accounts, and I do not have an account in Aylesbury!"

"Right. We'll have to deal with that one at a later date. Now, Mike, perhaps you can tell us why ..." Maynard thought it was a good time to nip to the loo.

"Er ... I hope you don't mind, but I need the toilet ... I assume you have one here?"

"Yes, of course, on the ground-floor."

"Okay, I'll find it. I'll be about ten minutes or so. Thanks." Maynard left the office and took the stairs to the ground-floor. He hoped the lawyers would open up to each other about the whole bloody scam they were involved in. When the door closed behind Maynard, Justin spoke up

"The bank girl, Jane, Jane Dawson, how will she recognise Maynard in court?"

"That's easy, 'cos the cops are going to point him out as he arrives at court on a hearing day. And she also has a copy of his driving licence which Ian copied when Maynard was offered the job. So, that's not a problem."

"Good. We've been here before on this kind of job, haven't we?"

"Yeah! that little shit … Nick Forrester! Got him six months, and a successful claim on his boss's insurance! Cracknell and Williams, wasn't it? The firm? That guy Cracknell was a total arsehole, and we only got twenty thousand for that one! Cheap. What was the first one you did, remember, the one about four or five years before?"

"That one! Twenty grand that was worth! We managed to delay the trial for over three years, so we could destroy all the documents the bloke never asked for, and he got six months an' all!"

"And the client? Didn't he actually kill someone?"

"More than one … and his bent clients got hold of him and got most of their cash, and then they burnt him alive! He was actually a nasty bit of work, so I have no sympathy for him! But this one is a whole different kettle of fish! Even if Collins cannot claim on the insurance, he could ask for a charge on this guy's property … according to Ian, Maynard has an unencumbered property worth over two million!"

"Bloody hell! How do you know that?"

"Cos Ian went to have a look at it, then 'phoned round all the local estate agents, and the estimate was just over two mill, and according to the land registry, no mortgage!"

"And we get just fifty grand each for this one!" There was other banter, useful but not as useful as what had been already recorded. Maynard returned to the office.

"Thanks, for that. Had a bit too much to drink last night!"

"Okay. Anyway, we have to tell you, Mike, that this is gonna be a bit tough for us to crack, but we'll manage it. Do you have any questions for us?"

"Er … no. But I might have a few for you later. I assume I can …"

"Mike, you can call Justin at any time. The trial I believe is set for March?"

"Yes."

The charade continued for another forty minutes or so with the barrister constantly hinting at how difficult the case was, and Maynard denying every accusation put to him.

"Well, Noël, I think that about covers everything?"

"Yes. Mike, just bear in mind that the case might not have the outcome you are expecting!" Maynard thought, really? Well, it will certainly not be the outcome you are expecting! The party said their goodbyes, Maynard picked up his bag and made his way back to the Butts centre to find Karen. She was where he left her, and by the looks of it had been nibbling some stickies. Well, he mused, better than smoking! He bent down and kissed her.

"How'd it go, darling?"

"Much as I suspected! Anyway, hopefully I have some good stuff on the recorder, so I'll call Terry and get him to do the usual. And I really ought to give him some money!"

"Yeah, love, you can use your Cayman island account!"

"Hey, careful darling, somebody could be recording us!"

"Maybe! But another thing occurred to me … have to get the low-down on that bank woman, Dawson. Maybe talk to DCI Ellis? He seems like a good guy!"

"Right, let's do some shopping!"

TWENTY FIVE

The following day, Maynard called Ellis.

"Mike, I wonder if the name Dawson, Jane Dawson means anything to you. According to my barrister, she is the person who says she saw me when I allegedly I opened an account at the Aylesbury branch, but I have never been to the place! Any idea?"

"That's interesting! When Dent moved all those drugs from your office, they used a van registered to her. We haven't done any checks on her yet, but I think maybe Dent might have something on her. Leave it with me, and I'll check her out. I'll let you know." Next on Maynard's list was to get the bag recordings to Terry to do the usual. He called, and agreed to drop the bag off at the laboratory. After all, he was not working, so the next day, when he was told the stuff was ready, and that there was some very useful information to be gleaned from the lawyers' indiscretion, he again dropped into see Terry and collect the material. Terry obliged by playing the CD and he was correct; it was really useful. Then he had a thought. Bearing in mind what the lawyers said about Dawson, it might not be a good idea if DCI Ellis were to approach her, as it might mean that she would not be used as the 'unimpeachable' witness regarding him and the bank account. He called Ellis again to set out his concerns.

"Actually, Mike, that might be a good idea to not mention her involvement with Dent and Forbear until after she has given the identity evidence! Which of course, will be before they call you to give evidence in your defence!"

"True! But clearly, my barrister won't question her evidence 'cos it wouldn't be in his intertest to do so!"

"But once you are in the box, you can bring the court's attention to the connection. If we approached her now, she would undoubtedly tell Dent and Forbear, so they will know we are onto them, and that might not be a good idea!"

"Got it! Maybe you might just see what if anything you've got on her."

"Will do, but we will not approach her! And you'll never guess, but I've had a nod and a wink from a publican friend of mine, ex DCI and he knows Dent of old, and when he's up to something! Apparently, Dent and Forbear are having a meeting with the lawyers in his pub, and we've already bugged the place, their private little room. Using your mate Terry! A damn good chap!"

"Wow! A bonus!"

"Sure is! As soon as we have any results, I'll let you know!"

Emma Collins called to her husband who was just finishing his evening meal.

"Any word from Beth? She should be back by now!"

"No, love, and remember she would tell us when she can meet us again. I assume she's got a few things to organise first, like getting all the trustees to free-up for the meeting. And as soon as I know, I'll book some more days off!"

"Makes sense. Any word about Ian?"

"Actually, yes! Chris tells me that the trial is fixed for march, and he and Arnie have been going through all the stuff which Mike might find useful, and by God he's got a pretty formidable pile of documents to show at the trial! And the whole office is keeping their fingers crossed!"

"Will Chris or Arnie give evidence for Mike?"

"I asked that ... they said they will if it looks like slipping away from Mike, but at the moment, they reckon Mike has got it sewn up!"

"I've heard that before! Let's hope they are right!"

"Yeah. Maybe you can do a google direction search and see how long it'll take us to get to the JaworInt offices! Don't want a last minute rush!" Emma moved up to the dining table and sat down opposite her husband.

"You know love, that Cedric guy seems to me to exhibit all the or some of the same issues as Ian does ... what did you think!"

"I think we've been here before. But of course, Cedric has by all accounts never had to work, ergo, Ian's obvious issues all emerged when he had to tackle the business of working for a living. Either way, and that by the way is not trying to find excuses for him. But that's where his real problems manifested themselves. I wonder what would have become of Hitler it he didn't ever have to find a bloody job!"

"Good question, but when all this had died down? What then?"

"Maybe we should do the same for him as Beth's doing for Cedric! In fact, Cedric and Ian might get on well together!"

"Well, that might not be a bad idea!"

"I dunno, love! It will become pretty obvious that Ian has more of Cedric in him that I do!"

"Yeah … maybe keep them apart for a good few years! Maybe until Ian gets out of jail?"

"If he ever does! He might piss off the other inmates so much, they might top him!"

"That might save us a great deal of trouble!"

Noël Sowerby-Newton and Justin Weatherby had called the meeting with Dent and Forbear. It was with the intention of establishing that they had covered everything ready for the trial, and while they still had time to sort out any holes in their case. The two cops arranged the venue at a pub on the road out of Reading in the direction of High Wycombe. They had arranged a private room, so they could arrive and depart without being seen by anybody in the public or saloon bars. From the other direction, Dent was driving, again in their white van. Noël still had something to say about the cops.

"I bloody tell yer, mate, the biggest bloody worry I've got is those cops! It cannot have escaped the attention of the higher-ups that those two are up to something. They've been doing drug runs, they were involved in that case with the Forrester kid, and

I bet the silly buggers are banking all that dosh from Collins! Imagine the IPCC will have a field-day!"

"So, what the hell can we do about it? I mean, if the shit hits the fan, they ain't gonna blag on us, 'cos if they do we'll well and truly stuff them! I mean, whose gonna listen to a couple of bent cops trying to finger a couple of decent, law-abiding lawyers?" Noël gave his mate a sideways glance, to see in there was any indication of him being facetious. There wasn't. maybe the guy was a bit stupid.

"Yeah, true!" Just humour the guy. He knew that if and when it all turned to worms, he had his own arse covered. They pulled up outside the pub, and as directed, nipped round the back where the deliveries were off-loaded, then into the private room. Dent and Forbear were already there.

"Hi, you two! What you having?" Orders taken, Dent closed the door. He didn't want anybody earwigging their conversation. "Right. We have a trial date. It appears that all the footwork has been done. Any issues?" Noël spoke first.

"Don't think so. The prosecution will give us the chance to pick-up on any weaknesses in Collins' story, which I reckon he's bound to cock-up, so I'll steer away from the obvious ones. Maynard is I think, a bit too cocky, maybe thinks he's got all the avenues covered. That Aylesbury bank account … one of you guys is gonna have to point out thy guy before the girl gets into the court, 'cos, as you know, witnesses are not allowed into the court-room until called. And don't forget you two are supposed to be assisting us, so anything you hear that will be of interest, either prosecution or defence, I need to know first!"

"Any points?"

"Yeah, just one! Have you two been fully paid up yet?"

"Got fifty grand between the two of us. That still leaves Collins with what, three-hundred thousand? And he'll get the insurance pay-out I expect, once Maynard is convicted, so he's onto a winner. The insurance half a mill plus the three hundred thousand! Wouldn't mind a few more of these cases!"

Half way through Mark's working day, Bethany called Emma.

"Emma? Trust you and Mark are fully recovered after Christmas! Just to tell you, if you give me a few dates for the meeting I mentioned, we can get this thing off the ground. Frankly. I'm looking forward to getting it all done and dusted!"

"Thanks, Beth! Yes, we'd like to move on with our lives. I'll get Mark to call you on this number as soon as he has managed to get time off agreed by his boss. How's Cedric?"

"Oh, Emma, you'd never believe it! I think as the days pass he seems to be more brain-dead than alive. He's going to overdo things if he's not careful, and I can't physically restrain him! I do not know how it's going to end … maybe like the princes in the tower, like you mentioned! Him being locked away for his own safety!"

"That's awful! However, I'm sure you have what it takes to keep him on the straight and narrow!"

"I never have in the past, maybe that's the problem! Anyway, I look forward to hearing from Mark!" Emma sent a text to Mark to see if he could arrange a few days off. Again, cite personal problems. Since returning from Spain, Mark had been on a bit of a high, and in anticipation of a somewhat dramatic change in lifestyle, he had become a bit contemptuous of his present life, far better than Ian had even achieved, but he knew he had it in him to do far better. He had a degree in business studies, which he took whilst still under training for promotion to the higher echelons of the prison service, but felt that his full ability was not appreciated by his bosses, one in particular, who happened to be on duty today, but Mark knew he had to approach him. He could not really blame the service for his lack of promotion. With his years in service, he had a great deal of experience which would probably be lost to the service if he were promoted, and the whole world knew that there were far too many people in prison, too many because they did not qualify for parole unless the inmate admitted to having committed the crime. Many were innocent, he knew, and were decent people and many had exhausted the appeals process, which, due in particular to the Criminal Cases Review Commission, was not functioning as it should. Again, this was a well-known fact, but for some reason the government was turning a blind-eye to it, and it grieved Mark that he had to keep them in jail. He knocked on his boss's open door.

"Yes, Mark!"

"Sir, I'm afraid I need another day off. I have …"

"Mark, for fuck's sake! What now?"

"Again family. Firstly, you know Ian is in the shit up to his eyeballs, and I need to give him a day to go through his case, and secondly Emma and I are looking at the idea of selling up and buying a place closer to here, after all the commuting is a waste of time and …"

"So you keep telling me!"

"Anyway, I suppose you did work over Christmas. Very well, but this will have to be the last non-scheduled time off! We are very busy here …"

"Sir, all prisons are busy with too many prisoners …"

"Don't get political, mate! What day did you want off?"

"The day after tomorrow?"

"Okay. Mark it on the board behind you. *Collins off … again!*" Mark would be delighted when, and if, he could return in a few days and tell Governor Wallace to stuff his job.   During a break, he called Emma to tell her that he had managed to get the day off, and would she tell Beth and sort out the sat nav for the trip. Job done.

Emma had been right. The JaworInt building was an impressive structure on the outskirts of Oxford, and as Emma and Mark entered the reception they were greeted and escorted to some inner sanctum.

"Thank you for coming. The others will call for you when they are ready, and Bethany will also be here. Can I get you anything ? Tea? Coffee? Soft drinks?" Emma responded.

"No thanks, were fine." Within a very few minutes, the visitors, both dressed very formally, were escorted up to the top floor and ushered into a very palatial conference room. The recognised Beth instantly, looking very healthy after her sojourn in Spain. She rushed over to then and hugged Emma and took Mark's hand. She was definitely overjoyed to see them.

"Come in! Meet the trustees!" The gentlemen and one lady Beth indicated were now all standing, and Emma and Mark went round the table shaking hands, then sat in the chairs indicated. The man at the end of the table who had introduced himself as Martin Sweeney, welcomed the visitors.

"Right, let me tell you a little about the business ..." He took some ten minutes to tell the whole room what they and the visitors already knew, especially as Mark had done his own research on the company. He then had each trustee set out their own individual functions within the organisations. The human resources manager, the lady, Frances Dyer, had some good news. She was also tasked with the board's families welfare, and undertook to arrange schooling, holidays, children's savings plans, accounts and estate planning for all those who needed those services.

"And," she added, ... "that means if you move here I will be tasked with finding schools for your two children!" Well, that was good news. Sweeney took over.

"Right, here's the deal ..." Firstly, the guy was not in the least interested in the relationship with the Cedric person. He made it clear that as far as that went, Bethany had satisfied herself that Mark and Emma were qualifiers, and that side of the deal was tied up. He then explained then remuneration package, the terms, duties.

"And, Mark, with your qualifications we may well find you a position on the board, and Emma, as a former director in a travel business, perhaps you can assist Frances here with her travel planning for our overseas visits to suppliers and growers! How does that sound!"

"Well, I must say, it sounds pretty good to us!"

There was a refreshment break after the best part of an hour, and afterwards the time was filled with questions and answer sessions, most of the questions being asked by the visitors. Then, as the meeting drew to a close, Sweeney again.

"Right, I have here a contract ... please take it away with you and if you are happy with the terms, let us have it back completed within ten days. Now, Bethany would like to show you the accommodation ... which is where I expect you and your children will be living if you come on board." That was a surprise!

"Er ... well, we had been thinking of selling our Reading property and ..."

"Much as I suspected! But first let's see how you feel about our little place!" With that, the meeting was over and Beth took charge of the next step.

"We have a car waiting when you're ready to go!" It did not take long to arrive at the residence. It looked like the place everybody wants to own, but is way out of their league. Beth explained. "This is basically an annex to the main house, almost next door, which is where I and Cedric live with a small live-in staff, and the trustees also have accommodation there when needed. This place is now empty, it is a six-bed, four bathroom property with many family-friendly features. The company owns the property as with next door, and as it is a private company, as you know, it will pay for the upkeep and will have it fully furnished to your requirements. It keeps the tax bill down! The only issue is the swimming pool. You might wish to have it covered in view of the children, or reduce the water-level to just lie-down depth. Mark and Emma were speechless.

"Wow! Beth, what can I say?"
"How about 'can we look inside!"
"Can we look inside please!" They all laughed.

Back in the company conference room, Sweeney posed a question.

"Well what do you think of them? Hands up for yes!" All the hands went up. "Thanks. It was a bit touch and go, with Cedric getting ever more of a problem, we didn't have much time, but a far as I'm concerned, as Beth is more than happy, I think we have little choice anyway. At least, the business and our futures seem secure, and as they have two young children, I think they will, between them, see us out! And as the master contract says that we have a very wide discretion who we appoint. I think it is a done deal."

The meeting was a resounding success for Mark and Emma. On the drive back to Reading, Emma was in tears most of the way.

"I can't believe it! Honestly, love, I don't think the Sweeney bloke really cared about the DNA stuff, just relieved that somebody slips into the slot!"

"Well, that may be the case. We'll go through the contract and get it returned to the company bosses. Now let's get home and have a celebratory drink!"

"Darling, this is a turning-point in our lives! If we hadn't gone for this DNA thing, we'd be in a right mess … Ian nicking his clients' cash, your job problems, mum and her being robbed by Ian as well…we can do so much to put those problems right! And the children, going to get the best education money can buy, a lovely house for lifetime occupation …!"

"Don't count your chickens! Have to get this contract signed, then endorsed by the company before we do anything!"

"When is Mike Maynard's' trial?"

"In about a week or so, I think!"
"Are you going to go?"
"I can't … you may be able to if you want!"
"Yeah, maybe I ought to go!"
"Well, don't start shouting out, *'He didn't do it! It was Ian bloody Collins what done it!'* or words to that effect, will you!"
"How did you know? That was exactly what I was gonna do!"

TWENTY SIX

The first day of Maynard's trial was warm one for March so most people including Maynard and his defence team were in quite a good mood. Justin and Noël damn well should be, Maynard mused, as they had quite a lot of money out of the stuff Ian had stolen. Maynard had gone through all the ANWisecurity stuff, and the sound and the transcription was excellent. The video stuff was also first-class and it was one hundred percent clear from the first recording when Ian met the two cops, exactly what they were up to, including the drug-deal. And in particular, the forged ID for the false bank account set up, Ian's discussion about the Cayman account, it was all so good, it was almost like a scene from a feature-film. It was clear that the parties were in it up to their necks. Further, the so-called-defence lawyers had been a little too open about their role-play and their collusion with the cops, Chip and Pin, their discussions with Ian Collins and, the cream on the cake, was when they mentioned the lad Nick Forrester, whom they referred to as 'that little shit' and who had netted them thirty thousand pounds several years ago for deliberately botching the defence case. In fact, they laughed about it, suggesting that the six-month jail-time might do him some good.

Maynard was under no illusions; it was going to be tough and although he expected the corrupt cops and lawyers would fight like alley-cats to have the footage disallowed, every bit of research he had done resulted in a positive result for Maynard. He had also done some research on likely sentences when the four conspirators were sentenced after trial and conviction, and it turned out that the offences were severely punished, with terms without parole of ten to fifteen years. Well, maybe jail-time would do them all some good. Maynard had not shared his thoughts or actions with either Nick or his uncle Sam, but he did however tell them that the prospects were good. He had not brought any of his defence documents with him, but they were secured in his safe at home, and the baby-sitter and her boyfriend were staying at the house. The stakes were high, and if any of the other parties had any notion of what he had amassed for his own defence, he knew that there would be quite a degree of interest shown by the wrong people, people who would doubtless be well-paid to get hold of it and destroy it, and no doubt they would not stop at violence. Maynard slipped into the bench at the front of the court next to Justin. The barrister was still in the robing room, no doubt passing the time of day with the prosecution barrister, Nigel Willis, who would be pressing for a guilty plea.

"Cummon, mate! You know damn well the evidence against him is very substantial!" Just what Justin wanted to hear because it fitted in with his plan.

"Come off it, Nigel, you know I like a fight! Certainly, I and Justin have made that clear to him, but he ain't gonna budge!"

"Well, Noël, I will of course have to tell the judge that he continued against good advice … you know Graham Coppins can be a bit hard on sentencing! All the crap about expense, wasted time …!"

"You just do your best, mate!" Right I suppose we'd better get into court!"

The first and tedious business was the swearing-in of the jury, achieved once the usher asked the members of the jury if they had had any dealing with the firm Collins and Goodrich; none had. Then, when all done and dusted, a court usher took over.

"All stand for His Honour Judge Coppins!" The court usher stood by the door at the front of the court, and when the court was on its feet, he opened the door and Coppins came in and sat down. "Be seated!" Maynard was led to the defendant's box. The judge fiddled about with some papers on his desk then looked at Maynard, still standing.

"Mister Maynard, please state your full name, address and date of birth." Maynard obliged. "Thank you. You are charged that between diverse dates you stole the sum of five hundred thousand pounds or thereabouts from the accounts of your employer, Messrs Collins and Goodrich, solicitors. How do you plead, guilty or not guilty?"

"Not guilty your Honour."

"Thank you. You may be seated. The judge then looked at the CPS barrister, who got to his feet. "Yes Mister Willis."

"Thank you your Honour. I call my first witness. Mister Ian Collins." An usher standing near back of the court slipped out into the lobby, and was heard calling out, 'Call Mister Ian Collins'. Collins wandered in and was led to the witness box where the oath was administered. He did not look at Maynard. Willis was still on his feet. "Mister Collins, Please state your full name."

"Ian Mackenzie Basil Collins."

"Thank you. What do you do Mister Collins?"

"I am the senior partner in the law firm Collins and Goodrich."

"Thank you. That is a successful, busy business?"

"Yes, it is." Maynard noted on his counsels' notebook, another fib. According to the copies of the firm's office account that

Maynard had, it was well overdrawn, at one stage by as much as seventy thousand pounds.

"And you employed the defendant. In what capacity?"

"He was engaged as a conveyancing solicitor."

"And I believe you had occasion to address him on the matter of one of your client's account?"

"Yes, I did. It was the account …" Willis interrupted.

"Just answer the questions, Mister Collins. And you do not need to mention the name of the client whose account the defendant was concerned with. Will you now please tell the jury what your concerns were and what you did regarding the same."

"Yes…" Maynard looked at Collins. He appeared to be nervous, so maybe he had not learned his lines too well, that is, of the four or five he had drafted then trashed, and which were now stashed away with all the other evidence Maynard had. Maybe it was the police-drafted statement which he was going to refer to. "I was completing the work on a probate matter and there was going to be a substantial delay in paying out to the estate beneficiaries, so I decided to put the funds into a separate trust account, a high-interest account, which is what I did."

"Thank you. And when did you realise that funds were missing from that account?"

"Almost immediately … I checked all my client accounts every day and I saw that a hundred thousand pounds was missing."

"And what did you do then?"

"I went onto the account on my PC and saw that the missing funds appeared to have been sent to an account in the name of the defendant, Maynard." Mike realised, as no doubt Collins did too, that Collins had made a big mistake. Willis picked up on it.

"Er … Mister Collins, what did you do having found out where the missing money had gone to?"

"I called the police." Getting in deeper, thought Maynard.

"Mister Collins, can we go over than again please? You say you saw a hundred thousand had gone missing …"

"Sorry, I should have said five hundred thousand …"

"Missing immediately?" Collins was in trouble. "Mister Collins, according to your statement, the one you gave to the police, you say that the money up to the level you just mentioned, went missing over quite a period of time yet now you say a hundred thousand …" Collins saw the error. He interrupted the prosecution counsel, who had no interest in the case beyond asking questions.

"Sorry, I was … I am a little confused. It was over a period that I noticed the cash was missing. The trust account had mistakenly been opened in my satellite office, and I did not check that one every day." Another problem for Collins; he must have checked it least twice every week! Maynard knew damn well that the extractions by Collins ran over three months, September to November. He had a print-out of the account.

"Very well, thank you for clearing that up. So what did you do then? I think you said that you called the police?"

"Yeah, then I let them get on with it."

"Chasing the half million pounds?"

"Yes!" There were more questions and answers most of it tedious detail about what Collins did or did not do. Overall, he did not come over as a particularly good witness, but to Maynard that was not an issue. It took about an hour to finish with the witness.

"No further questions your Honour. Wait there Mister Collins!"

"Mister Newton. Your witness." Noël SN stood up.

"Thank you your Honour … Mister Collins, you must have been surprised that your trusted employee, a solicitor, was stealing money? Sorry, allegedly stealing money?"

"Yeah, of course I was!"

"Did you ever approach him? Ask what he was doing?"

"Yes. But my fear was that he would disappear with all the money but at least, if he still had it we might be able to recover it all."

"Thank you …" To Maynard's mind, the questioning was inane. "Didn't you move the account to another office to get him away from the temptation?"

"No. Every office has all the account details so they can access all the accounts … it would otherwise be difficult to operate. It's the way we have to work …"

"When you discovered the thefts, didn't you sack Maynard?"

"No. I might have been wrong about him …"

"Thank you, no further questions." Maynard got the distinct impression that the prosecuting barrister thought he had it in the bag, and despite Collins' obvious cock-ups. The judge again.

"Mister Willis do you wish to …" Willis raised his butt off the seat by about six inched and replied.

"No further questions, thank you."

"Mister Collins, you may stand down." Maynard wondered about the obvious points he had noted; didn't his barrister pick up on them? Maybe he did, maybe he did not, but as Maynard already knew, the barrister was not exactly on his side, and so far he had not been taking any notes. During the questioning, the usher was handed a note by someone who had just entered the court, and after a very brief discussion, the note was conveyed to Justin. He read it and looked at Noël. The note said that the woman who was to identify the defendant as the person who opened the Aylesbury bank account was not now going to attend. There followed a whispered exchange between the two men. They did not look pleased. Collins' evidence now finished, the judge spoke again. "Mister Willis call your next witness."

"I call Mister David Brooks!" The usher again did his bit outside the door of the court, and the Brooks guy entered the court, nodded to the judge, and went straight to the witness box, and took the oath. Obviously well acquainted with court work. Willis was onto him immediately.

"Mister Brooks your full name please."

"David Edward Brooks."

"And you are a forensic accountant?"

"I am. I have been for over thirty-years."

"Thank you. Please tell the jury how you are involved in this case and your findings."

"Of course. I was engaged by a Mister Ian Collins to look at the various movements of cash from his clients' account and from the information supplied, I discovered that over a period late September to December of last year, a substantial amount of money close to five hundred thousand pounds was moved into an Aylesbury account in the name of the Defendant, I was ..."

"Mister Brooks, were you able to establish for a fact that the account was opened by the defendant?"

"No, but going by information supplied by the bank, we were unable to establish that it was not."

"Thank you, please continue ..."

The opening day of the case was pretty short, due to the swearing in of the jury, and the ramblings of the witnesses various. Maynard made notes, which to him seemed necessary, as, during the entire proceedings, neither Justin nor Noël had made any. When the judge rose and asked the parties to be ready for a ten am start the following day, Maynard approached his solicitor.

"Well, how are we doing so far?"

"Don't look too good, does it? I'm afraid that you might be in for a disappointing result!"

"Well, that's something we just might have to live with! I'll see you tomorrow." On his way home, Maynard's 'phone rang. He took the call on his hands-free.

"Mike? ... Terry Thorne. Can you talk?"

"Yeah, go ahead."

"Got some good news ... I have a good mate who is pretty high-up in Crimestoppers, and he nipped over to the lab ... I invited him ... and he was absolutely outraged at the stuff I showed him about your case! He also reckoned that there was no way you would be prevented from showing that evidence at the trial, and in fact, he offered to assist, if necessary, by appearing on your behalf! How does that sound!"

" Great ... and my bloody lawyers, as you would expect, showed absolutely no interest in today's' proceedings!"

"As expected!"

"Right. And this evening I'm going to write-up my notes, and go over some stuff ready for tomorrow!" When Maynard arrived home, Karen met him at the door.

"How was the day, love?" They both walked to the kitchen.

"Good. It's clear to me that neither of my lawyers know what they are doing, but I'm just going to let them dig a big hole for themselves!

TWENTY SEVEN

It was obvious to Maynard that the prosecution were going to throw the book at him, or in the alternative, were stringing it out because they had no better cases to attend to. Maynard sat through nearly two weeks of rubbish evidence about a solicitor's duties to his clients, and how the accounts process worked. He could see that the jury was bored. It was not a murder trial or anything as nearly exciting as a bloody murder, and it must have come as a relief to everybody when the CPS finished presenting their case. The judge then finished the day early, informing the court that the case for the defence would open the following day. He disappeared into his room behind the court, the court then emptied. The solicitor, Justin, approached Maynard.

"You ready for tomorrow?"

"I am, are you?" Maynard knew what was coming next.

"You know, Mike, there is one hell of a case against you ... you would be doing yourself a great favour, and I think the judge would be very pleased if you were to plead guilty tomorrow, and I could do one hell of a good plea in mitigation if you did! I mean, in terms of sentencing, you could save yourself years of prison time, and let's be reasonable about this, it will definitely mean a custodial ..."

"Justin, look. You just turn up tomorrow, and you never know, you might be in for a surprise. I'm off home now. See you tomorrow." The solicitor shouted after him.

"Mike! ... I think you are being very silly!" Maynard just waved his hand in response, and under his breath muttered

'Well, mate, you are gonna have to earn your fifty thousand, aren't you, arsehole!'

The next day, Maynard met his barrister Noël and solicitor Justin.

"I hope you brought your overnight kit!" was the greeting from the barrister. "Justin tells me that you're going the distance ... won't do you any good, you know!"

"We'll see. Thanks for the advice." Maynard picked his bulging briefcase off the floor, and went to the café for a coffee.

"What the fuck has he got in that case, Justin?"

"No idea ... what do you think!"

"Dunno. I just hope he's not gonna spring a surprise on us! Do think he knows anything? About our little job?"

"Na! There's just no bloody way! Relax mate!"

"I wish I could feel as confident as you! He seems to, I dunno, be a little to unconcerned about the case?"

"Always was. Just let's see what turns up! Let's get into court!"

"All stand!" The judge entered the court, looked briefly at the defendant, dropped his notebook onto his bench and sat down. He looked at Noël Sowerby-Newton.

"Are we ready, Mister Newton?" The barrister stood up.

"Yes, your honour."

"Mister Maynard take the stand please." Mike Maynard moved to the witness box, and the oath was administered and as before, he chose to affirm.

"Thank you Mister Maynard, remain standing please." The usher moved away. The judge looked at Newton again, who stood up.

"Your witness, Mister Newton"

"Thank you, your Honour." Newton faced the defendant. "Mister Maynard, did you steal the sum of five-hundred thousand pounds from your employer?"

"No I did not."

"But Mister Maynard, you were the only person in the firm who had both motive and opportunity to steal the money, so I have to ask, if it was not you who stole it, who was it?" Maynard looked at the judge who looked a bit bemused by the

question, as indeed he was. "Maybe you can tell the court?" Newton turned to face the jury as if to bathe in their undoubted admiration in his posing such a stunningly incisive question. For a moment, Maynard said nothing, allowing his counsel to wallow in the admiration he saw on the faces of the jury, and also for Maynard to use the silence to wind up the anticipation of his reply.

"Sir, I will most certainly tell the court. The money was stolen not by me, buy by my employer, Mister Ian Collins!" The judge was the first to react.

"Mister Maynard! Do you have any evidence to support this slander?"

"I do indeed your Honour, and what is more, the police officers, Messrs Dent and Forbear as well as Mister Newton and solicitor Justin Weatherby know it to be true as they were all conspirators …" The judge again. He raised his voice this time.

"What evidence do you have of this! We must see the evidence!"

"Very well your Honour." Maynard reached down to his briefcase, and placed it on the bench in front of him.

"Any evidence you had should have been given to your defence lawyers! This is a disgraceful way to behave! Why didn't you hand it over months ago?"

"Your Honour, if you are concerned about disgraceful behaviour, then I respectfully suggest that you see the evidence I have here then if you are so inclined hand it over to the Crown Prosecution Service …!" Maynard glanced over to his lawyers. They looked a bit shell-shocked, unsurprisingly. The judge turned his attention to Weatherby and Sowerby-Newton.

"Mister Newton!" Newton shot to his feet.

"Your Honour?"

"Were you aware of this?"

"No, your Honour, I was not, but I can tell you that the defendant is a desperate man and nothing he says would surprise me! I … I suggest that it might be worth your Honour's while to see what evidence if any he has to support these outrageous claims!" He was calling Maynard's bluff. Weatherby looked shocked. Clearly, he was of the opinion that Maynard had something; Newton was clearly not convinced. The judge turned again to Maynard.

"Mister Maynard, hand your documents to the usher … I can call a recess and read them in chambers."

"Your Honour … what I have here will take hours to go through … I am in no position to tell you how to utilise your time, but I think you may need to maybe close today's proceedings and discuss the information I have here …" Maynard pointed to his files … "and then take whatever action you deem appropriate."

"Mister Johns" the judge addressed the usher, "bring me those documents or whatever they are please!" Johns obliged, somewhat taken aback by the weight of the paperwork. He placed it all onto the judge's bench. "We shall adjourn for an hour."

"All stand!" As the courtroom emptied, with many making for the café, Maynard's lawyers marched up to the witness box.

"What the bloody hell are you up to!" It was Newton. You are not doing yourself any good you know! This judge will crucify you!"

It was less that thirty minutes before a Tannoy announcement recalled participants to court two, Crown versus Maynard. When all settled, the judge entered and sat down.

"Mr Newton … I am adjourning this hearing until the day after tomorrow., We will meet here again at oh-nine thirty hours on Thursday. The court is now adjourned. HH Judge Coppins rose and was gone in a moment. Clearly something was up. Maynard noticed the usher Johns approach the prosecution barrister, Willis, and it seemed he was being asked to meet the judge in chambers. That, thought Maynard, was a good sign.

Back in their office, Maynard's lawyers were worried.

"Justin, you and I know damn well that Maynard knows something … maybe it's Collins trying to buy time, but I don't see how his helping Maynard is gonna save his skin!"

"No, mate, it ain't Collins. He's too damn stupid to do anything fancy like this!"

"Well, I suggest we look seriously at our escape plans! If old Coppins picks up anything from what Maynard's told him, we could really be in the shit!"

"For God's sake, calm down! Clearly the guy is gonna blame everybody he can, there's no way he can have anything on us, I don't suppose …"

"What about those goons, the cops Dent and Forbear?"

"Or worse, what about Roger, Roger Cracknell?"

"What if he's opened up to Maynard?"

"He won't! His little plan worked, he got back all his money didn't he?"

"I suppose, yes, so he won't blab!"

"I'm still worried ... let's keep our fingers crossed for Thursday! But in the meantime, talk to those two coppers! They might be the Achilles heel in all this! I'll call them now ..."

Weatherby tried several times to call but there was no answer.

There was no answer, because Dent and Forbear were in a meeting with their superior, DCI Wignall.

"Now, I suppose you got the feedback from the Maynard trial today?"

"Yes Sir, a little. By all accounts, the guy is blaming us! You remember, Johnny, he said he would, so we kinda expected it. I mean, the bloke is clutching at straws, and who can blame him?"

Wignall knew better. He had been tipped off and the reason for the meeting was to make sure that on the day the case commenced, both were on other duties and would not be free until the verdict was due. Wignall was surprised at their over-confidence, and at the enormity of the evidence against them as delivered from a nearby station. He had his own misgivings about the two, and was still looking into the murder of the drug-runner Toady, shot dead in Prospect park. Also, he had been asked by the neighbouring station to provide any information on a female, name of Jane Dawson. That was his next call. He dismissed the two officers, and they fortunately seemed to be unaware that they were basically, on 'open arrest' pending the outcome of the Maynard trial. The officer was still waiting to get the report from the banks of the two officers, and their spouses, which he was told would show unexplained deposits of substantial sums of cash. Apparently, this was linked to the Dawson woman. He accessed the file. It showed a case of a death at home, and It was a seven-year old case, a coroner had ruled that the death was a suicide. The Dawson woman was then living in Marlow, her husband had been the manager of a large engineering business, and the widow received a substantial pay-out on his life insurance and pension. The investigating officers were Dent and Forbear. Wignall decided he would go and visit the woman to see what her connections were with Chip and Pin, aka Dent and Forbear.

The following day, Wignall parked up outside the Dawson residence at Weedon Hill. There was no answer at the door, so he chose not to park up and wait, as his presence would be too conspicuous, so he drove away and waited until a car passed him going towards the house. He did not have very long to wait. He had in the meantime been on his mobile looking at house prices in the area, an established that the house was in the million pound plus bracket. Very nice for a widow, who was no doubt fending off boy-friends looking for opportunities for a predatory marriage. Wignall left it for a few minutes, then drove back to the house. He parked up and left the car. The front door was still open, so he approached and called out.

"Hello!" There came a response from inside.

"Yes? Can I help you?" The lady approached the front door, then stood looking at the visitor. Wignall took out his warrant card.

"Missus Dawson? I am Inspector Andy Wignall ..." He got no further.

"Look, I have already said, I am not going to do this again! Those two coppers ..."

"I'm sorry, Madam, I am nothing to do with those two, those two being I assume Dent and Forbear! And I want to reassure you that they will not be bothering you again. May I come in and have a chat with you please!"

"Oh, very well."

"Thank you ..."

"Come through to the kitchen please ... the lounge is in a bit of a mess...now, what is this all about?"

"It's about Dent and Forbear. I understand that they have been using you for what I would call illegal purposes, in particular to do with your job in the bank. Would you care to explain, from the beginning."

"It all started about five years ago, when my husband committed suicide. He had terminal cancer. We then lived in Marlow. Anyway, when I found Gerry, in the garage, he had shot himself. He was the holder of a gun licence. Those two arrived when I called the police. To cut a long story short, they accused me of shooting him and went on to say that they could make it look like suicide, and told me that to save a trial and probably a life sentence, I could help them. Then they said it didn't matter how long it took, if I did not help them, the offence was not subject to any statute of limits or something like than ..."

"Statute of limitations?"

"Yes, that was it, then they took a load of photographs and stuff, rearranged everything, then the scene of crime people came in and later with the medical people confirmed it was suicide. Dent told me it was because of what he had done, otherwise it would be regarded as murder, which I did to get his insurance pay-out."

"So, what did you do for them?"

"Mainly bank stuff. I moved here about a year after Gerry died, and worked for the same bank, different branch. Then the last job, which I told them I was not going to do, was about some guy called Maynard ... I opened the account but when they wanted ne to go to court I just said enough was enough and I refused. I told them only the other day!"

"And the van?"

"My husband bought a van which he was going to convert into a holiday thing for me and my daughters, but he never finished it. Dent said he would like it, I said no, I wanted to keep it then he offered me fifty pounds per week if he could use it, so I said yes. And I can give you all the details of money paid to me and which I had to pay out ... the names are here ... the two police officers, a Mister Weatherby and a guy called Sowerby-Newton ..."

"My goodness!" Wignall looked at the statements. " ... they had one hell of a lot of money!"

"They did, and I was getting more amd more involved ... and it was also a few years back, the same four and another guy ... let me see now ..." Dawson flicked through her file. " ... yeah, a guy called Cracknell!"

In all, the meeting took over two hours, and finished coincidently when the two daughters returned from school. Wignall had made copious notes, and eventually declared himself satisfied.

"Well, thank you. You have been very helpful. I can assure you that this will be the end of contact with Dent and Forbear. You might be asked to give a formal statement when we deal with these people, and we will, but apart from that you may ignore them if they call again. Here, take my card and call me personally if you hear from them again." They said their goodbyes, with Dawson looking very relieved, a weight off her mind. And Wignall departed Aylesbury for the CPS offices to hand over the bank statement and a write-up of his meeting with Ms. Dawson.

TWENTY SEVEN

When judge Coppins opened the files Maynard had provided, he knew immediately that he was looking at something serious. He had not got the facility to view the CDs contained in the files, so he asked his usher to get hold of the CPS barrister. Willis was there within minutes. The judge and Willis once worked from the same chambers.

"Nigel ... look at this lot! I think Maynard is on to something, and frankly, I can't read all this but I think we ought to look at these CD things. Can you arrange it? Maybe we can get a couple of clerks in to keep up with the paperwork. We can view, they can get the relevant scripts. What do you think?"

"Let me have a quick whizz through!"

"Nigel, it ain't a quick whizz job, I'm afraid! It's hours!"

"The stuff is very professionally done, but we have to beware that it isn't a load of fiction! Let's get started straight away!"

"Okay! I'll get the stuff we need for the viewing. I'll be back shortly!" The judge called after him.

"Nigel! Not a word to anybody about this! I have a feeling this stuff is explosive!"

"Okay! No problem! My lips are sealed!" Willis was back in the judge's office inn no time, followed by two clerks between them carrying a large TV set and a number of black boxes which they arranged non the table, connected to a power supply.

"Sir, give us a CD and we'll just explain what you have to do ..." Willis handed over the one Coppins offered him, marked as number one, and dated. The clerks did their bit and got the first few frames on the screen, explaining the pause, rewind stop and volume facilities. Coppins was happy.

"Nigel! Do we have anybody yet to deal with the paperwork?"

"No, but may I suggest that we both go through a couple of CDs first, just in case it is patent rubbish ... don't want to waste anybody's time, least of all ours!"

"I'll second that! Lets give it a whirl!" Willis took the handset and pointed it at the screen.

"Ready?"

"Yeah! Let's go for it!" Willis read the label.

"Video one; meeting between Ian Collins and police officers DS Dent and DC Forbear; location the Green office. Then the date. Right, here we go!" Willis pressed 'play'. The picture was of an empty room, then Collins walked in followed by the two officers. The picture was clear, so was the audio. They saw Forbear pull out a pack of cigarettes and light one.   Willis pressed 'pause'.

"I recognise the police officers! And Collins, the complainant!"

"I recognise Collins as well." Willis pressed 'play' and Dent spoke.

'Right, some ground-rules. One. Nothing gets writ down. Two, you and I do as we say we'll do. Three, we get paid once a job's finished. Four We'll always deny we ever met and we tell nobody we've met you today, right? Right, mate wassyer problem?' Then it was Collins, leaning forward elbows on the table. He looked at the two cops on the other side of the table then spoke.

'I owe my brother some money, to repay him the dosh I used to set up this business. He has set a deadline, which will really get me into the shit unless I pay him, so I want to make it look like one of my employees has stolen a lot of money ...' Dent;

'Ow much.' Collins;

'He's going to steal three hundred thousand.' Dent;

'Hey, are you sure you're gonna get it back? I mean if there's no compensation order ...' Collins;

'No prob with that! The bloke lives in a house worth over two million, and it ain't mortgaged, either!' Dent;

'Bloody hell, mate, he has to be a crook!' Dent then raised his eyes to the ceiling, pointing to the loft hatch. *'Hey, Ian ... anything in there?'*

'No. Shouldn't be, anyway. Why? What's up?' Dent;
'Hey, Johnny, what about using that place for our you-know-what?' 'Better have a butchers first! Ian, can we have a look up there?' Collins;

'Yeah, of course. If you put a chair on the table you might be able to reach it!' Dent, with his head poking up into the loft.

'Hey! Looks okay to me! Plenty of room! Er ... can we kinda borrow the place? Just got some stuff to stash away for a few days, will that be okay?' Collins;

'Yeah, of course. When do you wanna put it up there?' Dent;

'Now! If you organise the take-aways and some beers, Johnny and I can stash it there.' Then there was the pantomime of Dent and Forbear stashing what was obviously drug packages into the loft-space. Coppins waved to Willis.

"Stop!" Willis pressed the stop button. "I've seen enough! Nigel, I want you to take all this and give me a report by the time I sit again the day after tomorrow! I don't know about you, but as far as I'm concerned this is a smoking gun! And I also want from the CPS an indication of the offences committed which I will pass on to the chief constables office who will arrest those three! And of course, anybody else you see in the videos. I'll fully support your recommendations! Okay?"

"Yeah, but I still can't see why Maynard didn't produce all this stuff before trial? Unless he was concerned about his safety! And of course, we might well have to address the question of admissibility ...!"

"No we won't, Nigel, as far as I am concerned at least as a senior judge I reckon it's fully admissible ... public interest!"

"Okay! Let me take all the stuff back to the office. We have sufficient staff to get the stuff sorted in time for the continued hearing!" Willis collected all the files, packed them away in Maynard's own case, and returned to his office. As soon as he arrived, he collared three of his senior prosecuting clerks and briefed them. Within the hour, the tapes were being played, and after each tape, they checked the transcription, then made a note of the likely offences committed by each of the parties. There was plenty of pausing, playbacks and discussion. It was a long job. Finally, Willis had a list of offenders and likely charges. It included Roger Cracknell of the firm Cracknell and Williams. Officers Dent and Forbear looked like the biggest offenders, willfully neglecting to perform their duty and willfully misconducting themselves to such a degree as to amount to an abuse of the public's trust in the office holders without reasonable excuse or justification. Then there was conspiracy, handling stolen goods, failing to account to HMRC for payments received, money laundering, drug dealing and perverting the course of justice. Willis summed up their position with his team. Basically, guys, the cops are in deep shit! Misfeasance in public office, guys, is an offence at common law dating back to the thirteenth century, often grounds for removal of an elected official by statute or recall election!"

"Hey, Nige, I'll remember that! it might be useful sometime in the future!" The lawyers, Messrs. Cracknell, Collins, Weatherby and Sowerby-Newton also had quite a lot to answer for.

"Yeah, it might, Sue, but I can't quite work out why Maynard didn't produce all the evidence to another legal team once he had gone to all the trouble of amassing it all. Maybe judge Coppins would be told in due course."

"I think I can work it out!"

"Go on then, Sue, tell us!"

"I think it is due to the bloke Cracknell screwed up! I bet Maynard wanted to bring it up in court once the judge had decided that his team were all crooks, and get the Forrester lad's conviction overturned!"

"Why didn't the lad appeal to the CCRC?"

"He probably did, but we all know that the CCRC is totally bloody useless! In fact, the obvious issue is, how can anybody steal two hundred thousand or even ninety thousand pounds of clients' money over what, three years, without anybody noticing, no client complaining, I mean, that alone is a good start for the CCRC to work on, but they ignored it. If any client had complained, the business would have come to light years earlier!

It just does not add up! To me, a mere clerk, it is bloody obvious that things do not stack up! Nor did the cops or defence team ask to look at his private accounts. It stinks, frankly!"

"True, it does! Anyway, when you have all finished your write-ups, let's get all the stuff over to judge Coppins! He sits again tomorrow morning! Maybe, Sue, you can drop it off with all the other bits of paper, like Collins' office account any statements which show it was never a viable business ... bloody hell, it really is gonna knock old Coppins for six! the stuff about the Cayman Islands accounts, the transfers to the Dawson's bank account from the Caymans and payments out, all the stuff that DCI Wignall had provided."

It was late morning when the CPS file landed on Coppin's table. He carried his coffee into his room, then opened the file. He was transfixed. It was a solid read for three hours, with the judge making notes on his pad. By the time he had finished, he was livid. He knew that as soon as the guilty parties learned of the tsunami of evidence against them, they would probably go into hiding or make for the airport and, with some of the offences punishable by a long period of imprisonment, it was a likely scenario, and it may be the case that some of them would have overseas bank accounts holding their stolen cash. He picked up his 'phone and dialled a number.

"Stan? Judge Coppins here ... can you drop in to see me please? Right away I need to get something sorted out by first thing tomorrow!" Stan Elder was in Coppin's office in no time.

"You wanted to see me?"

"Yes, sit down. Here, look at this list please. In court tomorrow, I am going to order the arrest of all these people ... and I don't want them to know beforehand that they could be facing arrest. You can speak to DCIs Ellis and Wignall ... they both know what's going on. The police officers ... Dent and Forbear may not be in court, so I want them under surveillance from first thing tomorrow, because as soon as they know what I am going to do or have done, they may well flee to some bolt-hole somewhere, and I want to prevent that happening. And when I sit tomorrow, say nine-thirty … no, say ten, I want them taken into custody."

"Got it! I will treat this as a top-secret operation!" Stan Elder knew this was hot information. He also knew that information is, at its essence, a resource; information has always been valuable throughout history, from covert meetings to strategic placement, the side with the most information, the best understanding of the playing field, and the ability to alter their tactics in response to that knowledge will win. He also knew that people pay good money for Information especially the type of stuff he picked up in his job. And he had many customers for the stuff he dealt with daily. What he had just learned was worth a lot. And he intended to cash in, and he had to be quick. On his way back to his office, he nipped into the 'HotStuff' café for a toasted ham and cheese sandwich and a hot chocolate, and when tucked away in a quite corner away from anybody's casual gaze, he dialled a number. It was a number he had in his memory, not in his contacts. He put his mouth close to the mobile, in case of lip-readers. He had to be cautious with what he was doing and had done many times before. It was answered.

"Yeah?"

"It's me, Elder …"

"I can see that. What do you have for me?"

"Hot stuff. It's gonna cost you a thousand pounds. Cash. Payable on delivery. Want it or not?"

"What is it? Give me a clue!"

"No clues … it's about Chip and Pin. Want it or not?"

"Okay. A deal. Meet usual place, usual time. Tomorrow."

"Tomorrow is too late. This info is hot off the press. It has to be today!"

"Okay. See you then." Then the connection was cut. Stack swiveled round in his chair.

"'Arry!"

"Yeah, Boss!"

"Meeting with Elder. Same time, same place as usual. Get a thousand quid from the kennels and as soon as you get the info call me, right?"

"Yeah, will do!" In the café, Stan Elder finished his snack, then walked to his office to call DCIs Ellis and Wignall.

The 'usual' meeting place was the local library, there it was safe, dry and warm, safe against raised voices and kidnap and beatings. Elder saw Harry walk in . He took a seat at the same table as Elder.

"Okay, Stan, what's the gen?"

"Money first." Harry slid an envelope across the table. Elder looked inside and did a rough count.

"Okay." He leaned forward and started talking. "Those bent cops, Dent and his shadow. There's a court hearing tomorrow, when judge Coppins is going to order their arrest, and they are gonna be under surveillance from first thing tomorrow morning, then picked up by the cops and held in the station cells."

"Is that it?"

"No, shuddup and listen. This is the good bit! A couple of months ago, they had a big drug delivery to do ..." And here, Elder was injecting a bit of fiction of his own to make the whole story a really bad deal from Stack's point of view, and he hoped worth every penny of the thousand quid. "... and in order to get into their boss's good books, they had the forensics guys tag every package with a tracker, so ..."

"Bloody hell ! You know, Stack ..."

"Hey, keep yer voice down! ... and when they delivered the gear, the cops could track every package of brown and every bundle of cash to their final destinations, and ... "

"Hey, mate this is hot stuff! So, these …"

"Harry! Keep yer voice down!"

"Sorry! So that explains how our couriers all got picked up! Jesus, mate, Stack's gonna love this!" Then more fiction from Elder.

"Hey, that's not all! They also got a load of gen on the bank accounts, names, points of import, methods, vehicles including those specially adopted mobile homes, you name it, mate, so Stack is getting very close to the front of the queue for a visit from the fuzz!" Harry already knew that there had just been a seizure of cocaine which had been due to hit the UK mainland. Was that down to the two cops? He wondered.

"Bloody hell! Is that it?"

"No, not quite! Tell Stack to pick up those two cops, like now, and get them out of the country or something, 'cos the rumour is, that to save their miserable hides, they're gonna turn Kings Evidence on the whole shebang! In a word, Stack and his buddies are gonna get shafted!" It was enough for Harry.

"Hey, Stan, you've earned yer cash today! I'd better get back!" The legman for the drug baron Stack, was gone in an instant. He was also aware that if things got bad for his boss, things would be equally bad for him.

TWENTY EIGHT

Emma Collins heard the letterbox snap shut as the postman dropped the mail onto their doormat. She slipped through from the kitchen and picked up two letters. One was a bill and the other was from JaworInt, which she could tell from the little insignia on the back of the envelope. She decided to wait until her husband got home from work before she opened it. They had signed the contract and returned it in good time and she now hoped that the envelope contained good news about their future. She felt in limbo a bit, looking forward to moving on, getting her Mark away from his job and the boss he didn't like to work for, giving him and the children some long-term security and maybe herself having a bit more to her life than as a stay-at-home housewife and mother. She knew she was not alone, as there must be thousands of women in the same position, but they had to deal with their own issues. She had loved working for a major travel firm, dealing with the drama of the travel industry. She did not in any way regret their approach to the DNA results. She was almost euphoric, intensely excited by the prospects facing her and her family. She also felt very sorry for her husband, a man who had devoted most of his life to public service, but who had to deal with poor conditions and lousy pay, the ever-present danger of assault, abuse from his unpredictable boss. He deserved better.

Mark Collins was again in the library. He had another two hours before he could sign off and drive back home, an hour and a half drive on a good day. As usual, Smudge was seated there working on his education. The inmate looked up.

"Hey, Sir! Your bro ain't doing too good is he!" Collins veered off towards him, and as usual, appeared to be engrossed in the book shelves rather than talking to the man. It was the protective measure, more than anything to ensure that the inmate was not seen to be cosying up to the management. That could be fatal.

"Go on, Smudge, what've you heard now?" It was common knowledge that Smudge was the best-informed old lag than anybody else in the place.

"The trial ... everybody knows your Ian is on a loser! He's a real case, he is. Kinda not human by all accounts!"

"Well, mate, it didn't help much you giving me the names of those bent cops, Dent and bloody Forbear!"

"Only bent goods come outer jail, Boss!"

"What else have those two been up to, then, Smudge?"

"Quite a bit! But me life ain't worth a light if I tell yer!"

"Like drugs!"

"Yeah, but that's just the start of it! I tell you, if those two get a long stretch the whole of humanity'll be grateful. But, and this is in confidence …" Smudge looked around the library, never well attended at the best of times, but now just he and Mark Collins were present. "If they get to do time, and if they've opened up to the cops to get a lighter sentence, and I'll tell you now, it is them who're gonna feel some rough justice, so their best bet is to bugger off and they ain't got too much time to do it, either and old Graham Coppins'll get them both into custody as soon as 'e sits the day after tomorrow, guaranteed!" Collins was rather taken aback by the extent of Smudge's familiarity with the case, and just how up-to-date he was.

"Bloody hell, Smudge …" Mark Collins was about to say something which might put the guy on notice that there must be somebody in the CPS office handing out information, but he just stopped himself. The info he had himself was older than what Smudge had told him. "…You are a mine of information!" But it was what Smudge had not told the prison officer which would really have caused a flurry of activity at the CPS and in the offices of DCIs Ellis and Wignall.

"Yeah, so I am, Guv'nor! It's a matter of survival in 'ere … what I know keeps me alive!" Collins thought that what Smudge knows could also get him killed. However, the information he had passed to him made it clear that somebody in the CPS building was passing information to the wrong people, and he decided to pursue the matters raised by Smudge without revealing his source of information. He finished his shift and booked out to begin his drive home. Tomorrow, he was off to Oxford with Emma and the kids for a final brief on his new job.

When Harry reported back to his boss, the guy went ballistic. He smashed up his table with a baseball bat, and when he cooled down he knew he had to act. He got on to Harry again.

"'Arry! I'm getting the cleaners in on this now! Apitz and Ziff will do! They're gonna pick up them bloody cops, tell them the bad news, and that they're being taken to the airport, and to sort out their bank accounts and to get the fuck out of the UK unless they want to see a minimum fifteen-year stretch, got it? Once the guys have done the job they can both piss of back to Albania or wherever they come from until the hoo-ha has died down." Stack knew that both Dent and Forbear had been moving cash overseas into a Málaga account, and by now with all the crooked stuff they'd been up to they must have quite a bit stashed there. Harry knew that bringing in the cleaners meant a bullet for each of them, just like Toady had got not all that long ago. "Go on, what are yer waiting for?" Harry did not like it. He left the office and made as if to ready the red mini-bus and ducking down inside made a call. It was not often that he called Stan Elder, but this was a matter of life and death. He knew neither of the cops would be missed. Dent had been beating his wife for years, but she knew life could be worse without him, and she was used to it. Forbear lived on his own in a grotty old flat, and never had any family or friends to speak of. Back in the CPS offices, Elder glanced at his 'phone. It was on silent, but as soon as he saw the number flash up he knew it had to be an emergency. Information between the men was a two-way thing, always had been. He moved into the corridor and as he slowly descended the steps down to ground-floor level, he answered the call.

"This better be serious stuff, Harry!"

"It bloody is! Stack has black-spotted the two cops … they're gonna get wasted unless you call in the cops. Like bloody now! Look for a red minibus!" Then Harry rang off and deleted the call from his mobile. Stan Elder ran up the stairs to the office, and as he entered he called out to anybody who would listen.

"Call the cops! The officers Dent and Forbear are gonna get killed! It's bloody urgent! Someone call the police now!" Two clerks reached for their 'phones.

The cleaners were informed of the deadline; the two cops had to be picked up within the hour and they were to be called beforehand and told to get cabin-luggage only, their passports and all their money stuff ready, as there was to be no going back. It had to look real. The red minibus collected Dent first. He was a bit difficult about it, but his wife told him to get the hell out of the house. As the small group exited the house she called out to her husband.

"Don't bother to write and don't bother to come back, either!" Missus Dent had, some time ago, obtained all the information she needed to access her husband's account in Málaga as well as Forebear's, and she fully intended to empty them both as soon as her hubby had left. She had known for years that her hubby was a wrong'un. Apitz, Ziff and Dent drove to Forbear's. The minibus was parked well away from the house, Ziff being concerned about Ring cameras. Forbear was in his pyjamas for some reason.

"What's this all about, mate? Was his first question to the driver.

"We're just the drivers! You should have been told already! There's a list here of stuff you're gonna need." He ran through the list with the policeman. Then Dent pushed in.

"Johnny, just get it! It's the same stuff I've got and we ain't got much time, so get a shift on …! We're being met at Málaga airport and looked after by Stack's guys. I think he wants us to work for him. We're gonna get new identities, all accommodation's been sorted out …"

"What's the rush?"

"There's a warrant for our arrests being made tomorrow morning, at about ten. Judge Coppins has told the Crown Prosecution Service that we and those bloody lawyers are …"

"Oh, shit! I knew it would happen some time! We'd better get going, hadn't we?"

"Yeah. I'll give you a hand! We're short of time but first thing, we're gonna get some photographs for our new identities, okay?" The two police officers disappeared into Forbear's bedroom. That was when Apitz and Ziff pulled out their Ruger mark four 22/45 SSH small, silenced automatics and entered the bedroom. After being shot, each cop had a *coup de grâce* administered to the back of the head just to make sure. Ziff picked both bags the officers had packed, slung them over his shoulder, and pulled Forbear's flat door behind him and returned to the minibus with Apitz. Then they made a call to Stack.

"Job done. We're off to the airport now, we've got all the kit and our cash, okay?" Stack called his gofer, Harry Swanley.

"Get to the airport. Bring the minibus back here and get the 'phones off those two plonkers. Make sure they're turned off … usual stuff, okay?"

"Yeah. Consider it done." Stacks oppo moved into a side-office where his buddy was watching TV. "Off yer arse, Si, you're taking me to the airport, like now!" Stack was still in a shit mood. He knew it was only a matter of time before the cops turned up mob-handed. He got his men together.

"Right, we're off! Away from here! Back to the Amersham address, so get all the kit and 'phones and stuff together now and leave!" Stack had eighteen of his top couriers and half a dozen of his money-launderers picked up because of Dent, or so he thought, and as was usual in the drugs game, punishment can be severe.

At the CPS HQ, the clerks got through to the emergency switchboard. It took the operator some time to react, but she had to track down DCIs Ellis and Wignall. They put out an APB for the stopping and holding of a red minibus believed to be travelling between Reading and Heathrow; two male occupants believed to be armed. They also send cars to the addresses of Forbear and Dent. At Dent's residence, Missus Dent answered the battering on her door.

"Where's Ronnie?"

"Gone! He left here about an hour and a half ago with a couple of dodgy-looking blokes. Apparently they were gonna go to Spain, for good I hope!"

"Was Johnny Forbear with them?"

"Na! I think they were on the way to pick him up as well!" With that the cops retuned to their car and sped off to Forbear's flat. When they arrived, they got no answer at the door, so it was kicked in. They found two bodies, and called for an ambulance, then backed out of the crime scene, with one of them radioing HQ. All possible manpower was now
stretched between Reading and Heathrow looking for a red minibus. It was chaos..

Apitz and Ziff were not stupid, but very street-wise. They knew their old boss too well. Instead of driving east to Heathrow, they drove west towards Bristol. With Ziff driving, Apitz rummaged through each of the cabin bags they stole from the police officers. Anything with their names on was put to one side, all money and clothing was kept. They had their own cash and debit cards to pay for a flight to Málaga, then on to wherever they felt save. They had been well paid working for Stack, and had no complaints. But they knew that they would be pursued now that Stack knew or thought he knew their itinerary. They were right. Now was the time to dump the red minibus. Hiring a car was a bit too complicated, so they drove into the town centre in Swindon and dumped the van in a multi-story car park, and the stuff they moved from the bags they stuffed into a waste bin.

There was not much. Then they casually approached a private-hire taxi and asked to be taken to Bristol airport. The driver called to base to get the job properly booked, and a bit reluctant to accept the job, he asked for the cash, two hundred pounds, in advance, which he got. He stopped off at his office and dropped the cash off just to be on the safe side. During the journey, Ziff convinced the driver that they were trying to get a flight to Paris, with some cock-and-bull story about a late wedding invitation, a ruse to put anyone off the scent once the minibus had been located. At the airport, they found a suitable flight, but it would be a morning departure. As far as they knew, neither of them were yet listed as fugitives. And anyway, their names were not Ziff and Apitz.

Much earlier in the day, back in Oxford Road, Emma, Mark and their two children, piled into their little car.
"Where are we going, Daddy?" Both parents knew it might be unwise to talk about daddy's new job, so they answered with a simple shopping trip excuse. They arrived early, and walked into the centre of town for a bit of refreshment and a look at the shops.
"Hey, Daddy ... this place is super! I wished we lived here!"
"Well, you had better talk to your daddy then, hadn't you!" Then it was time to head out to the JaworInt HQ. The whole family was ushered up to the beautifully appointed meeting room, where a little spread was set out for them, with the accent on treating the children.
"Wow, Mummy! Is all this for us?" Then Martin Sweeney, the senior trustee entered the room, followed by Frances Dyer, human resources, and Bethany. It was hugs all-round, then down to business while the children filled in some colouring books at the far end of the table.
"Right, if it is okay with you, we have pencilled in a date for your move to the city. The house is being given the once-over, and then it's yours."

"That's fine … we'll put our house on the market …"

"Mark, our estates manager will look after all that! And if you tell him what you want shifted up here, we'll do that as well. We can't have your attention being diverted from your new position with us on what are, at best, minor diversions, do we!"

"Well, that sounds pretty reasonable! And do we get to look at the local schools?"

"We go for the private schools, and as you would expect, there are some pretty good ones here in Oxford. We will make sure than our HR manager … Frances here … will go through all that with you. All we need to do now is give you a date for the move to Oxford and perhaps you can tell us what you expect your house to achieve and then let our people deal with it." That signified the end of the meeting. It had lasted a good hour, with the children still engrossed in their colouring tasks. The family returned to their car and headed home.

"Daddy, can we live there please? It's much nicer than Reading!"

"What does your mum think, Tracey?"

"I think it is a good idea! Any where's better than Reading! Let's work on it shall we?"

"Oh, yummy!"

"But you'll have to wait for two weeks, love, before the move!"

"And, darling, don't forget to hand in your notice! I think they'll want one month's notice, so maybe we can move up there in two weeks and you can manage on your own here!"

"Okay. And what do you think the house will fetch on the open market?"

"I've been looking .. I think about four hundred and fifty? Three bed, one ensuite, two bath, garage with forecourt parking …"

"Sounds good to me! Now, when I get in, I'm going to call Mike, Mike Maynard. I have some news for him!"

Once home. Mark called Mike's mobile.

"Mike! Mark. I have to tell you that there's somebody from the CPS who is leaking information … it's serious stuff!"

"Go on, tell me!" Mark Collins repeated what he had heard from Smudge. "I cannot tell you the source, but apparently, judge Coppins is going to have Dent end Forbear arrested, together with the two lawyers you have working for you, and is going to dismiss the charges against you …!"

"Bloody hell, Mark, if you know that, it must be somebody really close to Coppins! I won't say a thing to anybody, but pretend it's all a surprise to me. What the hell else can I do?"

"You're right! Nothing! I'll tell Ellis and Wignall and let them work something out! I have to tell somebody!"

TWENTY NINE

Maynard got up early as her wanted once again to check he had done all he could do prepare for the recommencement of his trial. He realised that it was going to be make-or-break time, but he was confident that it would turn out okay for him. Amongst other things, he was keen to see exactly how his legal team would get through the day. He drove to court and entered the building to see his two lawyers deep in conversation. They looked worried. Maynard sidled up to them.

"Morning! You to don't look too happy? What's the problem?"

"No problem. We just think Dent might be having a spot of bother, that's all. Anyway, we'll see what happens this morning, okay?"

"Yeah, I suppose so!" Maynard knew damn well that Dent, Forbear and the two lawyers were going to be in a spot of bother, which was a gross understatement. He had a quick coffee, then wandered into court. It seemed to him to be a lot busier than usual, and he recognised Ellis sitting near the front with a group of people who looked to him to be police officers. As he walked towards his usual spot in the court, he was approached by an usher.

"Good morning! Can I help you?"

"Yes … can you please take a seat at the front of the court? Thanks." Maynard did as he was asked, which put him close to Ellis, who acknowledge his presence, but made no move to speak to him. In fact, thought Maynard, he looked a bit grim. The court was now filling, almost to capacity. There was something going on, he felt. And hoped that whatever it was, it was something to his advantage. From a row near the back of the court, Harry Swanley had watched Maynard from the moment he walked into the court. Stan Elder had pointed him out. Swanley had dumped his boss's idea of collecting the red minibus, because he knew damn well that sooner or later the cops would be looking for it, and he did not intend to finish up sprawled face-down on some motorway, with about a dozen armed cops pointing guns at him only get shot if he so much as blew his nose or broke wind. His mobile was switched to 'silent' mode. He smiled to himself, imagining what would happen if he took a call from the two fugitives while the court was in session, then put his hand up to tell the judge that the cop-killers were on his 'phone and wanted to speak to him!

At nine-thirty precisely, the CPS barrister entered the courtroom, and the little door at the back of the court opened and the usher stepped out.

"Will the court stand for His Honour Judge Coppins!" Coppins entered and sat down, looked up and gestured the court so be seated. For a moment, that seemed to the assembled court more like an age, the judge just sat and stared at his notebook. Eventually, the usher, standing beside him, looked down at the honourable judge, which movement seemed to galvanise him into action. He looked up.

"Ladies and gentlemen of the jury, I have some terrible news. I was informed this morning that the two police officers who had been investigating this matter, the case you are here to give a judgement on, were both murdered ... last night I believe. But I hasten to say that the facts indicate that the deaths are nothing to do with the defendant, Mister Maynard, but rather regarding other matters which those officers were investigating. Thank you!" The silence was such that you could have heard a pin drop. Then the members of the jury started whispering to each other, then the jury foreman stood up.

"Your honour ... If I may on behalf of all the members of the jury, express our condolences to the families of the deceased officers. Thank you."

"Thank you, Mister Sewell. I now have another duty to fulfil. I have seen new evidence which I have now shared with the prosecuting authorities, and I have with their guidance, concluded that the case against the accused is fabricated in its entirety." Maynard turned in his seat to look at the two lawyers, who were now hurriedly collecting their papers together, as if to make a run for it. The judge continued. "Mister Maynard ... stand please." He stood. Coppins gestured towards him. "Mister Maynard, notwithstanding the awful news regarding the police officers, I have pleasure in telling you that all charges against you have been dropped, you are hereby released from your bail and are now a free man. Doubtless you will wish to pursue a case for compensation against the police authority. Thank you. You may be seated." He judge then turned to the jury. "Members of the jury, may I thank you for the time you have attended here on this case, and you are now all formally discharged. You may either leave the court now or stay for the remainder of this sitting which I assure you will not be for very much longer. Thank you." Then it was Ellis's turn. "Detective Chief Inspector Ellis ..." Ellis stood. "You know your next move. By the power invested in me, I hereby issue a bench warrant for the arrest of Messrs Weatherby and

Sowerby-Newton. Will you please arrest them and take them into custody." The two lawyers half-stood up, as a couple of police officers in mufti approached them. Sowerby-Newton had something to say.

"This is appalling!" Weatherby put a hand on the barrister's shoulder and pulled him to a seating position.

"Can it, Noël ... this is all Maynard's doing!"

"Can it nothing!" The barrister sat just the same. "This is outrageous!" The rest of the court watched as the plain-clothes officers escorted the two lawyers from the court leaving all their papers on the bench in front of them, all of which were collected by the police. As soon as they had left the court, the judge again spoke to Ellis, who stood.

"Mister Ellis ... I now formally issue a warrant for the arrests of Mister Ian Collins, Roger Cracknell and a Jane Dawson . Thank you." Ellis responded, acknowledging the instructions, then DCI Wignall leaned in towards Ellis.

"Mike, we need to chat about her, Jane Dawson. I went to see her the other day. I think she is prepared to be very helpful to our cause! I think she is a bit vulnerable as well."

"Okay, Andy ... maybe we ought to go together to see her first, then try and get any charges against her dropped. We can talk to the CPS later."

Ziff and Apitz departed Bristol for Paris at seven fifteen on morning of the day the court sat. They arrived in Paris at eight thirty-five UK time, and boarded the flight for Málaga at quarter to three UK time. Not once during their journeys did the pair acknowledge each other's presence, and did not sit close to one another. To all intents and purposes, they did not know each other. It was another measure the couple had often taken to put off pursuers who were looking for two men. Their flight landed at just after four pm UK time. The first thing each of the men did was to approach an ATM to see how much cash each of the police-officers accounts held. It should have been, according not their calculations, tens of thousands of pounds UK equivalent. To their horror, both accounts held between them only a few hundred Euros. Missus Dent had got their first, and she was now sitting on approximately a hundred and fifty thousand pounds.

"Fuck!"

"Wasser matter, bro?"

"Matter! We're stuffed mate! There's no cash in the fuckin' machine! How much cash 'ave we got?"

"Only what 'Arry gave us, and we paid the air fares, so I suppose about ten thousand, less what we spent, so, say seven grand?"

"That ain't gonna last long! What are we gonna do? Weren't we supposed get a job working for Stack's mate? Better get a bloody 'phone and call 'Arry!" The two killers had been wise enough not to have their mobiles on since they left Reading, and were not going to turn them on now. Anyway, they knew Harry Swanley's number. All they needed was a 'phone. That wasn't a problem. They purchased a burner 'phone locally, then made it to the nearest café. Ziff made the call.

Harry Swanley and Stan Elder had just settled into their seats at the HotStuff café for their usual when Harry's mobile rang. He didn't recognise the number, and was minded to ignore it, but he didn't. He looked up at Elder as he accepted the call.

"Hello ..."

"'Arry ... Ziff!"

"Ziff! Where the hell are you ..." He wisely lowered his voice just so Elder, but not any of the other fifty or so within earshot could hear the exchange. "The cops are all over the place looking ..."

"We're safe. Flew out of Bristol! Couldn't trust Stack to not shop us! We need to know how to contact Stack's guys here in Spain. Can you help?"

"Er … yeah! I'll get one of the guys to call you. Give me half an hour and I'll get back to you, okay?"

"Have to be. We 'ave no other choice mate! Speak soon!" Harry turned to Elder again.

"Youn get all that?"

"Yeah! Leave it with me … just give me the 'phone number and I'll get the real cops to deal with it. Need an EAW first … a European Arrest Warrant … er … call them later and tell them that somebody called Davis, 'Acker Davis … will get in touch with them, meet them and look after them, okay?" Elder was thinking on his feet. But he knew the system, and knew what to do.

"Okay, Stan! Finish your sandwich. I'll jot down the number and send a text to Ziff. Wait to be contacted by a bloke called Davis … 'Acker Davis!"

"You got it! Who's this Davis bloke?"

"Just someone I knew yonks ago. Total arsehole. Can't even read! But don't worry, I know what I'm doing!"

Back in the office, it was getting late but still Stan Elder insisted on calling Ellis.

"DCI Ellis? Stan Elder, CPS. Have some info on the two cop-killers."

"Okay, where from?"

"Can't tell you that, but very reliable. The two guys flew out of Bristol to Paris, then Paris to Málaga. They were supposed to be contacted by one of the drug dealers there, according to Stack, but were given no information, so currently they are at a bit of a loose end … I have a number for them, and what I propose is that they are contacted out there by a person supposedly to employ them. We've told them some guy called Acker Davis will meet them out there, and they will respond to that name…" Elder explained the plan. " … but as you have no names for them, whoever makes contact must get a copy of their passports, supposedly to get new passports for them, but so you can issue an arrest warrant … EAW job …" Ellis asked a few questions, then rang off, called his HQ and got the wheels in motion. Within the hour, a plot was hatched. It was late in the day, but a call was made to the number Ziff had given to Harry.

It was answered almost immediately.

"Ziff?"

"Who is this?"

"I'm calling on behalf of Acker … Acker Davis. Harry asked me to call you. Are you all okay for accommodation tonight?"

"Yeah."

"Okay. Tomorrow Acker will meet with you. Go to the marina, there's a great café there. Ask for Fidel. Tell him you are gonna meet with Acker, and he'll call you on your number and to make sure that you recognise him, he'll tell you what he'll be carrying. You also tell him how he'll recognise you. We need to have a copy of your passports so we can arrange for new ones for you 'cos the airlines will have copied yours on the way out so don't mess about with our lot please! Do as we ask. We do it a lot for fugitives, and whether you stay with us or take off for somewhere else is up to you, but if you do go, then we will not spend any more time on your case, we only do it once. We'll also book you into a hotel and as soon as we have sorted your bona-fides we'll let you into the business, got it? Okay with that? We are going to look after you so show some respect, okay?"

"Yeah. No problem. Let's get things going please." Ziff had no idea what 'bona-fides' meant, but is sounded pretty good to him. "Yeah … and thanks." The caller made sure he had cut the connection to the killers then turned to the two men standing next to him.

"You heard that … get onto the Málaga lot to organise it all. Chase-up the EAW 'cos we do not want them to have time to bugger-off again. I suggest you get a heavy mob to be in the background just in case. And if necessary shoot them both. Cop-killers are the scum of the earth! Even killers of Dent and

Forbear!"

THIRTY

The CPS and the cops were having a good day. They had four lawyers in custody all screaming like stuck pigs. Ian Collins was visited by his brother Mark.

"Mark, you bastard! Is this all your doing?"

"Ian! Shut up! You have been watched from the moment you started this bloody stupid exercise, it's all your doing! Everything has been recorded and is filed with the CPS. In a nutshell, you are in the shit!" Then Mark Collins lowered his voice. "Look, if you play ball, I am sure I can help you … I want to tell your defence team that you were not … are not … of full capacity, and plead guilty but we get a good plea in mitigation. Those bent cops, the …"

"The dead ones?"

"Yes, Ian, the dead ones! We must be able to make up some scenario that fits the bill. That's what I plan for you and you had better act along. And when you get out of jail …"

"Wadderya mean, 'get out of jail'?"

"Exactly as I say!"

"What about my business?"

"Ian, you never had any business to speak of … Chris and Mike are going to take it on and work it the way it should have been worked in the first place!"

"They are going to steal it …!"

"Ian, there's nowt to steal! Wise up! You're all washed up. Anyway, as I was saying,, when you get out of jail, I and Emma will look after you … if you let us. If you piss us about then you will be left out in the cold. We won't want to know you! Right that's it. I'm off now. I'll find some real lawyers to look after your case, okay?" Mark Collins stood up and knocked on the door of then interview room, and without a backward glance, left Ian Collins to himself.

Back in the police station, Ellis got a call from Nottingham. The caller had some information on the police-officers' deaths and by all accounts he had the whole shooting thing on camera. He was reluctant to say exactly the circumstances, but by his account Forbear was engaging in some sexual exercise and videoing it live, when he left the room briefly, before returning later with another guy, the other one who was shot, then the gunmen entered the room and shot them both, picked up a couple of bags then left. The caller then said that if the policer wanted to have the recording, all they had to do was collect it. He gave an address. The call ended once the address had been noted. The man did not give his name. With this and the Malaga business, Ellis was having a good day.

In Málaga, Fidel the café waiter-cum-USFDA operative had been fully briefed. He knew what the two killers would be carrying as a way of identifying them. It would be a big red and white sun umbrella. He knew that the cop impersonating the drug contact would be carrying a Sainsbury's orange shopping bag, with a copy of the London Times in it. He knew too that there would be at least five armed officers hanging around just in case. The plan was to talk to the killers, book them into a local hotel where they were supposed to stay until their new passports were processed, which would be never, and as soon mas the EAW had been processed and agreed with the Spanish authorities, the two would be lured into a trap and arrested. It all looked good to him. All he had to do was wait until he was told date and approximate time.

At the Reading police HQ, the arrested lawyers were all squealing to talk to their lawyers, but the moment their names were mentioned, most backed out with some rather uncomplimentary remarks. Eventually, two solicitors agreed to act provided it was for all the arrested parties, and that the deal was privately funded and not legally aided, with a bonus for any not-guilty outcomes. Once all were released on police bail, and had all gone home to change and smarten-up, they arranged to meet at the old Ramada hotel for a conference. In the meantime, the two solicitors then popped into the police station for a cop-brief. Mike Ellis agreed to see them.

"Okay, gentlemen, how can I help you?" The lawyers knew Ellis and had s good deal of respect for him.

"Okay, Mike, what's the issue with this lot?" As if they didn't already have a good idea. It took a long time to go through the files, but ultimately the lawyers were convinced. They tried every angle; entrapment; that the evidence would be deemed not admissible; that the solicitors set up the barrister and vice-versa. But it all failed. One of the solicitors said he would try to take sides with the barrister and blame the solicitors, the other would blame the barrister. It was all they could do.

In Málaga, Fidel had two customers. He spoke in Spanish.

"Hola, ¿qué queréis tomar?" Ziff answered.

"Sorry. No Spanish. Speak English? Romanian?" That was a give-away!

"English. Can I get you anything?" Ziff turned to Apitz.

"Stop pissing about with the brolly! What do you want?"

"English breakfast and coffee for me. You American?"

"No. I lived there for a few years. That's all. And you Sir?" Fidel turned to Ziff.

"Same mas 'es 'avin please!" Fidel scribbled the order.

"Scrambled fried or poached egg?"

"As it comes!" Fidel looked at his watch. Thirty minutes before Davis turned up. Easy. Fidel went in to make up the order and watched as more customers arrived. He recognized a few of them; they were his own people. No problem. They knew what was going on. Asd the full English breakfasts were delivered, the Acker Davis guy arrived, and seeing the big brolly, sat at the same table as Ziff and co. Fidel moved in to take an order.

"Yeah ... just a coffee please mate!" Done. Fidel observed the exchange between the killers and his man. They were getting on okay. 'Acker Davis' continued with his meeting. "Right ... down to business! I assume you're meeting here due to the stuff Stack got you involved in?" 'Davis' had been well briefed. He was in effect a Met police officer, serious crime division, and doing what he was doing now was not particularly unusual for him. He had an impressive force of officers behind him as well as being able to call on a variety of sister organizations including the Spanish police. He was never alone on these jobs. There were at least six of his men watching him now. "Always to assist anybody who we think can be useful to us. First thing, need to get you some new passports ... so let me have sight of your current documents ... I'll need to copy them of course. I suppose you brought them?" Ziff handed them over, and 'Davis opened them, then using his mobile, copied the photographs and dates of birth. Nationality shown as Romanian, also the place of issue. "Thanks. Right, as soon as we have got you fully legit, we'll meet the boss. He lives in a bloody great house not far from here, and initially you will be accommodated in the old farm property. And a word of warning. Always do what you are asked to do. We run a multi-million-dollar business, and we pay our people well. For the moment you will be accommodated in our place ..." Davis handed out information. "It's our hotel." In fact, it was an establishment operated by the security services and was totally secure. Just as the visitors finished eating, they seemed to have also finished their business. Davis got up, bade them goodbye, and took his leave. Job done. Fidel moved in with a tray.

"Hey, mate, where's this 'otel, any idea?" Apitz showed him the little card. Fidel looked.

"Yes ... behind the café, walk away from the centre, with the sea on your left that is, and it comes up in about two to three-hundred yards. Nice place, small, but with sea views!"

"Thanks mate!" The two then picked up their bags and moved in the direction indicated.

Within the hour, the information on the two fugitives was in London, and an EAW was applied for. The idea was that the two killers would be observed but otherwise left alone. The authorities needed at least forty-eight hours to get the warrant to the Spanish authorities, then the two would be arrested and taken to the airport to be deported to the UK. Neither Ziff nor Apitz suspected anything and spent a lot of time in the hotel bar, where a Romanian national listened to their conversations. Nothing alarming arose at least, nothing to give any concern, except their determination to get back to their home town, Bucharest, and the feel of Romanian Leu in their pockets. At no time did either of then express any regret for the three killings they had done for Stack. They had very little free time left. It was at four am the next day that the door to their suite of rooms was opened, and six armed officers of the Policia Nacional quietly entered their room and tipped them out of their beds. The cops had already checked that there were no firearms in their room. The operation went smoothly, and as far as the Metropolitan police were concerned, the men were as good as in a UK jail. Mike Ellis and Andy Wignall were delighted with the news, and with the evidence they now had the killers and the lawyers were as good as toast, as good as in jail, the killers for life and the others at a possible six to ten year stretch. Their next job was to put an end to Stack's business. Stan Elder suggested they pick up Harry Swanley, and provided he faced no charges, he could prove to be extremely helpful, so things were looking up for the Drug Squad, and while the Nigel Willis of the Crown Prosecution Service and his team processed the information from Wignall and Ellis to decide on the charges facing the three solicitors and the barrister, Stack and his crew were having a rough time at the hands of the drug squad.

With Ian Collins on bail, and ordered to live at home, Mark took it upon himself to look after mum, mainly because his brother had increased his drinking to the point that his mum's carers were getting fed-up with his behaviour, and was in serious danger of being locked up in one of the disused farm buildings, and as far as Mark was concerned it was not a bad idea. On this particular day, he had to go to work and hand in his notice, an event he had been looking forward to for years. He tapped on the door of his boss, Wallace. As usual, the door was open.

"Yes, Ian. What now?" Wallace was still face-down engrossed in his daily copy of The Sun.

"I'm moving … so I want to hand in my notice. Here." Mark Collins proffered his written resignation, just as the rules stipulated. Wallace looked up at his officer, slammed the paper shut.

"And just where the fuck do you think you're' going to work now? Eh?"

"Oxford."

"Don't be an arse! Oxford closed about thirty years ago! and anyway, it opened in the eleventh century, so it's a lot older than this one!"

"I will not be working in the prison, I have …"

"Oh, Mark, just piss off please! I have not got any time for this crap. Just go now and I'll get your pay sent on. Just go. I do not want to see you round my jail for another month with some stupid grin on your face. Go to admin and tell them then just go home, okay?" Mark Collins backed out of the office.

"Yes, Sir, thank you!" Under his breath, Mark expressed what he thought of his boss., and proceeded to HR department to give them the news of his resigning, and what Wallace had said. It was over pretty quickly, and the HR boss promised to forward the P45 and the pension details to the Oxford Road address.. Then he went to the library to see if Smudge was in. He was.

"Hi, Smudge! How's things?"

"Good. I've passed my Open University course, and I have to go to a ceremony in London, at the Barbican, to receive my award. And I'm going to work for the Prison Reform Trust … it's all kinda agreed!"

"You've done well, one of the system's few successes! And I am sure you will be an effective member of that organisation. And I have some news for you. I'm leaving here and getting another job. Not, I might add, in another jail!"

"I don't suppose that Wallace guy had anything to do with that did he?"

"That would be telling! However, I expect that pretty soon you'll have all the information!"

"Well, Sir, wherever you go, look me up. You've been one of the good guys, and we'll all be very sorry to see you go!"

"Yeah, Smudge – or should I say, Mister Steven Burcham, BSc., Hons, OU., keep out of trouble!"

"Oh, I will, Sir, I will!"

Shortly before Mark Collins climbed into his car to drive home, he turned to look at the prison building. He would regret leaving the job, but there were many positives on the horizon, especially for his family. In his mind he knew he had to do what he could for Ian, and he would do that by drafting a confidential mitigation plea on his behalf, setting out all the things Ian did not know about his origins, and there were other issues he would touch on which arose directly out of his parentage. Within a few hours he was back at home with Emma and the children, the rooms pretty well stripped of stuff they were taking to Oxford with them. Emma had told the school about their move, so everything was well in hand.

THIRTY ONE

With the end of the trials of the crooked lawyers imminent, Mark decided he should draft a plea in mitigation to do all he could for Ian. Emma agreed, if only to not upset mum, who had made it plain that he wanted her first son to treat Ian as a member of the family, and to take account of all his failings. Now with time on his hands, he sat at his PC and started writing. Every draft he did he ran past Emm, until finally they agreed on a final draft. Mark read it out loud to see how it sounded and to recognise any glaring errors.

FAO of His Honour Judge Graham Coppins, KC.
May it please Your Honour, herewith the plea on behalf of defendant Ian Mackenzie Basil Collins, which I submit on the basis that it will not be read in open court as the defendant is not aware of the issues I raise in his defence, and if he were to be made aware of them, I fear it would have a substantial deleterious effect on his already unstable psyche, as evidenced by Ms Goodrich, a psychiatric professional in the employ of the NHS.
I am not Ian's brother or half-brother, and his adoptive mother, I call her thus even though no formal adoption process was ever applied for, is the only other person in the family who knows this. My mother gave birth to my brother, still-born, and in the hospital, the Royal Berks, another boy was born to a young lady being the result of an affair with either her employer or her employer's son, I do not know which. She had come under a lot of pressure to have the child aborted, but instead she went full-term and knowing of my mother's distress at losing her child, handed the baby to my mother, and then disappeared. My mother took him home as her own. Even at the time of his death, my father never knew of the deceit. Ian proved to be a difficult child, categorised

as psychotic, but my father managed to get him, at age eighteen, into the Army, where he was attached to the Royal Military Police as an acting corporal dog-handler. However, the arrangement with the Army was short-lived, such was his attitude towards his superiors that he was discharged; and at Ian's behest we, we being the whole family, managed to get him to study for a degree and then persuade him to undertake articles to qualify him as a solicitor. We know that without our support and that of his principal, who did not find it easy working with Ian, he managed nevertheless to complete the necessary period to qualify, and he then took on occasional locum work. Being unhappy as an employee-cum-assistant solicitor, we agreed with Ian that we would finance the establishment of his own firm, but it was never a paying concern and mum undertook to finance it out of her and her late husband's savings, and when they ran low Ian was determined to repay her, and took some very bad advice which had a serious impact on his by then very fragile mental state engendered principally by the unprofitable business. He knows he has done wrong, and the firm is no longer a business he is involved in. I am now in the fortunate position that on Ian's release from his inevitable prison term, I will undertake to provide accommodation and care for Ian as long as it is needed.

I trust that Your Honour will take these matters into consideration, and give them the weight I believe they deserve in view of his difficult start in life and his continuing mental state.

I am, Your Honour,

Signed……………………………………..
Mark Adrian Collins, MBA
[HM Prison Service].
Dated this ……….. day of ……………... 2024

It sounded okay.

The trials of the killers had been a no-contest. Ziff and Apitz pleaded guilty to three murders and were sentenced to life with a minimum term of twenty-five years before parole, but on the advice of their lawyer who had spent hours going through the House of Commons paper 'Deportation and early removal of foreign national offenders', they thought they had a good chance of being repatriated to a regime where they could bribe their way to freedom. As far as the barrister Sowerby-Newton and the solicitor Justin Weatherby each received twelve years; Roger Cracknell got six years. When it came to and Ian Collins, the judge had received the written mitigation plea, which Mark had handed to Ian's barrister, not to be read out in court, but to be handed to the judge, who had been given a note before he sat for the sentencing hearing. He stated in open court that it was a very moving plea, and as a consequence he was limiting Ian Collins' term to four years, to serve half and thereafter to be released into the custody of Mark Collins, his brother. Just before he entered the court to hand down the sentences on the lawyers, he read the note again.

The judge handed down the four-year custody order, to be released after two years subject to the usual conditions being satisfied. Mark, Emma and Chris and Arnie were very pleased with the outcome. Ian did not seem to show any emotion as he with the others was led down to the cells and the prison van. Mark caught up with Chris and Arnie outside the court.
"Well, Mark, a good result!"
"Yep, I'm pleased., How is Mike getting on?"
"Well. The practice is very busy, and apparently, Nick is being compensated by the police authority, one hundred thousand pounds plus lost earnings over a period of four years which they put at thirty-five thousand per annum, so all in all a tidy sum. And the Law Society is going to admit him to the Roll and he will soon receive his first practicing certificate, and he'll be working for

Mike! And the bonus … Nick and our Debbie are now an item."
"So, all in all, a good result!"

THE END

They know who they are.

Printed in Great Britain
by Amazon